IT'S ONLY THE ENEMY SCREAMING

IT'S ONLY THE ENEMY SCREAMING

SCREAMING

a novel

Christopher P. McEnroe

iUniverse, Inc.

New York Lincoln Shanghai

it's only the enemy screaming
a novel

iUniverse books may be ordered through booksellers or by contacting:

iUniverse
2021 Pine Lake Road, Suite 100
Lincoln, NE 68512
www.iuniverse.com
1-800-Authors (1-800-288-4677)

Selections from the Tao-te Ching by Lao Tzu are from A Source Book in Chinese
Philosophy, translated and compiled by Wing-Tsit Chan, copyright 1963, by
permission of Princeton University Press.

ISBN-13: 978-0-595-34769-8 (pbk)
ISBN-13: 978-0-595-67152-6 (cloth)
ISBN-13: 978-0-595-79510-9 (ebk)
ISBN-10: 0-595-34769-X (pbk)
ISBN-10: 0-595-67152-7 (cloth)
ISBN-10: 0-595-79510-2 (ebk)

Printed in the United States of America

To my teachers. Especially to: Millie, Richard, Dominic, Bernice, Tony, Marie, Mary, Paul, and Loretta, of Revere, MA, whose character and sincerity continue to nourish me each day.

When people scream in pain and terror stuff your ears:
it's only the enemy screaming, remember that....

Henry Miller, <u>The Air Conditioned Nightmare</u>

Acknowledgements

The first draft of this novel was written during the Persian Gulf War of 1991. Through its evolution, I have benefited from the input and encouragement of many to whom I owe much gratitude. Special thanks to: Dr. Michael P. Lynch for his careful reading and critique, to Michael C. Obel-Omia for his tenacious encouragement and support, and to John Heavey for his generous assistance with editing. Special thanks, also, to my friend and wife, Kathleen M. Bliss, for reasons too numerous for mention here.

Author's Note

While this novel is a work of fiction, the details pertaining to the Persian Gulf War were recorded while the war was ensuing. The information, including quotes from major figures in the war, was taken from various print, audio, and visual media sources and is accurate in so far as those sources were accurate.

The internet was not among those sources as it was both unavailable to me at the time and was also not a predominant source of information for the general public. Other news events, attributed to news sources, like the shooting of the delivery man in chapter 7, are also real events gleamed from these same media sources.

CHAPTER 1

▼

If it weren't for warfare after all, what would any of us have to talk about?

As I look back on that time now, all that happened, the war itself seemed simple enough to figure out. It was the rest of it. There are about eight pints of blood in a person. At the end of the two and a half months, about two hundred and sixty one thousand people were dead directly from the war. That's 261,000 gallons of blood. Some people think that's reason enough not to do something. I just think it's something you should know if you're going to get in a war.

I was just trying to do what I was told I should do. That wasn't easy. Who should I listen to with all the people talking? I figured it out though. That's what led me to do the things I did. It was all about being who I was supposed to be. I remember saying the pledge of allegiance in high school. Now I know what all that shit is about. It was the war that taught me. The war, the General, the President, the Voice, the Commentators, the office people and all that riff raff on the street.

It was seven days before the war. Overcast. Cold. It puts you in a mood. Emilia Fellulu had lived in the neighborhood for sixty-seven years. I didn't know much about her except that she had been born into an Italian immigrant family of seventeen children. The kids would say "That bitch's crazy." The kids didn't know that was what I often thought about them. As a counselor in the shelter, I could never say that. It would have been easy to get away with saying it, but it was a rule I made for myself. It kept me from giving up on them even when I really thought caring about them wasn't worth the disappointment. That's what they thought, too—it wasn't worth caring about themselves, because they were determined to be disappointments. They seemed to know that the choices they made doomed them, but they were unwilling to make different choices. They wouldn't try anything new, because they were sure they'd fail. They were scared of everything. The only way they knew to defend themselves was to become as mean and ugly and frightening as they could.

The best I could figure was that Emilia was just a little bit retarded. Her parents were poor, and with seventeen kids, I figured the malnutrition alone could have done it. They tried to marry her off at some point, but she wouldn't sleep with Franko. She said he was crazy. "He want to sleep in the bed with me. He's crazy." Emilia was everything the kids were afraid of. She was old, small, weak, she had moles on her face, and she was alone. I never saw anyone from outside of the neighborhood visit her. Sometimes the kids made fun of her when she wasn't around, but when she was, Emilia talked with the kids for hours. When they didn't want to talk, she would talk. To get her to stop, they would have to start. If they got belligerent with her, she ignored it, just kept on talking as if they were being nice.

If the kids wanted to smoke they had to do it outside, and they all smoked as if they were waiting on the devil. I was out there with a few of them when Emilia came out. She said she had to go to the bank, but she was worried about the traffic. She talked about the weather, too, and she wasn't moving. I knew she wanted company, and I thought this would be a great opportunity to be a role model for the kids. I offered to walk with her to the bank, help her cross the streets. We walked down to the corner, and I was congratulating myself because all the kids were watching. When the lights changed and the traffic stopped, Emilia took my arm, and we started to cross. Emilia was on my left, between me and a car with two huge white guys in it stopped at the light. It was a worn-out rag of a car, and the size of the men inside made it look like a toy. They were pointing at Emilia and laughing. Then the driver took his foot off the brake and pushed it down again. Emilia startled because she thought it was going to hit her. She kind of jumped and started hurrying me along. The men laughed hard. Emilia didn't know they had done that on purpose, but I was glaring at them. When they saw me looking at them, they started giving me the finger and mouthing the words "Fuck You" to me. Now I wanted to fight.

Part of it was living in the city, but a lot of it was these kids and their attitudes. You're there to help them. You get paid like beggar. They can be normal, but sometimes it's nothing but attitude, and you have no choice but to suck it up. You're the adult. You're the example. You ask nicely, they spit at you. It's a lot of discipline. They push your buttons, but you can't fight. For a long time, I had wanted to be in a fight, and this gave me more than enough to justify it. I stopped on the corner and turned to them. Emilia asked me what I was doing. I started thinking about how big they were, that there were two of them. The important thing was to be as violent as possible; kick them in the nuts; get inside; poke out the eyes. They weren't getting out of the car, but they were taunting me. They wanted me to start something, two guys twice my size against me. It was a typical bully trap. I gave them the finger and quickly glanced down toward the shelter. The kids were on their feet and staring. They saw me turn and stand. I tried to think of how I would justify this to my boss, getting into a street fight while I was supposed to be on duty at the shelter. Emilia never saw any of it. She tugged on my arm and said, "Come on." I wanted to get into it, but I couldn't figure out how to make it right. "Come on," she said. "There's Vinny. He's holding the door." Vinny was a retired engineer. He was a hospitality guy at the bank. Not a watch your back guy. I just turned around and walked with Emilia, feeling like a victim the whole way. I would have to lie to the kids about feeling that way. As I looked back on the situation over and over again, it was hard for me to imagine winning a fight with those guys, beating them as they deserved. It was hard to accept that I might be incapable of righting a wrong right there at my feet, clearly my responsibility. That's why I couldn't stop thinking about it. That's what bothered me about the lie.

CHAPTER 2

▼

You don't go to war without intentions.

Wednesday was the dawn of a new era in global conflict. As I was running around the Pond, I came upon three people running abreast from the opposite direction. They spanned the path. As we got closer, I moved to a definite path at the far right, assuming they would shift to allow me to pass. But none of them moved. They looked at me with blank faces. I had to jump and run in the snow. I said nothing. It is difficult for me to speak when I run. It disrupts my meditation. I wanted to scream. I wanted to run them down and beat them. My father once said while driving, "There are two kinds of people in this world, those that are courteous, and jerks." Those people were jerks, and when I saw them on my next trip around, I was going to run right through them, barrel through them. And because they were so shiftless and slow, they wouldn't be able to catch me even if they had the tenacity to try. Shiftless mongrels don't have tenacity. They did not go around again. Then as I came around to the boathouse, a strange man engaged the run around the Pond. He was wearing shorts over black Lycra tights. He was wearing just a sweatshirt and no gloves. It was winter. He had curly hair. He had big, fat red cheeks. He was scrawny and short with a cockeyed, mischievous smile. His gait was awkward but quick. I moved to the right, the very edge, and that bastard saw me well enough, but he ran to his left, right in my way. I didn't like him, and I was going to clothes-line him if he didn't move over. There was plenty of room on the path. He moved over a bit, but still ran close to me, and since I didn't like him already, I didn't like him twice as much for that. I thought of clothes-lining him on the next pass. He'd just started his run, and it would be absolute lunacy to go only halfway around. I had to assume a certain intelligence about him, a common intelligence. But why was he oblivious to the "move to the right" staple of our culture? If he were not going full circle, then there would be no point in thinking about it, so I assumed he would. As I would see him coming toward me, I would move to the right. And he, in his doltish manner, would move to his left, or simply not at all. I would not look at his elfin grin or frozen red cheeks, but as I stepped to within half a stride. I would stick out my arm stiff to my side, level with his neck. His grin would pop off his face, freeze in the air, and shatter as it hit the ground. His eyes would bulge. He'd make desperate guttural sounds and land flat on his back, the wind knocked out of him. This would immediately acquaint him with the rules of the road and the concept of "safe distance."

As I came upon him again, I could see from a distance that he still had his grin, and, too, that he remained in bad position in my way. I thought maybe I would just punch him. That would really hurt my hand. He's probably one of those people with a rock-hard head. Even the clothes-lining would mess up my rhythm and stride, my breathing. It would disturb my meditation even more drastically than his troll behavior. I ran past him imagining it fully, but without the excitement. Then came three feebleminded walkers with baby carriages with no conscience among them. They took up the entire path and kept moving around in slovenly backward stumbles so that every proposed trajectory through them had to be aborted. I couldn't run babies over, or assault their parents, but I could think about it. I had to run through the snow again.

The snow under my feet gave way at each step, like running on sand. I had run along the beach a few times, and this is what it felt like. If I were in the desert waiting to fight, I'd run all the time. I'd run in the sun to acclimate my body. I'd work out all the time and train. If I were a squad leader, I'd make my squad train all the time. I'd make them sing songs as loud as possible as we ran through the desert. I would instruct them in growling and make them growl loudly. I'd tell them to make the enemy hear them. Make them pee in their pants. I'd turn oil barrels into drums, and at night we would have war parties. We would bang on the drums in hordes and shout. We would engage the spirit of war. That's what I'd do if I were in charge of something or other. If not, I would do those things by myself. Perhaps, I would be called upon to fight, I thought. I did not want to go. I did not want to sacrifice my life. I felt remorse for the boys who had done so already. What would be my family's reaction if I were to go and die? But these are not things to consider if you are in the desert with sand slipping away under your feet, cleaning your gun, smelling the oil, staring in the face of your enemy. The preparations of a warrior do not include doubt. They do not include consideration of the life left behind. The preparations of a warrior consist of absolute commitment, undaunted determination, and complete sobriety. All other considerations are made before the decision to go to war. If they are not, the warrior is doomed. I jumped back onto the pavement, and the snow shook loose from my sneakers.

It had rained over the snow that had fallen the week before. The fog was rolling in while I ran, and it surrounded the Pond just around the trees that stood at the water's edge all around. There were ducks and gulls on the Pond. The water was frozen in very large pieces in some places and not at all in others. Much of the Pond had a thin sheet of ice lying just under the water's surface. Of course, the mist formed a dome, a bowl. I ran around the Pond three times, equaling four and a half miles. I did not throw up. I sat down to gaze at the Pond. The mist behaved as the Pond's breath and the water maintained visible, rigid substance. The Pond stood as peace and stillness before me. The demonstration was monstrous. I ran back to my house. I had decided to take a picture. Picture taking is often obscene. It puts you in mind of being at a freak show. But I wanted a trigger to help provoke memory; my intention was not to capture it. It was late in the afternoon, and I would be late for work. I got my camera with my zoom lens. There was a small island about fifty yards from shore in the Pond. On the island grew a tree. The branches reached out and spanned the island. It was not a very big tree but it was loaded with character. The mist had moved in on the lake and I could see only as far as the tree. It stood against an ominous wall of white water, a specter. I got the most absurd inclination to walk across the water to it. I began to take pictures, walking around, getting angles through the trees. There were the most faint reflections on the water. I took my pictures as I found them, knowing none would come out; the scene was too delicate, the relationships too sophisticated. I stepped down to the water and was overwhelmed by what I heard. The soft drizzle touched the water and made a sound on the ice just below the water's surface. The drops on the still water and then on the ice could only be heard right at the water's edge, yet there were ten hundred million instances of this happening, one billion voices in a quiet chorus.

Work was a chaotic influence in my life. I was an uncertified counselor in a youth shelter. It was my job to befriend dispossessed teenagers, not unlike trying to convince a shark to jump into your boat. There were times when I would work a forty-hour week in two days. There were other times when it was almost like having an office job. The boss sent me to a training at a community college near my house. We were mandated to have trainings and she picked this one for me. She had seen the guy giving it and thought he was good.

It was very much like going to college, this training. There was a two or three hundred person lecture hall. When I walked in, the few people already there were sitting in the back. Most of them were dead silent. I walked down to the front row. In the first two years of college I was one of the silent piles of clothes in the back. One day I decided I was doing that out of fear, and I lived by a rule since then to always sit in the front, even at movies.

The trainer came in holding a cup of coffee. He was thin, short, professionally dressed but in a way that pegged him as a Human Services administrator. He did his best with what he had. He confirmed with me that he was in the right room. He put his bag and coffee down and then he took out a stack of documents. He looked through his materials for ten more minutes as the room filled to about half. I didn't take a look behind me until he started talking. When I saw the number, I knew for sure they weren't all working in youth shelters. This was a lot of different programs represented here. I got skeptical right away because it wasn't program specific. This was a general presentation. I didn't like that.

The trainer started by introducing himself and telling us about his background. He had worked for various Human Service agencies in the city throughout his career in a bunch of different types of programs. He went back to school to get a masters degree and that enabled him to get a job with the state as a training coordinator. Part of that job was giving trainings. This particular training was about human behavior. He hoped to boil down what would be a college semester course to about ninety minutes. At the very least, he hoped to give us some tools to use on our jobs to understand the people we were working with better. Most important was to understand that their behavior was not a comment on us personally. He said the minute we take what they do personally we are not performing our jobs as we should. Understanding people's motivation from a clinical point of view would help with that.

Then he said that because many of us were responsible for implementing behavior modification plans, it would probably be helpful to understand the thinking behind creating those plans. Then he started talking about Sigmund Freud.

"Basically," he said, "Psychology, Psychiatry, all that stuff goes back to Freud. It starts with him. I want each of you to think of your problems, all the problems that you have now, that you have always had, especially those problems you have with relationships. Freud basically confirmed what you all knew instinctively as teenagers, that all your problems are your parents' fault." He got a pretty good laugh. "And Freud, being the little man that he was, pretty much felt it was more your mother's fault than your father's. You look to your mother for more things. When you're a baby, she actually feeds you with her body. She keeps you warm; she wipes your butt, she gives you comfort. If you're not happy as a baby, it's basically your mother's fault and you spend the rest of your life feeling like, 'You know, you could have done better, Ma'.

"Actually, to be more accurate, Freud came up with the idea that your childhood, the way you were raised, the relationship you had with your parents, that kind of thing, actually sets up patterns of behavior that you follow for the rest of your life, pretty much, unless you experience some extraordinary event, or you do something to identify and change those patterns. That's how psychoanalysis and psychoanalytic therapy were born. Do you all know what psychoanalysis is? Would somebody be willing to give a quick explanation?"

A guy behind me raised his hand. He said, "It's when you go and talk to a psychiatrist and he helps you figure out your problems."

"Right. Basically, that's the therapy part of it. Without getting technical, what you do is talk about your life and your relationships, and the doc will try to help you identify patterns and then you and he will look at your past to figure out where those patterns came from. And where those patterns came from for your clients is very important because you as staff need to know that they don't come from you. It's also important to be aware of your own patterns and know what you are bringing to the relationship with your clients.

"I'll give you an example. A guy I worked with, a colleague, came from a culture where pointing at someone is a sign of extreme disrespect. Well, one day he was interceding with a client who was becoming violent, and while he's talking to this guy all of a sudden the subject starts pointing at the guy, right in his face. Immediately, I could see this changed the whole dynamic because my colleague instinctively read this as a threat, first of all, and it was an insult that he was used to responding to emotionally. Now, he was a very bright guy, and he kept himself in check but had he not been so experienced, his own emotional response could have sent that confrontation into something much worse than it had to be. That's the kind of thing you want to be aware of. You have to do an internal survey while you're working with your folks. Know what might be setting off your internal triggers and find a way to keep that stuff out of what you do professionally.

"The second thing you should know is that if you're going to understand a person, or yourself for that matter, you really need to get behind what they are doing and try to figure out why they are doing it. You need to get into their heads. Especially in confrontational situations. How someone behaves in a confrontation can be predicted based on how they have responded in the past.

"Another big thing about Freud is symbols and dream analysis, how to interpret your dreams. Example, how many of you have ever dreamed that your teeth were falling out of your head? You're in the dream, you feel a loose tooth and all of a sudden they all just start coming out. Probably during a time of stress, according to some it means you're feeling out of control. I knew a guy once who was having these dreams and it was driving him nuts, so one night during the dream, after all of his teeth had fallen out, he scooped them up in his hand and shoved them back in his mouth. The dreams stopped.

"Anyway, for Freud, symbols mean something to us, and sometimes we have emotional reactions when we see something that is a symbol to us. Example, say I was beaten by my father with a belt as a child. Years later I'm having a great day chatting with my friends, we walk into a store, and I see a belt on the shelf exactly like my father's. Suddenly my whole day goes south. I get moody. My friends don't know why. I don't know why. That connection is made on an unconscious level and it affects my conscious thought years later. That kind of thing, especially for people with traumatic childhoods, happens all the time.

"A lot of times you have no idea what is going to trigger something. It could be anything. It could happen at anytime. Sometimes it's okay to pursue it with someone. Even if all you're doing is making them conscious of the way they're behaving. You say, hey, I noticed when you saw that lamp you kind of tightened up. Have you seen that lamp before? But if the person rushed the lamp and threw it out the window, that's when you need to refer it to a doc. Symbols can be very powerful for people."

After that we talked about human behavior briefly. Than we talked about behavior patterns, behavior plans, and behavior modifications. Then, I went to the shelter.

I was at work when I saw the television news reporting on the "Showdown in the Gulf", that Operation Desert Shield had turned into Desert Storm. In the week previous, as I listened to Congress debate the issue whether or not to give the President license to declare war, some Congress-persons referred to it as "Operation Desert Spear." I believe they were opposed to the idea of war, but I rather liked the imagery of that term better than "Desert Storm." A storm is generally a tremendous mess without plan or purpose. None but God controls a storm. From this I would have assumed that the President was asserting himself as the composer and conductor of a great mess, or as God. Conjecture had it that he had given up that claim of divine authority when he relinquished his position as head of the Central Intelligence Agency (CIA). A spear, as in "Desert Spear," rummages up images of directness, accuracy, piercing precision, sleek and well-forged weaponry. Of course, the great Dr. Sigmund Freud would have all sorts of things to say in his whimpering way, but his babble is not to be considered in the warrior's preparation. Freud was a tragic figure. His shoes used to wear out rapidly and cause him undaunted anguish. People would say to him, "Hey Freud, nice pants," and he would accuse them of being breast-fed. That is not much of a strategy for getting things done.

Walter Cronkite made the most interesting point of all. He said that there should be no mistake made, that the people demonstrating against war were as patriotic as those who were for it. Both sides were struggling with their beliefs, making them known, crying at the goings-on. One side of the issue was prevailing, both had their ideas for the country's best direction, and all were tied to its fate. Mr. Cronkite told this story: He was taking a cab to the studio after he heard the news. In the cab, he took his radio out. The cab driver protested, saying he wanted to hear his own radio. Mr. Cronkite said to him, "There's a war on." The cab driver turned to him and said, "What, are you a soldier?"

CHAPTER 3

▼

A pack of justice, unfiltered, please.

"Take to the streets!" I felt that impulse. "Yes. Take to the streets. Fly down the streets. Stomp and snarl. Let us scream to our heavens." But the traffic. The traffic wouldn't stop. I knew that. Who would stop it? Not in this town. They wouldn't stop for me. You'd need firepower. And these are my citizens. Take to the streets. It seemed like the next step. What was taking to the streets, anyway? No one would record my taking to the streets. No one would notice, unless I harmed the citizens.

I'm not the kind of guitar player who gnaws the strings with his teeth. I play rock songs, Woody Guthrie-style. There are three simple chords to everything. Four, if I'm showing off. I only know about three songs. I improvise on the rest; but I don't really know how to do that. The guitar, when I picked it up, was out of tune. It had been getting hot and cold in my room lately. The strings were nearly a year old. These conditions tend to make it go out of tune. I picked it up and played, meowing like a cat. What could words say, anyway?

Strings need to be tight. These were stretched, thinning, useless pieces of metal. Good to meow. Good to sing no-tongue words written for the feelings found in soup, to be played on a souped up screaming amplifier and delivered like a disheveled, uninspired Woody Guthrie. And so I was.

Jake was from the days when I sucked tequila like my mother's milk, rolled my own cigarettes, and stayed up for days to increase their effect, all the while maintaining a strange office job in one of the skyscrapers downtown. Jake was a street musician. I met him one Sunday night in a train station around Government Center. He said he was playing progressive rock, but he couldn't play the guitar for anything, and he was just making up things and screaming them out. He was a natural fanatic, and I suppose that served as the basis of our conversation. Oddly enough, he worked in the same office I did in another department. It was through work that we became friends. He had just thrown his last roommate out, and as I had been sleeping on a friend's floor for three months, I took the open room.

Jake had once been kind of an inspiration for me: he felt it was no extravagance to ask of the rest of the world the simple right to sleep through the night without being awakened by sirens or screaming from the street. He demanded simple justice that the world was not prepared to give. He complained about the world as though all that occurred was a direct attack on him. He wore black at all times. Though I never saw him take a drink, I would often see him crawl in just his underwear in the middle of the night from his room to the toilet, where he would puke up his guts. Even his underwear was black. Sometimes I'd have to drag him out by his foot in the morning so I could get ready for work.

Jake ranted, mostly about public figures. The only argument I ever gave him was to try to get him to shut up. He would insist, however, in drowning me in his whining and snorting. He always had a cold or the flu, and when he got worked up, it was as if the words were barreling through some obstacle course to get out. Sometimes he'd blow chunks of snot out of his nose in mid-sentence. It felt like getting the head dunk treatment that cops and mobsters perform on their victims. He'd stuff my head into that toilet of negativity, and just when I was about to suffocate, he'd pull me up; mention something about the weather or the landlord. The conspiracy theories about the landlord would keep him going forever. He'd have that dirty bastard hooked with everyone from the Mormons to Mussolini's granddaughter. But the landlord's mess, his stink, his tight fist, his laziness were profoundly unsophisticated.

Jake had a startling ability to speak his mind to strangers. The first time I noticed it was in a movie theatre, a suspense film I think. Some people a couple rows ahead of us had been talking for a few minutes when Jake stood up and screamed, "Will you shut up!" It was sudden and desperate. The usher came down to kick Jake out, but he refused to go. He told the guy he could go fuck himself and that if he were interested in doing his job, he would have told the other people to shut up instead of leaving it up to patrons. The young usher persisted in asking him to leave, but Jake kept responding, "Go back to high school you little shit."

"Sir, I'm going to have to call the police," the usher told him.

"Yeah, right. I'm sure this city is full of cops with nothing to do but patrol movie theatres. You'll be growing hair on your chin before they get here."

Jake was crass, and I admired that. It turned a lot of people off, but if you didn't take it personally, and you didn't stand next to him when he was doing it, it could be exciting. This was a particular time when his target did take it personally. The young usher reached down, grabbed Jake's ponytail, and dragged him out of the theater. Of course, I stayed to see the movie. He fumed about it when I came out an hour and a half later. He was barraging a couple of prostitutes with the story, paused just enough to introduce me to them and launched straight back into it. His manner was engaging, especially if you didn't listen to his words or try to follow the meaning. The prostitutes were not only sympathetic but encouraged him with exaggerated nods of their heads, throwing in things like, "I know just what you're saying, baby," and "Uh-huh! You got that right." It had the rhythm of Bible-speak, like a vulgar revival meeting ("that fucking mother-fucker grabbed me right by the motherfucking ponytail and fucking threw me right the fuck out to this fucking spot I'm standing on now. And I didn't get no motherfucking refund. What the fuck is that!").

Jake was convinced that he was destined for fame. By what deed he did not know, but felt certain that he'd earn at least an honorable mention in the history books in the same vein as the agriculturist Jethro Tull. The only talent he had acquired thus far was his mania. His only ambition was to yell at people who pissed him off, which was everybody. He especially wanted to yell at public figures, call them hypocrites, or at regular people who were stupid enough to state their opinions on television. Watching television with him was a tremendous pain in the ass because he would scream at it. A commercial would come on and, "I don't fucking care about your fucking douche bags and your feminine protection. Get back to my fucking show you dipshit capitalist motherfuckers. They didn't need that shit a hundred years ago. I don't care! Shut the fuck up!" And then he would talk all through the show. During political campaigns he'd get really heated. "That fat cat, backstabbing mother-fucker. He's got every special Nazi interest in the God damn country jacking him off. It's bastards like him…I'll vote for your God damn damnation," he'd shout. "It's bastards like him that are the reason I can't get a real job."

"Jake," I'd say, "You can't get a real job because nobody likes you. And nobody likes you because you're a crass, contentious son of a bitch."

Saying that was like scratching poison ivy. Jake would crawl right into your ear and stay there for days pounding his point of view into your head. Since I was on a binge anyway I would take it, trying to outlast him sometimes the way I did with liquor and fatigue. But he was more relentless than those things, and the headaches he gave me were worse. After a days-on-end tirade about some demon in the public eye, I would find myself late at night plotting on paper this person's assassination, half convinced myself that the figure was demonic but mostly just to shut Jake down. It would have been amusing if I ever had gotten arrested for anything, and the apartment had gotten searched. I had at least a dozen or so plans drawn up, several against the reigning President of the United States. I could imagine conversations with the Federal Bureau of Investigations (FBI), something about those squirrels in their pristine suits and white socks that intrigued me.

I forbade Jake to enter my room. That was the only place I could take refuge. At first he didn't listen to me, but I enforced my will by beating him with a four-foot rod of bamboo whenever he stepped across the threshold, even if by accident or just to borrow a pencil. The last time I was on edge, having been awake for fifty-one hours. He walked in suddenly and turning toward him, I kicked him hard in the chest. It threw him backward onto the floor in the hall, knocking the wind out of him. I told him I would cut his throat if he ever came in there again.

The Bible is what made me quit Jake for a while. One day he came home and put it on the table with some other books he was carrying while he got himself some juice. "Holy Christ," I thought to myself, "what have you done to me?" His rhetoric began to spring from the Old and New Testaments as well as the Koran. In the past, Jake espoused traditional religion as vulnerable to hypocrisy and contradiction. He bemoaned the idea of somebody entrenching himself in a traditional relationship with God in which he was not formally raised because of the inevitable jackass that such a person makes out of himself by his enthusiasm and unfamiliarity with the tradition, or even the topic. In Jake's case, this was multiplied by his relentless, neurotic drive to hear his own voice, and by the terror he had of being wrong.

So, he didn't choose a religious tradition. He wasn't meeting God through the texts that he read. He read them because he liked the idea of dueling with preachers. Jake's meeting was with God directly, without a mediator. Though it took several months, the day came. I was sitting with him on the couch watching a report on the great marriage between personal economic interest and government, the Savings and Loan Scam (SALS) of the 'eighties. I expected to be up for another twenty-four hour tirade before I'd have to lock myself in my room. I sat sullenly awaiting it. There was a moment of silence as he looked down. "My God," I thought. "I've never seen him do that. If his mouth opens, I'll be blown out the window." And then he lifted his head again and looked at the screen. I saw his lips part, and all that came out was, "Thank God."

From that day forward it was "Thank God" for every God damn injustice he came across—murder, rape, anything. One day I heard him coming toward my room, and as he stepped up to my threshold, I drew the bamboo. He stopped in the hall, look me straight in the eye and said, "Thank God." All action was God's action. We were only expressions of God and so, in turn, were all our expressions. Even the expressions of murder and deceit were cause for thanking Him. I told Jake that this was a license to commit atrocities. He maintained in a low-pitched voice that his point was a prescription for ingesting the world as it acted upon one, not a prescription of action that one should take. His obsession with black continued with the exception that he stopped dyeing his hair, which, though he was only twenty-four, turned completely grey. So did the late-night vomiting episodes continue.

After that I just couldn't handle him anymore. I started to think of ways I could rig the apartment to take him out, and I just didn't think that thinking was healthy for either one of us. I moved out. That was all before he had his bout with heroin, the thing that finally mellowed him out. He was strung out for months and was so skinny that just looking at him made me sick. At the end of it all, though, you could finally have a normal conversation with him and not feel as if you were running a marathon in the back of a tractor trailer.

About the war, he felt it was good that oil prices would go up so that people would learn to conserve. He said he had gotten a perspective on this from his addiction. He also thought it was good that we would be getting rid of a lot of weapons we didn't need.

I had recommended Jake for a job with my agency. He worked in one of the Mental Health residences, mostly with people suffering from natural chemical imbalances as well as chemical dependencies. He described the people he worked with as "totally fucked." His job, as he described it, consisted of listening to people's problems (many of which he had), making up quarterly notes, and supplying residents with his cigarettes. Since starting the job, he had advanced from purchasing two packs a week to two cartons.

When he called, he wanted to know if I'd go to the bar with him.

"Are you out of your fucking mind," I said. "There's a God damn war on."

"What are you, going to enlist?"

"I'm busy, Jake. I'll talk to you later." I hung up.

I turned on the radio and listened to accounts of the war. Time was hardly significant to the listening. A twenty-four-hour broadcasting melee had ensued. It was all microphones and radio waves. I was very hungry, but I consistently neglected to buy food. I ate Oreo cookies from a tin that came to me at Christmas. I take bites out of Oreos. I don't eat out the middle. Sometimes up to three bites. Sometimes I eat them whole. I don't dip them in milk either. I don't drink milk. I like these cookies, but when I eat them, I feel as if they are rotting my teeth. Freud would say the anxiety was a feeling that these cookies were bad, that they sapped my strength. But I never bought real food. Freud considered himself an excellent swimmer but nearly drowned on several undocumented occasions. Freud was also a staunchly serious man but was known to hire prostitutes to tie him down and tickle his much suffered feet. I had wrapped my ear around a radio wave. Don't analyze me you little Wiener.

The radio reported everything. The radio had interviews with experts and diplomats and very important officials. It broadcast the President making speeches, saying the attacks were going well but don't be euphoric. The premise was a good premise. Kick their ass quickly, avoid casualties, end the war. But no "euphorica." There were many, many more things to blow up: poison and gas; airplanes; missiles pointed in every which way; and people. The people, where did they come from? And not a single one out of uniform. The feelings of euphoria, they came to me; but I fought them back, gnashing my teeth but without weeping. I wondered what the Persian Gulf looked like. I wondered whether you could go swimming, or whether you could fish.

As the radio reported, I looked out my window with my eyebrows pushed together, my forehead wrinkled like my father's, and my lips pursed. I looked to see whether they'd sanded this little road I live on. This little out of the way road, which was now a knotty sheet of ice. And, no, those bastards had not. I had called them twice. I had offered them doughnuts if they would come, but they had not. All the other roads were cleared and concrete. My road was ice. I called again. I asked them to come. They said that they would try. I said what does that mean, "try?" When someone tries, they begin to do something, and some aspect of the task, if they fail, inhibits them. What does it mean to say you'll try to go sand the only road in the city that needs to be sanded? Does that mean that every day I've called, and you said you'd try that you got in your sand truck and halfway over or a quarter way or just beyond your driveway you ran out of gas; that when you walked the two blocks for gas and got back in your truck, you had just enough time to get the truck back to the city yard; or did your "try" mean you did drive over here, but your friend Larry didn't put any sand in your truck, and that this was one try and your union dues say you are not allowed to try anything more than once a day; or did Larry forget to latch the hatch closed, and you wound up sanding a path all the way from the city yard to my pathetic little street with not one grain left to be thrown here? Did you resent me as a taxpayer for paying people like Larry too much money? Was your shovel defective? Did your truck of sand overheat and turn into glass? Were you having hallucinations all day that you were sanding my road? Did the doughnuts not appeal to you? What does it mean, "you'll try?" You've done it before. You're sure you can do it. Have you ever tried and failed before?

"We'll try," he would say, and hang up.

During the winter, the wood rotting in the base of my desk had only a faint smell of mold. I kept my radio on the desktop right in front of me, pushed back against the wall. It was the only thing in the room that shined with newness. Foreign-made, plastic, black, duel cassette players, it was the only thing worth grabbing in a fire. I changed the station. I listened to commercials. Really loud commercials shouting at me to shop around in loud, gravel-packed voices, to get the best prices and then "Come in and Save!" Each commercial yelled at me. They went beyond pleading to ordering me around. They wished to be my Dictator. My friend. My big brother. Their demands, they felt, were reasonable and would surely bring me happiness. When I turned them down, they got louder. They played roaring engines behind them and guitars screaming in sour notes, like mine. These commercials kept playing. Then the music came on, and I turned the station to another where the commercials played. I listened to the commercials. I called up the city yard. I told them I would try not to slip and hurt my back on the street outside. I told them I would try not to sue them for scores of money. I told them I'd hate to spend my winters on the French Riviera at their expense, that I'd eaten the doughnuts. Of course, there were no doughnuts to begin with.

CHAPTER 4

▼

A Little Mystery and War Over Dinner

In the Theater of Operation, Thursday was the day when the war commenced, but their time was ahead of ours, so it was Wednesday to us. Our Thursday was the day after everything began. I was with a friend that night, and I directed him to drive down a small narrow street. As we came toward the end, a car turned onto it from the other direction and stopped in front of us. We tried to arrange a maneuver that would allow us to get by, but the car seemed unwilling to move over; it simply stood in front of us. I became very angry. I thought about getting out of the car and asking the problem. I remembered news reports of freaks who shot people over things like this or got into fights. And I didn't have a gun. I stayed in the car. My friend got angry.

"Fucker," he screamed. "Fucker, Fucker, Fucker!" He put his car halfway on to the snow bank and drove past the car in that way. The man in the other car was yelling at us through his closed window. He was gesturing for us to stop. As if we were going to let him delay us longer. I found out later we had gone the wrong way down a one-way street. That's hardly unusual in this city.

We were in a dinner-serving pub, there to dine. It was a famous old Irish place. It had been used to make movies, used to make mayors. It had the old Irish charm and that was included in the price tag. We sat in "no-smoking" and thought of the war. The service was horrendous. If you're going to make a person wait to order, you better damn well get his drink fast. No such luck. I stewed. I got up and waved my arms. I was anxious. We ordered drinks. They came. We drank them. The service was terrible. I got up and found her, the waitress. I ordered another pint. The war was on television in the front room. We were in the back, in the corner. I was nervous. I'd been eating cookies and chocolate all day. I listened to National Public Radio (NPR). There was a window near our table with an etching, a map of the Pond that I ran around. I ran around it nearly every day—sometimes until I threw up. I was trying to explain something about the Pond. The raining over the snow and the mist. I described it all with the use of that map in the window. For the most part I used the map to explain the position of the tree and the island.

"Where is the island?" said my friend.

"The island is here." I used my knife as a pointer so as not to obstruct my friend's view. I explained the position of the mist, its movement and the visibility it permitted and controlled. "The dimensions were indefinable," I said. The waitress had still not brought my last pint, and I was anxious.

"How far out is the tree?" my friend asked.

"About a hundred yards."

"The fog wasn't that thick then?"

"No. It was thick. Like a solid. A gas, but like a solid. It was very thick."

"Then how could you see the island?

"That's what I'm trying to tell you. It was different somehow over the water."

"You said you saw the water?"

"Yes. It was incredible."

"What happened to the ice? Where was the ice?"

"I told you. Under the water."

"That doesn't make any sense. Doesn't ice float?"

"That's exactly what I'm telling you! It was exceptional! It was a fucking supernatural experience! Take my word for it. You've never seen anything like that before! Imagine it!"

"What are you saying? That you had a supernatural experience, or that it just seemed that way?"

"I'm saying you have to open your ears and eyes and your imagination a little bit and you'll get it. The fucking ducks got it; why can't you?"

"I don't know why you give a shit why I get it or not!"

I couldn't answer him. I didn't know why I did either. I was very angry at the waitress. When she finally brought our beer, she told us about Israel. She had a son in boot camp and another my age. I didn't know why she told us that. She said they were bombing Israel. What kind of silly brat would do that? As she gave us the check, she said she hoped we didn't have to go. Maybe that's why she told us. The Irish meatball sandwich gave me indigestion. There were a lot of people dying all of a sudden. A lot. Everyone was wondering how many, but by the time we would all find out the numbers, no one would give a shit.

The day before the Wednesday of the mist, the Tuesday, was Martin Luther King's actual birthday, to be observed the following Monday. They played a speech on the radio. He said in the speech that he would not want to be remembered for his Nobel Peace Prize, nor for his academic degrees. He said he wanted his eulogist to be able to say that Martin Luther King, Jr. tried to feed the hungry; that he tried to clothe the naked; to comfort the grieving; that he tried to visit those who were imprisoned; to give shelter to those who were homeless. They say he knew that his being murdered was inevitable. That's the way to go to war.

CHAPTER 5

▼

A little respect, please

What is a "sortie?" Everyone on the news reported the number of sorties flown on whatever day. I had never heard of this word. I suppose it referred to a combat air mission since I never heard them mention it in conjunction with anything else. The Friday after the Wednesday of the mist was the first time I remember hearing that word. The following terms were new to me: sortie, Republican Guard, collateral damage, fighter planes prefixed with F with a particular number following it. Friday as I ran, I considered this problem of people not initiated to the "run on the right side of the road" school of thought. I could call to them in advance in a very authoritative voice: "Move to the Right." Many people would listen to me. I would question, though, my presumption in that role. I shouldn't have to do that. Then this guy that I could hear trailing me for the last half mile gradually came up even with me. He started running next to me. He looked like Wade Boggs, but what would he be doing here in the winter? I didn't want to slow down because that would release some of the pressure I was putting on my body. Then he started talking to me. How can somebody be so flagrantly uncomfortable with silence? He talked about the weather or something, running on the ice. It was kind of difficult. I said it was better than running on sand. He agreed and said that the streets too were quite hazardous. It was bad enough that he lingered on next to me even momentarily, but I was offended to have my meditation assaulted in this way. I let the conversation fall like a dead cannonball. He moved on. He did run around again, but I resented him anyway.

When I stopped running, I imagined the situation of running with staunch fortitude on the right, not budging under any circumstance. And that perhaps a guy is running on the left, and he does not move. There is a near collision, and this man yells at me, perhaps he curses me, and I yell at him. Perhaps his steroids are taking effect on him now, and he turns to engage in confrontation. I would accept. We would talk. I would ask him whether he felt my position was unreasonable. He would say something, but ultimately agree that it was not. He'd then accuse me of being hostile in my action and my tone. But I'd refer him to his own obscenities and lack of foresight. Then I would tell him that I felt justified in my action but apologized in the event that I'd offended him. I would extend my hand; he would take it. Perhaps, though, this would not settle the issue for him, perhaps he would take this opportunity to strike me. I would thrust the heel of my foot into his privates, and then I would use my grip on his hand to pull his arm forward, exposing his right midsection to attack, and I would strike him in the ribs with the leading knuckle on my left hand. Then I would run so as not to prolong the confrontation. I wondered whether the right-side-of-the road regulation was worth it. I was trying to preserve a way of life. It made me very angry.

The third day, a Friday, it was of great concern to me that the start of the U.S. casualties had occurred. An F something was shot down by antiaircraft guns and the pilot was killed. What disturbed me was that that pilot could have been me, and, too, that I'd be irritated as hell if my life ended at that moment in that way. I wondered whether that pilot had reconciled himself to this beforehand, or during, or after. That military commercial came to mind. "Be all that you can be..." For this guy, that was dead. I continued to be anxious throughout the day. I remember urinating a lot.

As I peered out the window, I saw the old woman who lived around the block. I wasn't sure, but I thought I knew the house. She didn't live on my street, but she sometimes wandered down here looking for home. She got confused. These houses all look the same. I understood what she felt. I had often thought when walking home through the cold, especially from the bar, "Why can't I just walk into one of these houses to sleep? They all look the same. They look just like the house I live in. And yet they are warm and convenient. Don't we all strive for convenience? Isn't that us? Isn't that our mantra?" I would ask and wonder. I believe she may have been thinking this, walking onto my street. "Why," she would think, "does it matter what home I walk in. So what if it isn't my own? Won't the people feed me? Won't their house keep me warm? Won't their children make me smile? Won't they listen to my stories, over and over, of the things I saw happen? Isn't that what they do with us, the old people? It is so cold in this city. This street is all ice. I could die on this street. I could slip and die, so I must walk slowly. I don't even remember why I came out here. And I don't know that it matters, now that I'm heading back indoors. But where is my home? They always seem to hide it on me. As if they don't want me." I wanted to call her Martha, but I didn't know her name. I wanted to talk with her, to tell her not to walk on this street, to tell her she was risking her life, though that, I felt sure, she already knew.

I shot darts in my room to improve my eye for accuracy. On this Friday, as I shot, the wrist I had injured the previous Sunday while shoveling snow was stiff. It pained me to shoot. It was useful to develop accuracy with the deficit of pain. Perhaps I'd walk into a bar someday with a sprained wrist and challenge somebody to a game. They'd insist on a money game. They'd threaten me. I'd accept to avoid conflict. Then my lesson would be well learned because I'd kick that person's ass in the game and come out that much richer. They say that Jesse James was a master dart player. I wondered whether his opponents were just afraid to beat him.

Reports began to come in that Americans should be on alert for terrorist attacks. Most likely targets would be airports, especially international airports, like Logan nearby and large spectator events like professional sports contests, most notably the upcoming Super Bowl, "Showdown in Miami."

I sat in my room eating Oreo cookies late into the night. I seriously considered going shopping. There were many things I could eat, but if I could remain content with Oreos, maybe I should just go on eating them. Maybe I should buy food anyway, give it to someone who is starving, and then continue eating Oreos. I wasn't certain how this affected my teeth, though, and I brushed regularly. That was my biggest fear, losing my teeth. In a fight I'd be as much interested in protecting my teeth as my nuts. Freud is snickering and dying to talk about that but a dead man is easy to ignore.

While running earlier that day, I had thought primarily of the prospect of my involvement in the war as a soldier. How would I handle the inevitability of a premature death. They made the soldiers write wills before they were shipped out. Mine would require that a plaque of steel be sewn into the skin of my chest. The plaque would say, "This person has been confirmed "Dead" by the State Department. Please do not disturb, his last thought being, "I'm exhausted." This would be for anybody stumbling upon my ancient bones someday. I would consider myself dead if I entered into the military. I would consider it suicide. The Austrian Professor, Freud, had similar plaques sown on to his feet, one to each which both read the same: "This dog is dead tired."

About mid-afternoon, I walked off my little unsanded street, or slid off it anyway, to the more significant street with the hill and on down to an even more significant street that runs from the train station on up to the most significant street, Centre Street. I was going to my car. Hordes of young kids were walking in the street, kids no older than fourteen. A car, a woman driving, tried to inch through them. They walked around the car, their crowd taking its shape. They hit the car; they yelled out, "Bitch" and as she drove away, they threw snow and ice, missing. As I walked by them, they didn't seem to notice me. They made a lot of noise. They spit and pushed each other. What is it that they were doing? Our youth, who was doing this to our youth? I wondered whether they'd heard the reports. Did they think about the war? Did they know there was anything going on? That evening I dashed out a letter to the Globe's editor. It read:

To All Parents:

Your children are undisciplined, unprincipled, uneducated, and impolite and so are many of you. Straighten up, and don't spare the rod!

I was late. I had to pick a kid up at the bus stop. It was a favor I was doing for him, Friday being my day off. He was coming back to the shelter from a correctional facility. He called the shelter Wednesday and asked me if I'd pick him up. I didn't want to pick him up. It was my day off. That's why he asked me. It was policy for staff not to pick kids up as a service of the shelter. I didn't even like this kid. He was kind of a jerk. But he'd asked for me specifically and there was some sense that I should do it, because you have to build a relationship with these kids, and to say "no" to them when they are in need didn't do much in that direction. But this kid knew I was supposed to build a relationship with him, and he knew I had the day off. He knew I'd be hard pressed to say "no" to him in the end. I asked if he could get anyone else. He was in jail for assaulting his brother, who was a teller for the Bank of New England. He wanted the brother to help him figure out a way he could steal money and get away with it. The brother refused. This kid wasn't normally violent, but I guess he had a lot of pent-up anger for his brother. The kid went into a park, drinking with his friends, and came out with fire on his mind. He kicked in the door of his brother's apartment and pounced on him in bed.

"What about your father?" I asked him. His father had been a somewhat stabilizing influence and had at odd times given the kid money when he needed it.

"He's gonna be in court."

"Oh," I said.

"Don't you want to know why?"

"Not really."

"He's being arraigned."

"Okay. What time do you want me to pick you up?"

"Don't you want to know why?"

"Why you want me to pick you up?"

"No. My dad."

"You just said he can't pick you up," I was trying to throw him off the trail.

"Yeah, because he beat up my brother."

"Swell. I'll see you Friday. What time?"

"Five o'clock."

"Swell."

This kid's name was Web. If you called him anything different from Web you were in danger of being attacked. His father learned that one day while he was trying to force Web to get his hair cut and called him his given name of "Wilhem." For a reason he refused to explain to me, the boy hated the name, and he tried to enforce his preferences.

At the bus station he jumped in my car and said, "What the fuck's up?"

"Hey, don't talk to me like that," I yelled at him. "I'm not a punk, and I don't like being talked to like that."

"Are you calling me a punk?"

I slammed on the brakes and stopped in the middle of traffic. "Web, I don't mind giving you a ride, but you can leave your attitude here."

"I'm not copping an attitude, man," he said more calmly. "I just want to know if you're calling me a punk or not. Dag, I just want to know."

I started driving again. I didn't like doing this shock stuff, but you had to let Web know you weren't taking any of his shit. "You make your choices is all I'm saying, Web. You make your choices and they make you. That's all I'm saying."

"What the fuck does that mean?"

"It means if you talk like a punk than you are a punk! Figure it out, God damn it. I'm not your God damn wet nurse."

"All right. Chill out. I didn't mean to start nothing with you."

"You did too! You know God damn well you did. I don't like being played, Web. I don't like that shit at all. Am I helping you out, here? Or are you just playing me?"

"You're copping the attitude, man. Yo, why you gotta cop an attitude?"

"Answer my God damn question." I slammed on the brakes again, and we skidded a little."

"Yo, watch it!"

"Answer my God damn question! Are you playin' me now? I don't like being played. I'll help you, God damn it, but I don't like being played!" Cars were honking their horns. We were in an intersection.

"Would you just drive," said Web. "I'm not playin' you. Dag!"

We sat there for a moment with the sound of traffic and rain. The light changed. As the cars came at us I turned toward the road and started driving. "I just like to know," I said.

I wasn't really angry with him. I remember that. I just wanted him to hear what I was saying. I had to say it in the manner he was used to. Sometimes you had to put a gun to these kids' heads just to get them to wipe their noses. I dropped Web off at the shelter. They knew he was coming. I'd set everything up when he first called. I didn't go in then. I just dropped him off. He said, "Thanks." Not all of them would.

In my car I turned on the radio to monitor the goings on. My hands were bitter cold and stung as I touched the wheel and the stick shift. The price of oil was jumping all over the place. Reports rode a wave of being very positive, "We are very optimistic, everything is going very well…" to "There is another air raid here in Tel Aviv…We have seen as yet no evidence of Scud missiles, but the government is telling people to keep their gas masks on…We, for the time being, will show restraint but there has been no greater victim in this conflict than Israel, aside from Kuwait itself…" I went to a full service gas station, many here offer nothing but full service. Gas was the cheapest I'd seen it in some time. I asked him to fill it. I asked if he could check the air in my tires. He said he didn't have a gauge. Nor could he clean my windshield because the water for that had solidified and when he tried to get the rubber thing out the handle had broken. I paid for the gas. How could anyone feel anything but sympathy for the oil companies? Those poor crummy bastards.

I drove around with a full tank and empty pockets, listening to the radio. There were vehicles everywhere. In some places people walked through the streets with no regard for traffic signals. What kind of example were these people setting for their children? What was all this chaos? With a full tank of gas I could drive for a long time without needing any money. My vehicle was a compact, five-gear sedan. It didn't have a lot of power, but I could manipulate it with the shift, and its size made it easy to weave in and out of traffic. It occurred to me that if ground forces were engaged there would probably be much fighting on urban battlegrounds. Now, that's a picture of chaos. It would be good then to know how to drive quickly through the streets, to provide maximum retreat and attack capability, and to be able to maneuver with absolute precision around and through obstacles, in preparation for bomb craters or debris, or just to avoid being an easy target. I was downshifting to third in preparation to stop for a yellow light when this thought dawned on me. I quickly threw it into second and gunned it through a barrage of perpendicular UPE's, Urban Practice Enemies. I was soon up to fifty, and I nearly felt pity for those I sped past. Some had ten times the horsepower but not the honed awareness. I fastened my lap belt and realized that I had to go to the bathroom. If this weren't a practice run, I might have just stopped the car and taken a leak. This would contribute to maximum fuel efficiency due to the discard of excess weight and also to MOMS, Maximum Operator's Mental State, because a loaded bladder under pressure is damn distracting. I began to resent the vehicles in front of me because they seemed to be slow and useless. In a combat situation, I would destroy them. At a red light a policeman drove past on the intersecting street. I wondered whether that rigid, insensitive, blue-necked crew cut would understand my reasoning. Certainly, I was testing my readiness for something military and steadfastly American. It would be illegal for him to give me a ticket. He might possibly even show me a few things. But perhaps he was one of those unenlightened policemen. Perhaps he was one of those who never washed his hands and who ate his lunch of tuna fish and sardine sandwiches in his squad car, all the while farting and picking his teeth with a switchblade. Is this the kind of man who would understand terms like "The New World Order?" Would I have to go to court on my meager salary to fight the atrocity of a moving violation issued in the midst of combat training? Would I have to regard these things with any sort of serious attitude? Of course I would, because a serious attitude is an aspect of the warrior's preparation. I determined efficiently that this would not be in the best interest of me or the Coalition forces, or any of the people that would be caught in the massive traffic jam caused by this self-indulgent cop in pulling me over.

I settled back into my own little anonymous driver's seat, with the windows shut in my own private atmosphere. I turned the tiny, plastic control of the radio all the way up with my two fingers. I couldn't even hear the sounds of the traffic around me. I had to look at them to know they were there. A talk show came on. There are many talk-radio shows in my city. One year or so before the war, I set out to build up a tolerance to these shows. I wished to join in the engaging conversation of my fellow citizens. I wished to reach out via the airwaves to my brethren. I wished for them to reach me. I saw myself holding the phone up to my ear with my shoulder, even though I don't like that. It can give you a sore neck. It can make your shoulder muscles tight. But you have to be on hold for a while, and you can't put the phone down, because you have to listen to the show through the phone because of the two second delay that's broadcast. But I sit there with the crunched up shoulder, because I have something to say. I want to be heard. I thought that maybe someday I would have this extraordinary conversation on the radio with one of those hosts. One of those conversations that really takes people listening into a deep and honest journey into themselves and into the makeup of what being a Human Being in this world is all about. Maybe some of them are sitting at home, sipping their Nescafé decaf without Sweet and Low, because somebody forgot to pick it up when they went shopping. They didn't make a list, but they got those special cookies you like, and you love them anyway. Maybe some of those folks with the furry socks on their feet, to keep them warm, would pause at the bottom of the bowl to finally wipe that soup off their chins. Some maybe start weeping a bit, and maybe the host of the show starts weeping too, right on the air. And maybe I start weeping on the phone and this weeping fills the airwaves. I lean forward and hold the phone with my right hand, because I don't want to drop it.

Then maybe some late night I'm in a coffee shop eating in a counter near the register. Maybe I'm reflecting on things, the world going round. And I overhear a guy talking as he pays his bill. I recognize his voice: he's the talk show host. I tell him who I am, and we start talking again about humanity or something. Maybe we start weeping again, though we're men, and we know the establishment doesn't like that, but we're comfortable enough with our masculinity to weep in public. We shake hands for real. Not like we're playing softball on Sunday, but like we're doing solo treks through the Congo, and our paths just happened to cross, and it's time to head separately back into the jungle alone. He tells me to call in anytime. We say goodbye. Then he does a whole show on men weeping in public.

So at that moment I was still trying to work up my tolerance for these shows, because they often make my stomach churn. My ears start ringing and pounding as though someone were hitting them with led pipes. My nose gets runny. I get bad gas, and my underarms sweat erratically.

The caller said, "I didn't have a gun, I'd be dead. These guys walk into my store. They had their guns out when they come in. Lucky I seen it."

"What'd you do?"

"I didn't ask no questions. I was right by the counter. Pulled it out and let go."

"You keep the gun under your counter?"

"I used to. I keep that thing on my hip now. People come in they know right off I ain't [*Bleep*] round. Oh, excuse me."

"Please, watch your language. We can't have that on the air. It offends people. You know this whole issue of self-defense and handguns, it seems to me we'd all want to live in a place where we don't feel threatened, where we don't feel the need to carry a handgun. The fact is that we don't, and I don't think we ever will. Man preys on man. It's always been that way. It seems to me that all we can try to do is contain it as much as possible. What do you think, Jan, you're on the air."

"Hello?"

"Yes. Go ahead. You're on the air."

"Am I on?"

"Yes, go ahead."

"Oh, sorry."

"That's okay. You have something to tell us?"

"Yes. I just want to say that if there weren't any guns then it wouldn't be so easy to kill people, and like when these gangs are holding up liquor stores, it wouldn't be so easy to kill the people, and maybe they'd still hurt them or something, but the only reason they kill them is because that's the easy, fastest way to make sure they don't give 'em any trouble. You know what I mean? If there weren't guns to begin with, it wouldn't be so bad."

"So, you're saying we should just stop making guns altogether, is that it?"

"Yeah and, you know, get rid of the ones we already have and all."

"Well, how do you propose to do this, Jan? I mean you have whole industries, a whole section of the economy, based on the manufacture of guns. You have millions of guns already manufactured dating back to the Revolution. How are you just going to clean all that up?"

"Well, I don't know I mean…"

"I mean it's nice to think about, but how are you going to do that? If we could just say to everyone, 'Don't hurt other people,' and everyone listened, that would be nice, but…I mean really, if I had wings I could fly. Gun control's our topic. Are we killing each other because of them, or is gun control a pipe dream in the annals of liberal folklore? More of your calls after these messages."

A commercial came on for a medical alert bracelet alarm. An elderly woman was scared to death of falling and not being able to get help, so scared in fact that her doctor noticed a rise in her blood pressure. Her doctor became immediately concerned and decided he'd better investigate. He had time to do things like this since his divorce. Before, he was always having to rush home to do this or that thing that his wife couldn't be bothered with. His wife was an insensitive fiend, married him for his advanced degree, and was intent on raping him of his fortune. But he had no fortune because it all went back into the practice, compensating for the mass of Medicare patients whose claims the government had stopped payment on, elderly patients like Mary. He asked Mary whether anything had been bothering her, or whether there had been any changes in her diet. "No," she said. But he knew she didn't have all her faculties so he asked, "Are ya' sure?" There was one thing she had on her mind, and she told him. God! What a relief that was for her—desperate, dilapidated soul that she was. She feared her next step might rifle her to the Earth and that no one on this vast planet would hear her cries, if she could indeed make them. He suggested this Medic Alert alarm bracelet, saying it was sound peace of mind at a nice price.

"We're back. The issue is gun control. Should we take the great equalizer out of the hands of honest citizens, or is this whole issue a waste of the taxpayers' money. Frank, how do the Southies feel?"

"Hello."

"You're on Frank."

"Am I on."

"Yes, go ahead please."

So, including this commercial, I listened to a talk radio show for a good ten minutes.

I kept driving to get away from that talk-radio show, and I put on the news station again. I was getting to know the names of the news people. I began to feel this intimacy with them. I used to listen to the newscasters as if they were just calling out the news to whatever ears, but now I got this feeling that these people knew I was personally concerned, so they spoke to me and remained on the air as my hosts, giving me all they could get me. They had the names of normal people and very nice voices. Israel had been bombed again, they said. The President was really mad but urged them to restrain themselves. The President issued further warnings against euphoria. Israel said they would, for now, not retaliate, but that they had the capability and resources to attack with devastating swiftness and force. I wasn't having any doubts about that. There were protests going on in the city. One, downtown, had stopped rush-hour traffic yesterday. Then a big spontaneous parade of protesters walked down Commonwealth Avenue while some protesters protesting those protesters gathered on the sidewalks, not unlike a lava flow through water. Yellow ribbons were going up in different areas of town. The news flooded my car like water when you drive off a bridge and land in a lake. I think I went to the store, some store for something. When I got home I ran into my room and flipped on the radio because they had an expert talking about the principal weapons being used. Tomahawks were our missiles that got their targets programmed into them, and searched the ground until they found them and blew them up. Patriots were self-guiding missiles which were used to take out incoming missiles. Scud missiles, which were theirs, or his, weren't smart at all, and their accuracy depended on good guesstimation. "I think it's *that* way," I imagined them saying. Carpet bombing was laying a carpet of bombs, which seemed as though it should be a deciding tactic, but I wasn't a member of the cult of "euphorica" so I kept that thought to myself. I didn't hear everything the expert said because some cretins were doing construction in the apartment above me and wiping out my radio signal with their tools.

I talked to my friend on the phone. He said he was looking for soap operas this day when the President broke in. He said, "We must be realistic. There will be losses. There will be obstacles along the way. And war is never cheap or easy." All my athletic coaches used to say, "You get what you put into it." Then "The Young and the Restless" came on. They were talking this day about the Ground War. This will be Part II of the war. Part I continued as the quest for air superiority. There were 450,000 people in the ground forces of this country in the Saudi Arabian desert. I used to associate the word Arabian with stallions. They say that it is the Ground Forces that will ultimately have to move in and win the war. Their leader seemed bent on inflicting casualties, and he had a lot of his own people that he was willing to throw at our guys to inflict those "heavy casualties" everybody was talking about. The average age over there was twenty-one or twenty-two. People were still hoping the air strikes would take most of them out. We had some great shit as far as bombs went. We had this bomber that used a laser beam from the plane to "paint" the target with a bright spot of light. The weapons officer in the plane used a hand control to keep the laser dot centered on the target, which he viewed on a TV monitor just like the one my friend watched "The Young and the Restless" on, as the pilot guided the plane toward it. Computerized devices automatically released the bomb at the proper time. A sighting telescope in the nose of the bomb would see the laser dot on the target, and a computerized steering system guided the bomb, which exploded upon hitting the target. The plane then banked away safely out of range of anti-aircraft defenses.

I think I would want to be the weapons officer on that kind of plane. That's the way I play darts. I send out this invisible laser through my eyes at the bull's eye. Then I make this telepathic connection with the dart, and I synchronize the sights. I tell the dart where to hit but only by my own singular concentration on the target. That's why it's important to use the same darts all the time. It's easier to make that communication, and I am not yet an aficionado. My success is in a constant state of flux. But if I were to add actual lasers to my game, I most certainly would be known as "Hombre de Ojo del Toro," or man of the bull's eye.

CHAPTER 6

▼

You Don't Want to Know

On Saturday morning my clock radio woke me up with a news conference. I was lying under fourteen pounds of covers listening as if my ears were the only part of me awake. There seemed to be no insulation in my room. I felt, with just my face, the chill in the air. I turned on my heater and put some socks on underneath the covers. I turned the big radio on and hit the off button of the alarm. Each morning brings the struggle for a new day of sobriety. I threw darts to force my attention, but my attention still rested. All I could hear was the radio. I walked into the kitchen. As I prepared my coffee in the Automatic Maker, I flipped on the radio there. The press conference wasn't saying anything that hadn't been reported. It was confirming reports. I enjoyed this confirming of reports; it made things concrete. Statements weren't prefaced with "It has been said" or modifiers like that. The State Department was making reports official. Air strikes were going extremely well, and everyone was very happy with the progress of the air campaign. Marines on a border had come under howitzer fire, but the Air Force was said to have blasted those artillery positions. My concept of carpet bombing was having a critical struggle with itself. Wouldn't carpet bombing entail complete destruction? Everyone was pleased to hear that Coalition forces were taking extreme precautions to ensure against unnecessary civilian casualties. I wondered what I would do if somebody were bombing my city and my house. I couldn't call the police or my dentist or anybody. I'd have to wait, in my room or somewhere. I'd have to wait for the bombing to stop, assume that somebody somewhere was doing some kind of thing about it. There were no reports from the other side, save from the ones issued by their government. I guess I would just wait until the bombing stopped one way or the other. The first attack hit only eleven of the Opposition's planes. This news didn't lend itself in a positive way to the view of air superiority as an objective and a priority. There was a continued effort on the part of the President to dampen the euphoria. A

Senator said that we had so damaged their nuclear capability as to render it virtually nonexistent. Further speculation came from Congresspersons that there was virtually no resistance to the raids, saying that they were perhaps saving their planes for another day. Eight more Opposition planes went down in dogfights yesterday. Saturday was a big news day. The television was on. The dust stood upright on the screen like the terra cotta warriors of Xi'an and dulled the glow of reporters' faces over the backdrop of warplanes and explosions and empty desert. They pointed to the horizon and told of the opposition troops buried and waiting for the boys from Scranton, PA and Pawtucket, Rhode Island. I listened to the radio. I felt more information from the radio. It processed better. I had no maps in front of me. I had to rely on the description of the terrain. I was developing my conceptual capabilities, my understanding of terrain and geography, and of the cartographic points.

I found out that day that laser-guided bombs can be foiled if the target is covered by fog, clouds, or dust. It hadn't been a factor as yet though. I was further worried as the morning and my coffee progressed that the objectives of the initial attack hadn't been achieved yet. The President, or the Chairman of the Joint Chiefs of Staff, or the Secretary of War, said that these goals were to control the air by destroying the Opposition's warplanes and antiaircraft sites, to cripple the lines of communication from their leader to his own forces, to wipe out their offensive missiles and weapons of mass destruction, and to soften up their troops and tanks on the battlefield before the ground war began. The war had been going on for every second of every minute of every day for four days, and I found this lack of accomplishment quite disturbing. I looked out the window at my rutted, gnarly street of ice. I wondered whether those guys from the City Yard were training in the reserves that weekend.

The air outside was in the arctic teens. As I began my run, my left leg began to hurt. This was common, and it simply meant that I'd have something else to block out. I ran the several blocks and came upon that heavy road that skirts the Pond. There weren't any traffic lights near where I stood, none close enough for which I'd go out of my way. These were irritating moments. The cars poured in from one direction driving at nonsensical speeds around furious curves, barely maintaining their lanes. Then the pour would become a trickle. The trickle would be about to stop when an onslaught from the other direction would occur. This infuriated me, because it disrupted the initial preparations for my meditation, and I would have to stop and jog tentatively in place, or worse, jog tentatively in one direction or the other, all the while viewing each direction for a common break in this escapade to thwart my progress. I could fell a tree, I was thinking, I could have made myself a clear path, or blown a large hole in the pavement. I pinpointed the best position for such a thing. It was in the center of the longest straightaway near me, about one-sixteenth of a mile. I would have to wait though, and it then occurred to me that part of the warrior's preparation is patience. This then was an exercise.

Knotted ice still covered the path. It was also an exercise to maintain concentration on the terrain. I have weak ankles, and this is a focus on which I work diligently. I purposely dressed very heavily to engage a deep sweat. There were not many people around. The Pond had frozen over, rather clearly. My island with the tree drew my attention according to its way. Ducks huddled together on the ice. One week before, I had dropped shirts off at a Laundromat which also did dry cleaning. I walked in and this mass of half-bearded flesh directed his TV remote at the television in the back of the room. I stationed myself in front of him. He glanced at me briefly with his hard boiled egg-shaped eyes as he turned channels. There must have been four hundred channels on that TV. My car was double-parked, and I wanted to punch his chubby nose, but I didn't. I put the shirts on the counter and pushed them toward him. He looked at me reluctantly and put his remote down. He filled out the slip without a word. I pointed to blood on one of my collars. He asked whether I wanted them laundered. I wanted them to try the blood. "You're the cleaner man. Do what you do and do what you can." During my meditation I was considering this person who wore rubber gloves as he did the laundry that was brought to him. I wondered about pulling one of those gloves over his head. I wondered whether he'd resist at all or whether he'd just stand there and finally drop from suffocation. I wondered if I went in there shouting at him and pushing him around, would he listen to me when I ordered him into one of the dryers. Would he protest when I put twenty-five quarters into it? Would he destroy my clothes? I wondered whether he could change to specific channels out of sequence without looking. Did he know the television schedule for all four hundred channels or was he oblivious even to that? What kind of alarm would it cause him when I turned the dryer temperature all the way up? He held a constant, sad, moping frown that melted into his chubby cheeks around the edges. I imagined that you could stuff important small things, transistors or microchips, into those cheeks and use him as a smuggler. His expression was impenetrable. It must cause him great anxiety to have to smile. I wondered whether he took any psycho-tropic medication in order to relieve himself from these battles with smiling. It didn't seem that the man read, not even Judith Krantz. The Austrian Professor, S.F., enjoyed very much the <u>Tibetan Book of the Dead</u> in a most peculiar way. He liked to sit on it while eating lentils. The laundry man's greatest irony was that, although he operated his own Laundromat and spent all his time there, he constantly walked around in soiled underpants. Later that day when I went to go pick up my clothes. He wasn't there. A woman told me to check in the store on the corner. It was a store where I was once charged one U.S. dollar for one unpackaged disposable razor. They said they didn't have them by the pack. He wasn't in there. There was an eating counter there but he wasn't. I saw my shirts and waited another minute. I walked in behind the counter and took them. I left the money and the slip under the counter. All those lost socks that disappear in the laundry, this bastard was stuffing them into his cheeks.

When I got back from running, I peeled off the clothes I was wearing and hung them up. With the cold air in my room, I felt that much colder. I had stolen a newspaper from my neighbors. I didn't know my neighbors. They were new. I had seen one woman and heard two men. In the paper was a picture of our General in Charge. I began to look at it as I switched on the radio. Our General looked like an encompassing man. He had very short hair and a big head. His hands were big with big knuckles. It was very frustrating to think that this perception could be the suffering of illusion created by photographic perspective. He didn't look pleased to be answering questions. If our country were a small South American country where military coups take place, this is the guy who would be in charge of that, who would become the leader of our country. Our General wore a wedding band and a huge watch on his right wrist. In the picture he was pointing with his left hand. His look said relentless toleration. I had never seen anybody with piercing eyes before. Our General had piercing eyes. His forearms were very long. He could have been a heavyweight boxer in his youth. Those were good forearms to throw hooks with. He had some flab under his chin and around his neck like a bulldog. Our General was a veteran of Vietnam, and it was said that he got angry about the number of the Opposition's casualties. "If I have anything to say about it, we are never going to get into a body count exercise. At best it's nothing more than a wild estimate, and it's ridiculous to do that." He said that the campaign was right on schedule. Our General had very clean fingernails. I imagined that he was the kind of man who cleaned them three times a day in his tent with a four and a half inch folding Buck knife that he'd gotten for Father's Day from his daughter. I was sure that he shaved with a straight-edge razor. There was a man who ran around the Pond who looked a lot like our General. He wore a bright red suit. The red man never ran very fast, but his hands were always clenched, and one eye was always closed while the other sat wide open. He always wore a knit skullcap, but never any hand protection regardless of the weather. I wondered whether the red man thought of running on the snow as I did. I wondered if he thought it felt like sand. I wondered whether the General ran in the desert. How did he invoke his own meditations and what kind were they? I looked into the eyes of that picture and wondered whether he understood the warrior's preparation of patience. Did he see his having to face the press as an exercise? He was controlled, but was he patient? I was glad to see that he was in fatigues. He looked like a man at work.

There was incredible talk about Israel on the radio. They had been bombed again on Friday and seemed to be very angry. Great emphasis was placed on the need for Israeli restraint. It seems that nobody in the area liked Israel anyway, and their getting into it could have disrupted the alliance. In some self-declared neutral countries, there were larger Allies in support of the bombing by the Opposition. Further talk revealed the point that the Opposition's skies were black with Allied bombers and fighters ready to blow the crap out of anything they didn't immediately recognize. Also, that there wouldn't be any room for Israeli fighters.

On Friday the Allies lost eight aircraft; the crews from all of them were missing and presumed dead or captured. The General was said to have said that two thousand combat sorties had been flown each day and that they had been able to drop their ordinance eighty percent of the time. There was further assurance that the Allies were taking particular care not to hit civilian targets or religious sites. The General said that the Scud missile launchers were a priority target but since they were mobile they were difficult to locate. He said six had been destroyed and that twenty or so remained, although Pentagon officials indicated that the number may be more like forty-five or fifty. A Lieutenant General said that early reports that the Opposition's air force was largely taken out of action may have been overstated. The first attacks were said to have destroyed only eleven of the Opposition's airplanes, eight of those on the ground.

I have mentioned the cold in my apartment. I was trying not to use the heat because it costs money and I didn't have much. The sweat in my clothes got cold quickly so it was a rush to get them off. The cold still affected the sweat on my skin. At the beginning of winter, it was a distressing thing. But as time went on, I adapted and, in fact, became invigorated by the cold. I felt the arctic winds outside were a challenge to me when I ran, and the cold in my apartment was an extension of that challenge. As the weather progressed, I had adapted, and now by this Saturday I had grown to appreciate and utilize the cold. I was encouraged to walk around naked in the chill of my room and in my sweat. Sometimes, after I finished the run, I'd stand at the edge of the Pond and look through cracks in the ice at the water there. Heated up as I was, I'd imagine lying down, sliding in through the cracks and wrapping that coolness around me. This was my substitute, this naked wading in the cool air. Obviously, half a mile from my house, it would be lunacy to jump into a half frozen over pond. And, of course, with all of those people around, regardless of my true mental state, I would be arrested for idiocy, maybe thrown in jail. So I settled for the air.

Reports began to come in about curbs imposed on press coverage. The Opposition had ordered all journalists out of their country. One report said that it was reported that the CIA and the Army had gotten secret authorization for a propaganda campaign that would assault the confidence of Iraqi troops and civilians. The announcement, though, of a secret propaganda campaign made me suspect that the announcement itself could be part of a propaganda campaign. No one could tell who the source was, though. Perhaps knowing that everything they said was suspect, the CIA decided to tell the truth about everything, knowing no one would believe it. Almost all the information coming to the press had come from U.S. Military officers. A very big Godfather type journalist was on, and he said that the government had an absolute control of information, and that the public wouldn't know the reliability of that information until sometime much further down the road. The expert said, because it was an all air war, reporters would have to remain dependent on the briefing officers, and that once the ground war started, it would be difficult to control information. He said that he assumed the government was telling the truth because if they didn't, it would completely destroy the confidence of the reporters and everything would fall all to hell. In the last war, he said, the government gave out so much erroneous information that the five o'clock briefings were referred to as the "five o'clock follies."

I remember way off in the distance, in this prototype suburban town on Long Island, standing in the yard on a sunny spring day. My Dad was doing something in the yard. I was behind him, planting a hedge. I wasn't more than five or six. That was during the last war. I wasn't really aware at that time that there was a war, so I don't know where this question came from. I asked him where the war was. I just asked him that, like "Where do babies come from?" I remember being really surprised when he answered me because his answer confirmed that there was a war. I didn't expect that at all. His answer was, "The war is everywhere." As if to say, "Babies grow inside the mommy's womb, and pop out her vagina." I looked around me quickly, in the front yard and out in the street. I asked him what he meant by that. I didn't see any soldiers. I didn't see anybody anywhere. "The war is everywhere," he said again. I was starting to see it. War happens in the mind first, then on the battlefield. If America was at war, then the war must first have been living in our minds. It was wherever American minds were.

I called my friends as the radio continued the reporting. I set it up that Tasha and I would meet Jake over at his place. I was feeling very on edge, and I didn't think I should be alone.

Tasha had a cat which I once took care of for a couple of weeks. The cat, whose name I have forgotten the way you forget the name of a bad stomach vermin, had a variety of nightly activities which began with insisting that it crawl under my blankets with me. That seemed okay, a warm furry cat in the bed. At one it began, possessed fits of running around the room jumping off the walls, as though it were being chased by spirits. What really put Tasha in debt to me, however, was when this domesticated varmint would sit in its litter box and throw all the litter, paw-full by paw-full, against the wall and onto the floor. It was not a sound that could put you to sleep.

Once, I sat with Tasha in a car as she sped up to frighten a pedestrian who had perniciously wandered into the street against the light. "I hate people who don't follow the rules," she said. She could also have outbreaks of extreme sensitivity. When she spoke, it seemed by coincidence, much of what she said would come out in rhyme. I don't mean the "see you later alligator" type either, it was uncommon and often seemed that Tasha was speaking in couplets too original for me to reproduce. Upon waking each morning, she would have an unfiltered Lucky Strike and a cappuccino. She preferred to start the day with a good strong buzz. Tasha cut her own hair and rode a bicycle in winter. She never said a word without its dose of emotion. She never uttered things. When she was too tired to say it properly, she'd not speak with words anyway. You'd have to interpret her eyes if you wanted anything. You'd have to interpret the sway of her hair. It was only at these times that the cut of her hair seemed to have purpose. She only wrote her thoughts down if they were going too fast for her to speak them. She'd write the surplus down and say what she had written at the end. Then she'd light the paper on fire with the end of a cigarette sitting in her mouth and throw it in the ash tray. Sometimes, if it were available, she'd pour wine on the flames.

One time, Tasha brought me home to her father's house. It was a cold afternoon and we sat around a table in a room heated by a pot belly stove, drinking scotch whisky. If you wanted to get a word into her father, you had to jump on that instant when he was drawing breath. You had to speak sharply with volume. He had a certain motion with his eyes which indicated he was registering what you were saying; or as he would put it, what you were *trying* to say. If he didn't make that motion then it was as though you hadn't spoken. He riveted it into me that he was a poet, that he had no purpose that was not subordinate to his poetry. That he ate, for example, was only so that he could live and create. His daughter, he said unabashedly, was an accident of lust but also the element of nature in his life, which was itself one long poem. To him, Tasha represented God's will. Tasha was not pleased at all by this. She was adept at making him shut his lips to listen, though he didn't heed her. She was angry that he maintained barriers like poetry and God between herself and him. He said, almost regretfully, that he was a poet first and then her father.

"What about obligations to yourself?" I parried.

He looked at me as if to pierce my skull. "I have no obligations to myself but to keep fed and healthy, so that I may fulfill the task of humanity. You're not a poet and neither is hardly anyone that you know, and it is up to men like myself to make up for you. I am a Knight who rides the four chambers of the heart, whose atmosphere is the soul which is my breath." He jumped up and ran over to the door, thrusting it open, letting in the cold. He let out a gigantic breath which was fully visible in the cold. Pointing to it and darting his look to me he said, "Do you see that, boy? In that breath lies the history of all our people, our species, of all time and all space." The breath he had used to make his point had quickly dissipated but was replenished by that used to speak his words.

Tasha's father slammed the door as he walked toward the table without looking back and sat down, again leering at me, challenging me to speak. I could think of nothing to say, but feeling the pressure to speak, that I was required to speak, I opened my mouth.

"Don't speak trash," he jumped on me. "You don't see. You're a babe. You walk around and see civilization before you, as if it meant something. People see structure, their lives as a structure moving from point A to point B on to the end of the alphabet which for most people like yourself is D. I could travel the scope of that alphabet, A to Z, bouncing on my head. But I am a poet and to do so would be blasphemy. For me, all that lies ahead is wilderness. It is not the incidental spots of trees encountered in even the most mundane life, like the parks in cities, but absolute virgin wilderness. I move without a compass, without my bearing, equipped with only the desire to move in a direction altered from which I came. I look out over a street or the city with a victim like you knowing what you see, wondering how you don't witness what I do, the trees, the snakes. I wonder how it is you stumble around these conveniently invisible hazards and escape walking into quicksand or into the mouth of a tiger. Sometimes I see that victims like yourself are part of the structure of that wilderness."

"Don't let him scare you," said Tasha. "He's as crazy as you think. Pay no attention to his poetry madness. He speaks more than he writes, but either one is harmless."

Again I was at a loss. "I think he's quite interesting," I said, adopting her manner. He ignored both of us as we spoke, and he poured whiskey. He smoked a dry Virginia leaf tobacco which he rolled flawlessly with one hand. The other hand moved around wildly in the air while he spoke, as if he were making a show of it but without saying any words whose meaning directed your attention. Tasha, too, smoked them while we were there. She rolled them expertly herself, rolled a few for me.

"He's full of bullshit," Tasha continued. Then to her father, "You hear that? You're a barrel down the slope from where the bulls shit!"

He darted his eyes at her when she slapped him on the shoulder. Then he darted them at me. "Have you ever seen a bull shit?" he said drawing heavily on his cigarette, then after holding it a moment, "It's beautiful!"

Tasha began, "He talks until his tongue falls off. It's forever falling off all day. Eventually his head falls off and wonders how he got this way."

Tasha's father quickly leaned across the table as he pulled his right sleeve up to his elbow. He pounded on the inside of his forearm and said to me, "Feel that." I did. "That's a farmer's arm. That comes from working the tools, wrestling the cattle. That's a farmer's arm, as hard as any lead pipe. I can walk around anywhere I like, and the hoodlums won't bother me because when they see that arm of mine they know that if I get them with that part of my arm on the front of their throat, they're gone. That's an arm only a farmer will have. But see here, anyway. I had a wife before Tasha's mother. She was killed in an automobile accident. I had abandoned myself to her. It was only a final dedication of my life," he motioned to his head and body, "my whole being and body, all of it dedicated to poetry which kept me alive and keeps me alive still. Before that I lived only for my wife—I dare not speak her name for the words mean too much—having no purpose in life before her. Oh, yes," he rolled his eyes and then back at me, "it is true. I had desire for purpose, yes, as big as the Sahara Desert, as big as the continent of Africa or the entire southern hemisphere. It was excruciating. Life was then a daily exercise in pain in the grand style of Prometheus, that sort of pain. She saw that, this woman. But she didn't see," he was rolling another cigarette and with this sentence raised his hand high to the ceiling, "how she filled me. She didn't see how I'd endured and then sucked up my purpose from her as a greedy starved waif." His voice flurried around the lower register.

He continued. "This woman, my wife, in many ways she's still around me, in the things around me, the plants and animals and air, I consider her there. She was the first to see inside me, that I was a poet. She encouraged it completely, selflessly. I had written a poem completely out of lust for a young woman we saw shopping one day. I had written it and showed it to her. I wondered whether I had done something wrong, but she was not offended or jealous. No, not at all. She told me, 'You are a poet and you must write what you feel. I don't mind that your mind lusts, but stick to writing!' She said that to me, yes."

"When do you write the most?" I asked him.

He said, "Oh," inhaled quickly and exhaled through his clenched teeth, "I'm writing all the time, I think of something anywhere and I put it on paper. Anywhere. While I'm driving, yes, I don't wait to pull over, just stop and write. Sometimes I don't stop if the driving is my inspiration but write while driving. It's very dangerous. But one must. Oh, yes, I'm constantly composing. Always thinking, breaking down, restructuring. A constant metamorphosis. There is no time to rest. One must make the journey."

Tasha was rolling her eyes. She poured the whiskey now. "And where are your poems?" I said.

"They are everywhere. I write them on everything. Paper when it is available, walls, buildings, trees, anything. I loose many poems that way but only from my own possession. They are out on the world where someone can read them. I don't hold back for decorum. No, you see, that would be blasphemy. No, if I had nothing else I'd rip the shirt off your back and write on that. I'd carve poetry into your skin. But I've gotten better at remembering these things over the years so that doesn't happen anymore. Have you ever been to prison?"

"No," I said. I hadn't.

"It is wrought with emotion, prison. But it is a bad place, yes. You wouldn't want to go there. It is very oppressive. Even to the poet."

As we got up to leave, Tasha was bringing wood for his fire. Her father grabbed me by the arm and shoved his face up into my own. "I'll give you a verse," he said. "How about that?" He had a powerful grip, which hurt my arm.

"Yes," I said. He had a pungent smell of whiskey and tobacco. He looked up into the air as if reading it.

> "Along the halls of heated moon
>   long walks to help me kinder
> As stones they've thrown upon the beach
>   The waves and ocean hinder."

With that, he rushed me to the door and, shoving me out, said "Goodbye." Tasha was waiting for me there by the car. I hadn't noticed her say goodbye to him. She said she'd see him again soon enough. He had always been that way, she said, "crazy." He worked the farm and sometimes odd jobs for money. When he was angry with her, he would rant on in verse unbound by measure.

Anyway, Tasha and I and Jake got together and had spaghetti and wine and bread, afterwards Irish coffees. I volunteered to sit on the large stump of wood in Jake's kitchen. We didn't listen to the news at all. We didn't talk about it either. We ate dinner and listened to music. We went through conversations and laughed quite a bit.

Later on we went to an all-night diner and stuffed ourselves with breakfast food and coffee. Tasha started getting sentimental again. We were in the middle of talking about eggs, and she broke out in tears over the mass slaughter of chicken embryos. She wasn't even religious. Jake yelled at Tasha as our waitress filled the coffee cups, "What's the problem? You drop one every month yourself." When Tasha told him that was different, Jake replied, "Bullshit! I'll prove there's no difference. Look, drop one right now, I'll fry it up and eat it." He didn't mean it, though. That was the religion talking.

CHAPTER 7

▼

Violence by Caliber

I hit my pillow like a dead weight. In what seemed like three seconds, the sun came up. I felt like Frankenstein coming to life, the alarm clock jolting me awake. It was extremely warm inside my covers and by comparison, damn cold beyond them. That I'd have to get naked and take a shower in that cold did not appeal to me. There was a livelihood to maintain. Electric currents went through my skull. There was a price to pay for the indulgence. I gritted my teeth and slid out. It was like birth. One second you're in a warm comfortable place. The next second, air hits you for the first time like a cold rake. I challenged the cold to assault me. It accepted. The half-pressure water in the shower made it difficult to maintain a warm bathroom without scalding my tender skin. I wanted to weep but didn't have the strength. I couldn't stand in one spot because the water felt like acid on my freezing feet.

I got into my car and yawned so hard I thought I would give birth. The car turned on. The radio followed. I was going to have to summon the strength to drive and that in itself would require holy attention. This was like one of those scenes in the movies. The guy's leg is hanging off him, or his arm, and he's gotten out of this place, or he's got to get to someplace before somebody catches up to him or somebody else blows up or something. So, I saw it as my task to see myself through this struggle with optimum tenacity. I engaged the warrior's preparation. I would disregard the assaults of my fatigue, my headache, the wicked cold, the absurd brightness of the sun and lack of protective gear, and the sickening stench of my own broken wind. It was on this occasion that I met my new neighbors, Georgia and Felix. As I backed out, he ran up to my car and asked me for a jump.

"Have you got cables?" I said.

"Oh yes!"

"I never learned how to do this," I said as I got out of my car. Georgia explained it to me. Red to red, black to black, don't blow yourself up. They explained that their kitchen was supposed to be getting redone and that the noise all day from upstairs was impossible. "I know," I told them. They were beginning to hate the landlord. "I don't know him," I said, "but I'm beginning to hate him, too. I'm glad to have you as neighbors though."

"Thanks for the jump," they said.

"No problem at all."

I furthered the challenge by steering and shifting my stick-shift with my right hand only and made it to work in record time.

A big fuss already brewed when I got there. I saw the cop car out front, and wondered whether I could ignore it. I really wanted to. I knew I needed to be there, but I didn't want to deal with that cop. It had to be one of the kids. I had to bite my lip to keep my eyes open. It doesn't matter what they do; it always made me feel uncomfortable to see a child in trouble for anything, and I never got over that feeling even working with these kids.

"Hi, Boss. What's going on?"

"Lawrence brought a gun in last night." Her eyes were all red.

"Lawrence?"

"Yeah, I couldn't believe it either."

"Are they going to arrest him?"

"They have no choice. I didn't want to call, but what are you going to do?"

"Why did he have the gun?"

"I guess one of the other kids threatened him. He wouldn't say who."

"It must have been a hell of a threat. Did he say what it was?"

"No, he wouldn't say anything about it."

"So he was gonna shoot the kid?"

"I guess so."

"Why didn't he just tell you what was up?"

"I don't know. Like I said, he wouldn't talk."

"So, his father has terrorized the fuck out of him, and chased him out of the house. He comes here for a week, some kid threatens him and now he's going to jail. He'll probably meet his dad in there."

"Too bad his father can't chase him out from there. I'd like to know where he got the gun."

"He probably found it in the fucking street. How did you find out about it?"

"Web told me. He said he couldn't sleep all night knowing there was someone in the room who had a gun when he didn't."

"Why didn't Lawrence just fucking tell you? Shit!"

"I just think he was scared."

"Fuck him if he's scared. If he's scared, he comes and tells you. That's your fucking job. That's your job. You get paid for that shit. Why does he have to go and bring a fucking gun in here for?"

"Be quiet. He can hear you."

I lowered my voice. "Well, why don't they take him out of here, for Christ's sake? How long does it take to arrest somebody?"

"They want to find out where the gun came from. Are you feeling all right? You know you look like shit."

"I feel great. I'm sorry. It's just a rude way to start a Sunday morning."

"Well, nobody knows it better than that kid. I have to go. You'll have to finish up the report when they leave and all. See if you can find anything out. I'll see you."

I knew damn well why Lawrence had brought that gun in. He'd been in the shelter before. I had never heard any mention of his mother from anyone but his father could be a raving maniac, and he was giving his kid a crash course on how to hide fear with salivating rage. He had put all his trust in that man. The world doesn't work the way it should when those who have been charged by God to protect you chase you around and scream for your blood. Lawrence was scared to go, but when he got old enough his father chased him with a baseball bat out into the street. The way he talked to me at fourteen you'd think he was born in Alcatraz. But when we fed him, and let him go to sleep for the first time without the worry of keeping one eye open, he started to lighten up. I didn't like seeing him go back home that first time. But that's the way they do it. That's the way they set it up. It's just a shelter. Three weeks and the kids go somewhere else, sometimes back home. I guess his father talked a good line to the social worker. I didn't know why he wanted the kid there, but he did. My guess was that he figured as long as the kid was allowed to stay with him, then he (the father) wasn't quite a werewolf. I guess he figured you needed state certification for that.

This time when Lawrence showed up, he seemed as if he had everything under control. His father had thrown him out again, and even though he got beaten up he connected a couple of his own punches to his father's head. His right hand was in a cast. I couldn't imagine what it would take for a son to hit his father. You take a poke at the strength from which you've built your world, you take a poke and you think that you're tearing it all down, to rebuild and never be what he was. That swipe seals your fate with the stick that was used to beat you. The bond is made. The only blind emotions you will ever share will be that of rage and anger. Feel anything else, channel it to anger and express yourself. Lawrence knew fear well and it was burning him out. He'd begun to understand that, ultimately, the only person who could protect him was himself. He'd begun to learn how to do that. The real trouble from him would begin when he learned that he could hurt people too, without them being able to hurt him back. But there's no room for that in a report.

It was a long day. At the shelter they try to look like teenagers with their cigarettes and their foul mouths and their violent attitudes. But they're just little kids in pre-adult bodies. It's like giving someone a car just because they turn sixteen. No driving school, no test. No license. Just give them a car. When they wind up cracking up, you tell them what shitheads they are and throw them in jail. We complain about the fruit, but no one tends the orchard. That's policy for you. Driving home, I hit the radio again. At the first traffic light, I was nearly captured by a nap. I opened the window and extended the antenna. It became apparent that to enhance the warrior's preparation a further step would need to be taken. It was dark and there was no traffic. I tucked my right hand underneath my butt and adjusted my position so as to give my left arm access to the stick-shift and the wheel. This procedure requires a vehicle with excellent alignment as it frequently entails short intervals of letting go the steering wheel. Turning at high speed was particularly tricky because it required a downshift during the turn. My new conditions would force the shift before the turn, unless, of course, I was simultaneously changing lanes. These circumstances required individual assessments and spontaneous POA's, or Plans of Action. I did not make it home in record time. I was not driving fast because I didn't want to engage any unnecessary danger. The warrior's preparation does not indulge frivolity.

Seven purported POW's, Prisoners of War, were displayed on the Opposition's television. The videotaped segments were then promptly played on our twenty-four hour all-news station. The men were said to be pilots but, even though everyone had seen pictures of them, officials were still using qualifiers in referring to them like "the alleged American pilots," as though they had a little doubt that the men were Americans. I didn't understand why the military would have any doubt about the identity of their own personnel. I mean, you sent them out in multi-million dollar aircraft, and you don't know what they look like? The pilots said things denouncing the war as crazy and a matter of simple aggression against the peaceful Opposition. Apparently, the men appeared to be badly bruised, with cuts on their faces. They all stated that they were being treated well. The point was issued that according to the 1949 Third Geneva Convention, POW's "will not be maltreated or misused to obtain information or for propaganda purposes." It was further stated by somebody official that assuming the airmen had been forced to say what was said, the Opposition's leader was in turn guilty of war crimes and would have to answer for them in a world court. Allied sorties against the Opposition totaled seven thousand in four days of the air war. The first and second Marine divisions were moving forward toward the Kuwaiti border in Northwest Saudi Arabia. There were six Opposition Scud missiles fired toward Dhahran; Patriot missiles destroyed five, and one fell into the Gulf. The second round of Scud missiles, four, were all destroyed by Patriot missiles before hitting Riyadh. Fifty-six Allied war planes bombed the Opposition from a base in Turkey. Our General, the big guy, asserted that there was heavy bomb damage to the Opposition's nuclear, chemical, and biological weapons production. I heard him speak on the radio. He just laid the information right out for you. "Here it is. Chomp on it and suck it down, cause we got another batch incoming at 16:00." I had a real affection for him, because he seemed to say it like it was. It was further reported that our B-52 and A-10 planes were continuing to bomb the Opposition's elite Republican Guard. There seemed to be this strange aura around that Guard. They were the best soldiers the Opposition had, a "world class fighting unit." There were a lot of them, apparently, and they were the source of devastating potential in ground-war scenarios. Our General said that the Opposition's supply lines to Kuwait and the logistical communication links had been broken. The Opposition had 270,000 troops in that area. A picture in the newspaper revealed that the General had very wide eye sockets and that he parted his hair on the left. The Opposition's anti-aircraft systems were said to have seemed "impotent." Congressional leaders called for a rigorous continuation of the air war and the House Speaker said that any pause would allow their leader to scheme and prolong the war. Public opinion polls found that we here at home were upbeat about the progress in the war, but that about two-thirds of us were worried that it would spread. Only thirty percent of us felt that we would stop fighting if the Opposition withdrew its troops from Kuwait, with the condition of their leader remaining in power. The President marked his second Inauguration anniversary at Camp David.

In a segment prefaced as "The Rest of the News," it was reported that four people had been killed in Latvia, in the Baltic region of the Soviet Union, formerly the Opposition. Government troops had seized Latvia's Interior Ministry after a four-hour-long gun battle. Latvia's deputy Prime Minister had declared the start of Civil War, but that apparently was premature. Earlier in the day, I had been on the phone with Tasha. She had just gotten off the phone with her sister. Her sister had ordered a pizza. After about an hour the pizza place called her back. They asked her whether she'd ordered a pizza. She said she had. They said their driver had just been shot once in the head. They said the pizza wasn't coming. So there was a report on the radio while I was driving home. This twenty-two year old father of a nine-month old child was shot with a semi-automatic weapon in the foyer of an apartment building just moments after dropping off a pizza to some college kid. The man lived with his wife and child and had moved to this country from El Salvador in 1984. He worked seven days a week. Pizza guys don't carry more than twenty bucks on them. Beyond that, the New York Giants and the Buffalo Bills were headed to the Super Bowl. Talk of canceling the Bowl so as to avoid providing a target for terrorism was dismissed by official people who said that it would provide a terrific boost in morale for service people and that the number one priority in dealing with terrorism or the threat of it is to not allow it to intimidate you. Cancel the Super Bowl? Yeah, right.

CHAPTER 8

▼

The Technology of Intimacy

I woke up Monday with the press conference ringing in my ears, storing the information for analysis. The cold held me down. I dressed underneath the covers and switched on the space heater. I got this intense sickly hunger pain as I continued to store information. I went out to the kitchen and made my coffee. For the last two and a half years, this had been the number one thing on my mind upon waking up, except when I had to go the bathroom badly. I turned on the big radio. I threw a few darts but couldn't focus at all. I really needed that laser system. I put some pants on because my hunger pain was persisting, and I felt a need to eat or throw up. Throwing up gives me a headache. I walked down to the supermarket which, if you walk in the right direction, is the third turn off of my street.

I noticed that it was cold, and it looked as if it might snow. I picked up this bread I like to eat and went to the line. These magazines on the counter talked about soap operas; movie stars; TV stars; cosmetics; love children; impotence; aliens; Adam and Eve; flying dogs; talking infants; royal adultery; relatives of movie stars who had contracted Acquired Immune Deficiency Disease (AIDS); diets; movie stars who needed diets; movie stars who had put their relatives and pets on diets; people who had seen Elvis; people who had talked to Elvis; people who wanted to talk to Elvis but only got as close as his late brother Jesse; people who had no respect for themselves; movie stars who were on the "lack of self respect" diet; how to find the man of your dreams and marry him; how to avoid being married; how to tell if your lover's faking it; how to tell if you're faking it; how to tell if your neighbors are faking it; how to get rid of the man whom you previously thought was the man of your dreams; how to avoid broccoli; how to get your hair cut; how tomorrow looks; how to prepare your astrological chart; how famous people are nearly all test tube babies; how the Austrian wore lifts;…and I paid for my bread.

The woman at the register moved very slowly. I said hello to her, but she didn't respond. I gave her exact change. She gave me a plastic bag. She had on a lot of makeup. She had a puffy grey hairdo. She handed me my receipt without looking. I said thank you. I stood for a moment with my receipt in hand, but she said nothing.

The wind was bringing incredible cold against my face. I walked down my slippery crooked roadway. I called the City Yard. The voice, the gruff one, answered. I told them that I had been calling them to get my street sanded for the last week and that this morning a poor elderly woman had fallen and broken her hip. Yes, she did indeed have an alarm bracelet, the expensive model, but her fall was so wild and drastic that she landed on the alarm and it was destroyed. She lay out there for hours approaching atrophy when I quite accidentally tripped over her head, suffering some bruises myself. She had even been assaulted by a tomcat. I said The Globe had been there, and I was sorry but the reporter had tied me to a tree and beat the story out of me—how I'd been calling for sand all this time. Of course, I wanted to keep my mouth shut out of civic responsibility. Who needs the entire Department of Public Works to lose their jobs? Who needs the drain on the public well-being? Who, after all, would then clear the roads? In whom could we then place our public faith? I was nearly in tears to him. But the reporters would not let me escape. They badgered me relentlessly. They told me story after story of children getting kidnapped, policemen on the take, satanic murders; they misspelled and used misplaced modifiers; they spoke with contempt, with an overwhelming perspective, driving me to madness like ten thousand eyes hidden by the thicket on a pass through the night. I saw no escape from them. They made me want to stuff my head into the nearest glass of water. But there was no water to be found. Only snow and ice. And though I tried to vanquish the urge, I had to stop when the banging of my head on the ice released blood from my forehead into my eyes and approximately tripled my dizziness and disorientation. I didn't want to tell them but now the press knew all about it, and I was sorry that it would be on the front page tomorrow. I said that since this had already happened anyway, could they at least come and sand the street now, if only to prevent further tragedies. The poor woman's sons were lawyers and now they would have to take time out of their schedules to visit her in the hospital. I wondered whether they would try to make that time profitable. In any case, could they please come and sand the road which had been turned into a homicidal maniac by the elements? They said they would try.

I ripped a big chunk off the bread and soaked it in my mouth with coffee. I turned on the news way up loud because of the noise of the people working upstairs. I put on my running clothes and began to prepare. There's a need to rock back and forth on my back to stretch it out. The biggest stretch is the leg stretch, sitting on the floor with legs spread forth like a V, kissing the nose to the ground. This is why I have clean floors. This tunes me to the texture of the muscle there. I generally yawn quite a bit during this. The stretches sometimes wrenched my knees. A friend told me a story from when he was in some foreign country where people drive too fast. He saw this guy get hit by a car and go flying through the air way on down the road and land on his head. Anybody with an IQ could see he had neck and spinal injuries. The driver of the car comes running from his car like he's Shazam, grabs the guy by the shoulders, and starts shaking him, yelling, "Are you all right! Are you all right?" Crippling pedestrians step one, step two.

I was trying to rub out this knot in my neck as this came to mind, and it made me think of Tasha. We were having dinner and talking about alarm bracelets, and I had told her that story in a matter-of-fact way. The light from the candles around us were shining on her face, and I was struck suddenly as I finished the story by the reflection of her tears. They piled briefly under her eyes and fell. She had the slightest look of pain. She blinked twice and said quietly, "That's so sad." Her slight weeping struck me as exquisite, and then she continued on in our conversation. I'd not thought of it since until the pain in my neck reminded me.

I put on my skullcap and the socks I wore to protect my hands from the biting cold and walked out the door. I had to walk down my street carefully. What would I do without an alarm bracelet? I couldn't afford it, and yet it seemed like such a good idea, almost necessary. As I began the run I thought of the General. I wondered what his wife was like. What effect was this having on their marriage? Did he have any children and if so did they suffer torrents of emotional trauma because of his militaristic attitude? Or was he able to separate the two? They said he had a near genius IQ. Does that mean he could foresee the danger in raising children as you would soldiers? Did he resent his children for not joining the military? Was this turmoil at home affecting his decision-making in the field? Or was it the case that his home and family consumed none of his thought while he was in the field? Did he forget to write home? Did he sometimes wonder what the ring on his finger was supposed to remind him of? Did his wife struggle desperately to understand this? Did she regret her decision to marry him? Did she long to have affairs with non-commissioned officers? Was the loneliness devastating, or was she the kind of person that could kick adversity in the teeth without flinching? Was she the kind of person who understood her husband's charge? Was she relieved to have him out of her hair for a while? Was she able to keep his military bent in line when it came to the children? Or, did he have to keep her's in line? The General was a mystery, and not yet had I heard or been able to surmise his elucidation on the warrior's preparation. A man who was as large as he seemed to me must need to have some concern about his weight. I wondered whether he ate extraordinary amounts of food or could his appetite be satiated with a Swanson's frozen Hungry Man dinner? If ever it were my duty to serve under this man, what kind of meaningful insights would he pass on to me? Could he make me a fine-tuned military machine? Would he ever invite me to dinner at his house, assuming I became an officer or something?

The Pond was again frozen over. The tones in it had shifted. Clear spots occurred in non-particular places around the edge. This is where the ducks would congregate. It smelled like snow. There was plenty of sand on the trail. The Pond guys were very on top of things like that. I wasn't thinking about swimming today. On my second turn around I saw the red man. He was about six foot three. His face and hands were all red. Not the wind red that my skin gets but the red skin one gets from having an uproarious blood flow. He had his skullcap on. I could just see the outline of his short-cut gray hair. His hands were clenched and his big knuckles were just a little whiter than the rest of his skin. The red man had his pale blue eye jutting out in front of him like the headlight on a locomotive, like the jab of a boxer in the later rounds. He ran a tired, constant gait. I was drawing good breath from the cold and ran hard past him. His look revealed nothing to me at all.

Freud was said to have said of big men, and especially military men, that he was sure they could beat him up, and he further asserted that this was the basis for at least three of his theories. When pressed, he refused to admit this of big women because he said that he "never forfeited the nodules of his strength to the grasp of a woman and was, therefore, invulnerable to them." He also made emotional pleas to be called "Sig" by his employees.

I did not listen to the radio because I just did not have the time. I needed to get to work, and I couldn't afford to be captured by some sudden burst of news. That type of thing could be dangerous. So I stripped off my sweat clothes and did pretend Tai Chi in the cold air. The shower was at half pressure again because of the clowns working upstairs. I became increasingly infuriated, as if I were showering in ferocity, and I yelled out loud several times.

I began to review the information that I'd received that morning. It was edible. An A-6 Intruder pilot was rescued in what was said to be a daring dash into enemy territory by an Air Force search and rescue helicopter. The rescue took place shortly after two A-10 ground support bombers strafed an Opposition army truck headed for the airman, the Air Force said. No word was given on the fate of the second crew member of the two-seat carrier-based bomber. The President condemned the Opposition's leader for using our captured pilots as human shields. The President was played on the radio saying, "If he thought this brutal treatment of pilots is a way to muster world support, he is dead wrong." The Opposition's radio said that they intended to place the prisoners at locations considered to be prime targets, but an Opposition diplomat denied that they would be used as shields. The armed forces listed twenty-one Allied servicemen as missing in the war, twelve of them from our country. The President was said to have said that the mistreatment of captured Allied servicemen would not affect our military strategy. The President again said that their guy would be held accountable should the POW's be mistreated, which everyone believed they had been. The International Red Cross was refused the right to inspect the conditions under which the prisoners were being held. This sparked a whole slew of references to the Geneva Convention. An army official stated that two Scud missiles were fired at them but were shot down by Patriots. Two other Scuds landed in the desert. The Pentagon reported that the Opposition had been successful in confusing Allied pilots with phony launchers. A Congressman said that his impression, based on what he was told, was that the Allied forces' plan was to continue bombing away. He said that their guy was "hunkering" down and didn't have much choice but to see whether he could wait it out. Experts were said to have said that the failure of our planes to knock out their Scud missile launchers had cast some doubt on our claims to have severely crippled the Opposition's war machine. The mobility of the launchers made them difficult to find. The Opposition reported that Allied bombers had hit a baby milk factory. They also said that they had destroyed 160 Allied aircraft. An Allied naval commander said the air war would take at least two more weeks. Three out of four of us in this country believed the war would take up to a month or more. A teenager somewhere in this country called somebody on the telephone, claimed to be the Opposition's leader and threatened a Scud attack. Later, he exploded a pipe bomb outside the person's home. People in my state were reported to be buying gas masks to protect themselves from the Opposition's chemical weapons. These were the things I'd retained.

Other news was reported that Rebels in El Salvador would try two guerrilla fighters accused of executing two U.S. servicemen whose helicopter was shot down at the beginning of this year. In a statement, the FMNL, or the Farabundo Marti National Liberation Front, said that the American soldiers were executed by order of a sub-zone commander, Dominguez, who was at the scene. They also said that "a court made up of members of the FMNL and independent people, to insure impartiality [will try both men]." I was glad that was settled. For the fourth time in a row, George Foreman had a child and named it George.

Further news came in about that pizza guy shot in the head. A source said that the guy was an innocent bystander. It said he was in the wrong place at the wrong time. This was an "investigative source." Then a neighbor was said to have said that the killers frequented that apartment building all the time to buy drugs. The investigative source further said that if the pizza guy had shown up ten minutes later or sooner he'd still be alive. It was said that the source's, the investigative one's, comments contradicted speculation that the killers were planning to rob the pizza guy, or settle a score. The pizza guy's car, which was stolen by his murderers, had not yet been found. The guy delivered a pizza, up to five guys shot him in the head and stole his car. The owner of the pizza place said he couldn't have had more than twenty bucks on him after delivering two of the three pizzas on the run. The owner of the restaurant expressed deep sorrow. He said that if those guys had wanted the car, he'd have told the pizza guy to give it to them and that he'd have picked up the cost. The pizza guy came to this country to work seven days a week. He spent the rest of his life raising a family. The pizza guy's widow didn't speak English and held her nine-month old daughter. English is the official language in Arizona. I was glad she didn't live there. The paper had this short thing. This nineteen-year-old woman was found in a dumpster. She had been shot multiple times in the head. I turned to my horoscope. I read those damn things every day, and they're never worth shit. My feet began to feel the cold as pain. I went into my room to get dressed. My underwear had holes in it again.

In my underwear and socks, I flipped on the radio. I felt a need to be heard suddenly. I felt a panic to be heard. There was nothing I could do with all this information. I needed to communicate with someone on the issue, and it would have to be someone who could have some impact. I believed in direct communication as the only means to settle disputes. It was a blatant necessity to write the leader of the Opposition. This was, of course, the answer. No one had thought of it because it was so simple. So, I sat down in my holed underwear and socks and wrote.

Dear Sir:

I bid thee greetings. It is the purpose of this writing to lend some further dimension to your present thinking which finds you at war with my country. Regardless of the reasoning behind your aggression, or for the stance which you now take, your enemy is the last power commonly referred to as a "world power." It is true that you're a formidable power in the Middle East. However, I will refer you to the world map which I've enclosed. The difference between your area of the world, which I have outlined in a single red line, and the world, outlined in double red lines, shouldn't be overlooked.

Further, your country and the one that you have acquired are battle grounds. If my government decided they wanted to take over Mexico, but Asia and Europe said they were going to bomb my house, I'd be adamant my government forget about Mexico. So, I will say that your thinking has not been very considerate of your citizens and that this is a good method by which to initiate a bloody coup. That's just food for thought.

It's been said that you come from a background of poverty. I can only imagine the kind of painful clawing and personal sacrifice it required to become the ruthless dictator that you are today. I imagine that times were hard as far back as your furthest memory; that hunger was an undaunted companion. I have seen your picture many times, and seen in your eyes that howling cry of loneliness and mistreatment, of pain and distance. Perhaps you were beaten as a child and meanness was branded on your backside with furious belt leather. Life must have been tough on the windswept sand dunes of Tikrit. But you survived it, and I have to say that many people, at least a few, would admire the tenacity you've shown in becoming a dictator: escaping a death sentence for the attempted assassination of your then leader, General Kassem; then your imprisonment for plotting the overthrow of the subsequent regime and your final success at ousting the 1968 civilian government, rising like the Phoenix, if you will. You must admit that your career has distinct similarities to that of Hitler.

You are obviously a victim of circumstance. Your depraved and meager background has left you unspeakably undereducated and, through no fault of your own, ignorance has led you to exploit and destroy the lives of thousands. In an effort to bridge this gap, perhaps to afford you some better honed tools by which you may govern your country and to bring an end to this thing going on there, I refer you to the thoughts of Lao Tzu on government as presented in the Tao-te-ching (The Classic of the Way and its Virtue) as translated by Wing-Tsit Chan. Lao Tzu was a Chinese thinker who had, and continues to have, profound influence on Chinese history, thought, and daily living. There is some dispute about which time he lived in. Some scholars place him at the third or fourth century B.C., but I'm sure you will find his thinking vital, provocative, and quite on target.

> Do not exalt the worthy, so that the people shall not compete
> Do not value rare treasures [as in your palace and other people's oil fields] so that the people shall not steal.
>
> Do not display objects of desire, so that the people's hearts shall not be disturbed.
>
> Therefore in the government of the sage,
>
> > He keeps their hearts vacuous [meaning absolute peace, pure minded]
> > Fills their bellies, [Builds support]
> > Weakens their ambitions, [Which avoids bloody coups]
> > And strengthens their bones,
> > He always causes his people to be without knowledge (cunning) or desire,
> > And the crafty to be afraid to act.
> > By acting without action, all things will be in order.

It is apparent that you do not hold a consideration of your country's citizens and their interests as a priority, so right from the start your thinking is awry and in discord with the Tao. Chan makes an interesting comment that "The philosophy of the Lao Tzu is not for the hermit, but for the sage-ruler, who does not desert the world but rules it with non-interference." You are an outgoing personality and, with some sound thinking such as this, you should be able to make the most essential changes; namely adjustment to the concept of ruling by non-interference. Because by following nature, as Chan says, "...man is not eliminated; instead his nature is fulfilled." Perhaps then that painful glint in your eye would clear itself up.

The following passage might serve as an excellent guideline to governing.

> The best (rulers) are those whose existence is (merely) known by the people.
> The next best are those who are loved and praised.

The next are those who are feared.

And the next are those who are despised.

It is only when one does not have enough faith in others that others will have no faith in him.

(The great rulers) value their words highly.

They accomplish their task; they complete their work.

Nevertheless their people say they simply follow nature.

As I read this, I become increasingly dismayed at the disparity between action of the Tao and your own. You will note the end of both these passages—order and nature. On the list of rulers, you're dropping rapidly from the third to the fourth category, and also that your country is right now in complete disarray and experiencing the quite unnatural effects of bombs and explosions. You are also on record as making bald-faced lies to the rest of the world on several occasions and, as I understand, repeatedly to your own people. My government at least promised it would not lie, but would refrain from saying whatsoever they didn't want me to know.

The next passage that I have selected does not deal specifically with government but with the individual. I think that you will find it useful.

To yield is to be preserved whole.

To be bent is to become straight.

To be empty is to be full.

To be worn out is to be renewed.

To have little is to possess.

To have plenty is to be perplexed.

Therefore the Sage embraces the One

And becomes the model of the world.

He does not show himself; therefore he is luminous.

He does not boast himself; therefore he becomes prominent.

He does not brag; therefore he can endure for long.

It is precisely because he does not compete that the world cannot compete with him.

Is the ancient saying, "To yield is to be preserved whole," empty words?

Truly he will be preserved and (prominence, etc.) will come to him."

I think even you would be hard pressed to deny that your actions of invading another country, calling for a holy war, trying to take over such a large portion of the world's major fuel source, threatening a bloodbath and attacks on civilian populations throughout the world, and expressing a willingness to sacrifice such a huge portion of your own forces to achieve these ends, classify you as boastful, ostentatious, fatally competitive, unyielding, and greedy. It is quite apparent to me, as I hope it is to you by now, that there is a wild misdirection of your values. One might think that you are intentionally leading your country on a rampage to suicide. If you do not yield to the resolutions put before you, your country will be bombed back into the stone age, and I can assure you that if our ground forces enter your country, their primary objective will be to chop you up, and they won't stop until they do. It is obvious that you must yield your violent stance to preserve the well-being, whatever is left of it, of your country and your own life.

> He who assists the ruler with Tao does not dominate the world with force.
> The use of force usually brings requital.
> Wherever armies are stationed, briers and thorns grow.
> Great wars are always followed by famines.
> A good (general) achieves his purpose and stops.
> But dares not seek to dominate the world.
> He achieves his purpose but does not brag about it.
> He achieves his purpose but does not boast about it.
> He achieves his purpose but is not proud of it.
> He achieves his purpose but only as an unavoidable step.
> He achieves his purpose but does not aim to dominate.
> (For) after things reach their prime, they begin to grow old,
> Which means being contrary to Tao
> Whatever is contrary to Tao will soon perish.

These are not the words of mystics or of self-importance, or of racism, or of religious or nationalistic zeal. These are the words of clear thinking. Although I am sure you will be able to find a copy of the Tao-Te-Ching in your country, I would gladly forward it to you if you cannot. I would also be glad to discuss these matters further with you. My address and telephone number are on the map next to where I've marked my location. Please feel free to contact me."

I signed it and typed out the envelope, "S. Hussein, The Dictator, The Royal Palace, Basement level 45, Baghdad, Iraq." I put on my clothes in a hurry. I was late for work but assumed lives were on the line and viewed this as a military mission. I ran to the large grocery store down the block. Inside I saw just one woman in her fifties at the register. I told her I needed two world maps. I needed them immediately. The lady looked at me in a disgusted way. She said, "A what?" I told her I needed two world maps. I was breathing very heavily. She yelled, "Hey, Manny, we got any maps?"

"World maps," I yelled.

Manny said, "What?"

"World maps. Any world maps?"

Manny said no, they had no maps at all. I dashed out of the store, nearly knocking an elderly gentleman into the street. There were a whole bunch of stationery stores down in the center. I ran the whole way, a half mile or so. The first store I went into had a food counter in it. It occurred to me to eat breakfast but I realized that breakfast at such a time is frivolous. I asked for two world maps. The man said their maps only went up as far as the state. I yelled at him that he would do well to have a more global outlook. "There's a war on you know!" The next store I went to had no maps at all. They had some good doughnuts though, and I bought one. The next store was a hardware store and they had no maps, but they told me that the travel agency across the street did have world maps. I gave the man there my doughnut and ran into traffic without looking, nearly hitting a Chevrolet. There was a middle-aged woman in the travel agency. I asked her whether they had world maps and she said yes.

"How much do they cost?" I just remembered I only had a couple dollars on me.

"What do you mean?"

"I mean to purchase two world maps."

"Do you want to go on a trip?"

"No. I just want the maps."

"We use the maps to help people plan world trips. We don't sell them."

"Do you give the maps to people who are going on world trips?"

"Of course."

"I've forgotten my wallet. Can we discuss the trip, maybe make some reservations now and then make financial arrangements later. I really need this vacation."

"Certainly. Do you really want to go on a trip?"

"Yes. A long one. I wish to leave in two days and make all the arrangements through this office. Can you do that?"

"Certainly," she said. "Do you have some idea of where you want to go?"

"Yes. I know exactly where. Please take this down." She picked up her pen. "I wish to go to Kansas City, Kansas, Eureka, California, Tokyo, Bangkok, Thailand, Ban Ban, Thailand, Sri Lanka, Bombay, Karachi, Teheran, that's all I've thought through. Could you show me that on the map?" She took out a world map, and it sure enough met my needs. "Of course, I'll need two world maps. I'm taking my ex-wife, sort of a going-away present, and I'm meeting with her attorney this afternoon for lunch. I want to give it to him to pass it on."

She said, "You need two maps?"

"Yes," I said, "Two will be necessary."

She pulled out another map and handed it to me. I asked her if she had a red marker which she did and handed to me. I asked to see the map she was holding, and I spread it on her desk. She pointed out Sri Lanka. I circled the Middle East. She began to talk about Thailand in slow, distracted speech. I told her that my markings were an obscure system I'd worked out to remember things. I told her I had a chemical imbalance in my brain which had sporadic effects on my memory. I asked her to please go on about Thailand. I made the other circles and markings, including my address and phone number. I asked the travel agent to hold the one I'd marked up and to please tell me about accommodations in Tokyo. As I spread out the other map on her desk and began to make the markings, I asked her about Japan. How accessible was the black market to foreigners? What was the availability of automatic weapons? She was upset by these questions. As I folded the maps, she told me that there was no way her agency would have access to such information. I thanked her and told her that I was late for my lunch date, that I would be back later, and that that information would be extremely valuable to a wealthy man like myself. I shoved a dollar into her hand and ran out of the store. I ran home as fast as I could, feeling extremely anxious about being late for work. I called the boss about it, but she seemed unfazed.

I surmised that the flow of regular mail into the war zone had probably been killed. I typed up another envelope addressed to the Opposition leader care of the King of Jordan. I drove to the copy store and made copies of the letter, filled the envelopes, and put three dollars worth of stamps to be sure the postal service would treat these letters with priority.

I wondered whether there were any mail boxes left in the Opposition's country. It struck me that you could probably make a pretty good bomb out of a mailbox if you filled it with gunpowder and loaded it up onto a catapult, like the ones the Romans had. You could really blow the hell out of something with that. When I was in college, my friend and I were out late and we stole a mailbox. It was easy as hell; we just picked it up off the street and threw it into the hatchback. We picked up a hitchhiker and put him next to the mailbox. After about ten minutes of driving around this kid in the back said, "What are you dudes doin' totin' around a mail box?" We told him that there were none near our house.

"It's the public's responsibility to initiate postal convenience. Haven't you heard of this? It's a big movement; it's been all over the papers. People are doing this kind of thing all over the country. It's kind of like streaking in the seventies. Only this is no fad. This thing is real. I feel really patriotic doing this, like a minuteman or something."

"No way," he said.

"Absolutely. This is the real thing, man. Haven't you noticed the ease of mailing lately?"

"No. I just mail everything in the Student Center at school."

"You see what I mean? That's convenience. So convenient, it's right under your nose and you didn't notice it. Wake up, boy! It's a brave new world out there! And convenience is King!"

The next day, though, as we stood around the mailbox in the living room discussing it, I made the point that the unwitting people who had mailed their mail in good faith in that mail box certainly didn't deserve to suffer as a result of our frivolity. I was adamant, and my friend agreed. We tried a vacuum cleaner with a hose. We tried gravity, a crow bar, a screwdriver and a hammer. We tried beating the crap out of that mail box with no result. I can say with all confidence that mail in a mailbox is generally safe. Its impenetrable nature forced us to return the box to the post office from which we took it. With some modification, a mailbox could really make a hell of a bang.

I pulled on to the highway and newscasts flowed from the radio.

They were finishing up talk about the pilot who had been rescued behind enemy lines. Japan condemned the Opposition for saying that POW's, Prisoners of War, would be held near potential targets. They said that this was blatant commitment of war crimes. The weather over the battleground was bad. There was massive cloud cover. An oil pump was burning unchecked in the occupied country, which may or may not have been a military maneuver with the consideration that smoke and clouds hamper the effectiveness of the laser-guided weapons systems of the Allies. There was an accidental launch of a Patriot in Turkey while planes were returning from successful sorties. The missile had to be detonated by transmission from the launcher as it had the capacity to blow up planes. That fuck-up cost us one million dollars. There were large pro-opposition demonstrations in Jordan outside our embassy. The Red Cross was investigating Britain's handling of Opposition nationals and Palestinians suspected of being a threat to National Security. The British maintained that the detained were free to leave the country but some did not want to and some plainly could not. Some wanted to but, of course, there were no flights to the land of the Opposition. This would hamper mail. The Opposition accused the Allies of purposefully hitting civilian targets. The Allied command was reported to be maintaining their pleasure at the progress of the war. No aircraft had been lost that day. Allied strikes were strikingly accurate. There was an Opposition boat, which had the capability of laying mines, left dead in the water. There was a Soviet military guy on the radio. The Soviets had trained a lot of the Opposition military and designed a lot of their weapons systems. This guy was saying that the Opposition was offering little defense against bombs because they knew the Allies' air force was superior, and it would be a waste. This Soviet guy said that the Opposition was saving his planes this way. This, he said, was a Soviet tactic. He said their leader is waiting for the Allies to attack his strength, his ground forces. He said the war would then turn ugly, and that then the blood would spill.

There was traffic at a stop light. The green said go, but there was little going. My attention was lost in the news and the waiting, the starting and the braking. I imagined the land war, and I remembered a dream from the night before. I was in the desert in this large bowl in the terrain. I was walking with somebody. Suddenly, there were people in tan jumpsuit uniforms and gas masks appearing at the tops of the dunes. They had automatic rifles. We thought to run but there was no cover. We hit the ground. We had no guns. I was screaming to troops behind me, "Shoot them!" I don't know how I knew there were soldiers behind me. Then there began the firing of weapons all at once. It was loud as all hell. It seemed from what I could see that we were hopelessly surrounded but for the guns behind us. I kept expecting to get shot and was perplexed that I wasn't. Whoever was firing the guns behind us was cutting into the tan guys pretty good. There was a lot of smoke around and, though they were getting shot up, the tan guys continued to advance. Whoever I was with, a woman I think, and I kept crawling back to get behind our troops. Then I saw this tremendous bomb go over our heads in the direction of our retreat. It looked like a huge bullet. I got this really sinking feeling and an intensifying of my expectations of getting shot. I thought, "Oh, shit. Here it goes." We hit the ground trying to burrow into it. I saw that the bomb would land just on the other side of a small dune not far from us. I was certain we'd be blown to bits. When the explosion came, though, we were only hit by a spattering of debris, and we weren't hurt at all. I looked up at where the bomb hit, and I just didn't understand it. That was the end.

I didn't get to work too late. The cycle was still in motion. My checks were directly deposited into my account. I never saw the money transfer. I went to a machine and took money from it. I wrote checks to pay my bills. I sent them through the mail. I never saw cash or people, and yet it all operated on the fact that I went to work each day. But if I were fired, it would not take a day to disrupt this entire system that depended on me. I felt possessive of my room, but it was rented. I'd never even met the property manager. I wrote my check to the landlord and mailed it to the property manager. I couldn't pull these people out of a crowd. And yet, this was my house, this was where I lived. I got approval for my car loan over the phone. I gave the bank some information, and they gave me the loan. I went in to pick up the check and the rude bank representative was the only person I saw. My payments were taken directly out of my account. I never wrote a check. And since my payments were made every month on the same day, somebody I didn't know said that I was a good risk. So, I got tons of credit-card offers in the mail. People were dying to lend me money and I could barely maintain a five-dollar checking account. All these transactions took place in my name, as if I were doing them. And in fact, I did nothing. I was here. I needed a job. I needed to eat and have a place to live. I needed a car to get to work. This circle existed like an ecosystem. I got mail almost every day as a result of this chain. My mailman looked at my name almost every day because of this, and it was all generated by the fact that I went to work. I'd never been to the office that generated payment of my salary. I didn't know anybody that worked there. I talked to a person on the phone sometimes, but that was the extent of my contact with them. This distant structure, though, would one day soon all fall to nothing.

I had hardly watched television coverage and not seen Walter Cronkite since that first night. He had looked extremely good, but I knew that he must be getting on the elderly side of things. He probably was not getting a lot of rest due to the coverage going on. I wondered whether he was doing all right. I hoped he wasn't overextending himself. He certainly shouldn't be putting his health in jeopardy. I remember someone saying that he was very into sailing. I thought it might be interesting to go sailing with him sometime. He probably knew a lot about it, and I figured he could tell good stories too.

At an intersection I saw a couple guys begging for change from cars stopped at the light. It was really cold, and I remember thinking that they must be in dire straits to be out on this night. They did have coats on but no gloves. They wore sneakers. I thought that they would freeze to death. They were moving around to keep warm. The cold had made the streets of the city deserted except for these two guys. If they'd come to my car, I'd have given them change or bills, whatever. But they were about fifty yards away and didn't come over. My car had just started to warm up at that point. It felt good. I'd be looking for a place to get warm if I were them.

I turned on the heater in my room, then the radio. It was jazz. I went to make myself some hot tea. I hadn't put my return address on the envelopes I'd sent to the Opposition, because I figured it would be too easy for some presumptuous somebody to just send it back to me.

There was a letter waiting when I got home which had come from a dating agency. This agency makes meeting people easier-quality, single people. They said I wouldn't waste my time with blind dates or meeting the wrong types if I used their exclusive video viewing approach. It opened "Dear Single." They alerted me to this trend that made it increasingly difficult with each passing year to meet new, interesting single people and develop special relationships. It said that we were just not exposed to enough of the right kind of fine quality singles. It said that we were locked into our work, our neighborhood, and our limited circle of friends. How did they know my friends were limited? I looked to see that the letter was written by the Founder and President who was apparently married and not dating anybody seriously. He said that the busier we get, the less time we have to look, and the fewer options we have. He knew I was concerned with options. Options interested me. He said that as a result of this condition of ourselves, we were trapped into hoping for the lucky chance encounter that rarely occurs, and into settling sometimes for second best. My friend asserted that this was not good enough. Not anymore. My friend offered me a better way. He had thousands of friends like myself. They were successful, selective singles, and they met and began fulfilling relationships. In fact, his success at this kind of thing had been featured on all kinds of cheesy talk shows which he was not embarrassed to mention, as well as in magazines. The Founder and President went on to mention his exclusive library of other selective singles. It was a nationwide organization and had the world's largest selection. Leisure and options. This man had identified me. He specified that I'd see and hear these videos of relaxed conversations in comfortable privacy in case I wanted to masturbate. Then I, and nobody else, would select whom I wanted to meet. He said it was efficient and dignified. Just like the Gentlemen's Clubs in downtown Paris. He said it was a way to find the kind of person I preferred to socialize with before agreeing to meet them. He said it was a way to avoid wasting my precious time on blind dates or with losers.

There was a profile form on the back. From it I would hear about how I could find the fulfilling relationship that was missing in my life. All I had to do was complete it. Or call the local office. The information was free and without obligation. Leisure, options, no obligations. These were what I wanted in a relationship.

The Founder and President made the point that my potential partner, that I might not otherwise meet, was possibly waiting for me in his library. Could it be that that certain someone, the love of my life, was sitting in the library of the Founder and President, a person whom I'd never met nor heard of, nor completely understood? Stranger things, movements if you will, of time, of events, sways of people's lives, breezes, whispers, wisps, apparitional warmth and mystery, had occurred. They were biblical occurrences. They had occurred in the ministries of Fundamentalist preachers. People who were the founders and benefactors of large universities and golf courses. People who had pursuits of supernatural proportions. One such person said that he had seen a nine-hundred-foot Jesus. How could he verify that kind of height? The Austrian would have had a field day with that. We'd have to shoot him up with lithium and lead just to bring him back down to Earth. The Founder and President nudged me to complete and return the Profile, to explore my options, and find out the ease with which I could meet successful, busy singles, people like myself who wanted that special relationship.

The survey was mostly multiple choice. For the person I was looking for they wanted to know her age, whether she smoked, where she lived, her education, her occupation, athletic interests, appearance, religion, whether she had children, her marital status, and cultural interests. I marked that I didn't care how old she was, or where she lived, that she should have an advanced degree, she should work as skilled office personnel, her athletic interests should be nil, her appearance should be "does not matter." I marked that she should have children, should at present be married, and have no cultural interests. In the blank space next to "other" I wrote "No warts, or STD's (Sexually Transmitted Diseases)."

Then I answered questions about myself—the Confidential Preliminary Profile. I checked "I am too busy to look for people." I heard about the company from the Founder and President. I was dating various people. I was single and never been married. My annual income was under $15,000. I had graduated high school. I was not planning on moving in the next six months. My primary social goal was marriage and to date a lot. My name was Theodore Ruzavelt. I was twenty-four. Male. I had no phone. I had no work. I looked up the name of the Founder and President in the phone book. I put his address and phone number down. I was 5'3". I was a tree inspector and had been for three years. I weighed one hundred and twenty pounds. I worked the late-night shift. There was a heart sticker that I had to place on a spot for free details. I ripped the heart in half and placed the pieces on the spot with a space in between them. I put the letter in the postage free envelope and put it in my coat pocket.

On the radio there was a man speaking about Martin Luther King, Jr. This day had been the day of observance for his birthday, which had actually been on the day before the day of the mist. There was conversation on the peace of the man, the timing of the Gulf War deadline being made his birthday. The man on the radio said that this was typical of the flagrant lack of awareness on the part of those in government and particularly at the higher levels of the concerns of minorities and of the goals and ideals behind not only the civil rights movement, but behind the present-day push for equality. This thinking was notoriously offensive, he said, and the administration never made recognition or apology of the situation. They moved right over it and maintained a complexion of disinterest. He quoted King from 1967: "A true revolution of values will lay hands on the world order and say of war: this business of burning human beings with napalm, of filling our nation's homes with orphans and widows, of injecting poisonous drugs of hate into veins of people normally humane, of sending men home from far and bloody battlefields, physically handicapped and psychologically deranged, cannot be reconciled with wisdom, justice, and love. A nation that continues year after year to spend more on military defense then on programs of social uplift is approaching spiritual death." The man, who was a contemporary and associate of King's, explained King's opposition to the Vietnam War. He said that King said he knew that "America would never invest the necessary funds or energies in rehabilitation of its poor so long as adventures like Vietnam continue to draw men and skills and money like some demonic destruction suction tube." He said that King said of his vision that "One day war will come to an end, then men will beat their swords into plowshares and their spears into pruning hooks, that nations will no longer rise up against nations, neither will they study war anymore." And then the news came on. It said nothing new.

CHAPTER 9

▼

She was one in half a million.

The clock radio woke me again, ringing with the press conference. My first thought was how I hated being awakened, and yet every night set the alarm. With my eyes closed, half awake, my attention reached out for the broadcast. The same voice as yesterday. No friendly aircraft had been lost in the last twenty-four hours. Two thousand sorties were flown. Approximately 10,000 sorties had been flown since commencement of operations. Seven Scud missiles had been launched. Six were sent to Saudi Arabia. Two of those were intercepted by Patriots, and the other four fell harmlessly in unoccupied lands or waters. After three nights of not being attacked, Israel experienced the launch of a missile at Tel Aviv. Patriot missiles were fired but did not intercept it. The missile landed in a densely populated area killing three and injuring seventy-one. Cloud cover was preventing proper evaluation of the damage inflicted by Allied air attacks. The Opposition was successfully rebuilding some bombed airstrips within twenty-four hours. The voice said that smoke from the burning wells could pose a problem for smart weapons and satellite photos but that they posed no long-term military significance. Reporters started asking questions. No more information was being elicited by them, so at that time I pulled my covers off and got out of bed. I turned on the space heater and accepted the chill as one might the pinch of a blood test. I put the big radio on and turned it up so I could hear it as I made coffee. There was a tremendous white fog that surrounded me in the mornings. It prevented thought. The actions I took were from a checklist I'd developed and made into a routine. I had to grasp each action mentally and then determine to do it. My actions were almost completely cerebral—getting out of bed, making coffee—for they each required a procedure of commands. Pull the blankets back, sit up, put your feet on the floor…in that fashion. I was so unfocused that I considered throwing darts a bit dangerous. It was not inconceivable that I would throw them into my foot. Certainly, the wall would take a beating. I continued through time in this state until the coffee was down eating the lining of my stomach. My taste for coffee was the only provision for accuracy. It had to be good and it had to be strong. It would have been insanity to face the morning in any other way. Among all the other aspects of my life, all the conditions, this was an essential ingredient that made much of it possible, stable, palatable.

I slowly became aware of the incredible noise coming from upstairs. I thought it was a headache, but it was, in fact, horrible banging and scraping. Things being dropped on the floor. Hammering. They were messing around with the plumbing, too. I was sitting on the toilet and the entire bathroom began shaking. Something was coming through the ceiling, I thought. Something big and it was going to fall on top of me. I'm gonna die while taking a crap, just like Elvis. My connection to the king would be that I die on the throne. I was once on the phone with a friend of mine who lived in a college dorm room in the Bronx. She suddenly screamed in the phone like a woman in flames. I screamed back to her, wondering what the hell was going on. The phone on her end sounded as if it were getting tossed around. For fifteen minutes I waited frantically, screamed when I thought it would do something, while all I could hear was the sound of screaming women and a phone dangling against the wall. "Are you still there?" she finally said. I was in a panic. "Yes! What happened?"

"You know how I hate cats?" She was out of breath.

"Yes! Yes! Just tell me!"

"A cat fell through the ceiling."

That's the kind of chaos I was feeling. I cleaned up my act and got it out of there. I sucked the coffee down like mother's milk. "Dynamite," I thought. "I'm gonna throw dynamite up there and blow those bastards home." They were relentless with their noise. They were terrorists. Among the few pleasures allowed for a person's indulgence, quiet should be one of them. Just then I heard a bit of a scream from outside. The road had gotten another one. I walked to the window and saw Georgia on the ground laughing, in a way, as Felix tried to help her up. This went on for two or three minutes until they finally stabilized each other and headed into the building. I listened as they walked through the front hall and into the apartment. They were having their kitchen redone so there was also construction right in their apartment. They seemed to be extremely tolerant people, and I discovered this while staring naked out the window like some voyeur. That's no way to get to know people.

I sat down at my desk to stare at the big blackness of the radio. I looked at the note in the left tape player, "This tape player is faulty." I listened to the press pool asking questions. There were questions based on previous questions, follow-ups, questions based on follow-ups, questions based on reports from somewhere else, questions based on rumors, questions based on reports from the Opposition's television. The voice said to many questions, that answering them would endanger Allied troops by giving information to the enemy. He said to other questions that answers on his part would be speculation and therefore he couldn't comment. He said to other questions that he didn't know, "I have no way of knowing." He said he couldn't confirm anything reported on the Opposition's broadcasts. He said that he "wouldn't dare guess" about such things.

It was nighttime there now, the end of the day. An extremely convenient aspect of time zones and physics allowed time to gather all the war information on one plate and eat it down. The fighting generally occurred while I was asleep, the forces slept or did their nighttime things while my day occurred and then again. This was rather neatly established, and I found it convenient.

At the start of my second cup of coffee, I pulled the darts from the board and began firing. I shot only bullseyes in the morning. It was an exercise to assemble my focus. After several rounds, I hit five bulls in a row. During college I had won a game like that. It was during the summer after work, playing a woman I'd spent the day training. I had worked for a political lobbying group as a door-to-door person, the infantry of politics, asking for money. I'd been doing that for a month when this woman was hired, and I had to train her. She was nice enough, had worked on the volunteer paramedic squad in her home town. It was a small town she'd come from, probably a small dot on a map of the county. She had a country glint in her talk, and I was sure she wasn't too well educated. I trained her as best I could. I told her about my technique. I gave her information. Information was a tool in that job. If you could firmly out-information somebody, it was like having their ATM card with the password written right on the back. I gave her a lot of information. I even gave her some good false information and I told her what kinds of people to use it on. She just didn't seem to have a clue about people. She seemed like someone who really needed help. Her hair was too short, and she wasn't attractive, actually. She seemed nice, I remember, so I gave her approach, technique, and information. It was overwhelming. I told her I knew it was, not to worry about it, and just take in what she could. Soon, I told her, it would click in the conversation as she got to know individuals in a neighborhood in a general way. That day was wickedly hot and humid. She told me she had been married. Her husband had left her without a word. They'd been married for a year and he left. He took all her money, some jewelry. He just left, she said. She reported this to me. She was living with her parents, because she had nothing. She'd joined the Army and would be entering in the fall. She said the

Army offered some good opportunities. I asked her whether she felt like she needed to get out of her town, go someplace to get away. She said no. She just didn't know what else to do. The Army had good opportunities. She wasn't very expressive in her movement or her eyes, and I could see no pain. She just told me these things as though she was talking about a cloudy day.

I thought she'd be eaten alive. The public can be cruel. The public doesn't like people coming to their door during dinner, talking to them, engaging them, their eyes, their talk, their thoughts, their whims, countering their generic responses to people they want to leave them alone. The public is not kind to those things, these people. If they agree with what you say, you can relax. You won't be abused. They may not give you money, but that's where ATI comes in: Approach, Technique, and Information. The people that agree with you are practice, like starving fish. If you can't get money from them you shouldn't be fishing. You should go to the market for it or better yet just not eat fish. "Save the Fish," get a bent like that. Beyond that was a range of increasingly hostile profiles: people who might be sympathetic but didn't care; people who didn't care; people who adamantly didn't care; people who disagreed and didn't care; people who adamantly disagreed and didn't care; people who disagreed and adamantly didn't care; people who disagreed; people who adamantly disagreed; and people with big dogs and guns. These were my worries. Legitimate worries. I tested her. She was skipping lines from the sheet, missing inflections and assertions. I questioned her and she had no information with which to respond. I told her not to worry; she'd pick it up in no time. I was worried but I couldn't let on. You can see this sometime when you're at a door. A person comes away from their dinner table still chewing. You tell them your name and the name of the lobbying group. You can see their teeth grow. You think they might spit their food at you. You're vulnerable. I worried. She made money, though. Lots of it. She raked it in. What was the secret? How was it so? I was surprised but glad. She needed the job. How she managed it, she never told. Some years later shooting darts in my room, I realized she was probably over there. That's when I hit the fifth bullseye.

I sat down at my desk to more news. They had two more pilots in their possession. They were accusing the Allies of deliberately hitting religious targets. This was denied by Pentagon people. They were calling for worldwide terrorist attacks against Western interests and for a Holy War. The Allied command continued to be pleased by the progress of the Operation. The search for a proper name for the conflict was still under way.

CHAPTER 10

▼

"To yield is to be preserved whole."

I got down on the floor and stretched my back, thinking of night in the battle zone—my morning. It was the end of the day there. What was the routine? I would write one letter a week to my family. "I am fine. Send food, please." Always said, "please." The rest of my time would be spent gauging myself. Would I have time to beat drums and scream to the Opposition? Would anyone join me? Would they tell me to shut up? Would the General tell me to shut up? Would he completely misread my preparation and shout at me in reprimand? Or, would he recognize it? Would he require the other troops to follow my example? What answer would the Voice on the radio give me to these questions? "I wouldn't dare to speculate." The General was a complex man with serious convictions. He may see my actions as a mockery. Or, he may see them as the method of tuning with the spirit of battle. Certainly, he did similar things himself. Certainly, he stood in front of the mirror and shouted, growled at the man he saw there. Surely he tried to pierce his own image with his glare, pointed his finger in its face, gritted his teeth at it. Did he ever strike himself while facing the mirror? Would he storm out of his office, up to me and my drums and tell me to go home? Would he grab a drum, paint his own face and start screaming louder than me? What were his dealings with the battle spirit? What were his commitments? I stretched my legs. "I would not dare to speculate." I know from movies that in army barracks the toilets are all just sitting there right next to each other. It would be like taking a crap in the middle of the town square, I thought. This would be the most difficult thing to get used to. Crapping with strangers. There is nothing in the warrior's preparation for this. I couldn't see ever getting used to it. That's one of the reasons I wouldn't want to go to prison, among others. If I could get over the open-door-crapping policy, I could adjust to the military. In the wake of sobriety, I viewed it as an equivalent to suicide, and who would make note of my crapping anyway? Who would make note of my adjustment at all? Who would make note?

I put on my running clothes. They smelled of the previous day's sweat. I took my steps carefully on the partly cloudy street. I pictured those men from the City Yard in the backs of their trucks hunched over marijuana cigars, playing cards, drinking English tea. They were filthy scoundrels. I ran up to the very main street without incident but there traffic was heavy, and no driver was willing to let me cross. I was prepared to dart across this five-street intersection where the lights were short (people curse at them all day long). I had to stop. I became infuriated waiting for a break which came when a bus stopped to admit passengers. The sidewalk was full of ice and snow. I ran in the street, jumping to the side as cars approached. These conditions I referred to as partly treacherous. Then I came up to the street that is the boundary of the ground that surrounds the Pond. Crossing this street is a spiritual exercise. It reminds you how close you are to death. Vehicles speed out of nowhere from behind curves, always in packs from both directions. The road has to be clear for fifty yards in both directions for a safe crossing. To cross under any other circumstances is insanity. Cars driving sixty in a twenty-five-mile-an-hour zone. This was a particularly harrowing day. My Pond lay in sight right before me but between us was this moat of frustrated, impatient, late, incontinent motorists. I growled at them and called them names, but they only sputtered exhaust at me. There are huge trees lining this road. If I could fell one into the road, my problem would be solved. I didn't drive this road. If I could push the tree over, it would be worth it. Finally, the break I needed came, and I was across, running the incline through the snow to the path. My fury had gotten me nothing, and I thought, "To yield is to be preserved whole." This was useful in the warrior's preparation.

The ducks were quiet. The wind coming off the water was cold. What would the Pond look like in a painting? I could not figure that out. The wind came from the Pond it seemed. The Pond, as if screaming at me to persevere, thrashed me with head winds. Two hundred years ago the Pond would have been isolated, and I would have lived here. I would have built my house on one of the small hills that surround it. I'd have fished and hunted. I'd have run around the Pond, swam it, at my leisure. I wouldn't worry about work or car insurance. My concerns would be focused to the concern of daily living. There would be no distraction from that focus. And then I'd die, I guess. The Pond would go on in its changes and duck floating. The Pond wouldn't take notice if I left now. One less person to run around it, to look at it, breathe the air around it, lash with the wind, one less image to reflect. I was not a condition of the Pond, it made that clear. It is part of the warrior's preparation to understand that all life is an exercise in death, that this fact is what makes the actions of life, the process, the living, so ensconced with significance. What thoughts would I have if I were going to die? If, for example, I was falling off a skyscraper, all the while down, knowing I would soon be dead, would I pass out? Would I just wait for it? Would I imagine the impact one hundred times over in excruciating detail? The wind hurling past me, through my hair. I'd turn my back to the ground. Would I tense up? I'd try to relax my body. I think I'd want to view the sky. My next step on the run could have been my death. This makes the impact of the moment on one's life immense. The warrior's preparation sets each moment equal to the next in importance and each, therefore, must be used in a productive, basic, natural motion. A commitment to war is a commitment to the last moment. A commitment to the last moment facilitates a striving for perfection. The Pond moved its water onto the shore and back. I thought a commitment to battle in any other way was a mistake. The difference between human beings and others is that we must choose to enact our moments with purpose, while other species simply do it. Would a duck ever commit suicide?

CHAPTER 11

▼

There is always a weapon around if you need one.

Some people feel a kind of kinship, some obligation, to say "hello" as they run past you in the opposite direction. It makes you feel as though you should respond. If I could resist it, I'd let their "hello" go right through me. I'd look at them, survey them, take them into my meditation. But I do feel that obligation, and it's hard to look. I don't like to talk, or grunt or wave on my run. I don't like to acknowledge to others that I'm there. I like to think I'm invisible in a way, not that I actually think that, but I don't like the idea of people taking notice of me. Their notice destroys part of my seclusion, the surrounding atmosphere of my meditation. I see people. I make surveys of them—runny nose, Adidas sneakers, bad runner, good runner, better then me runner—then perhaps I make assessments based on the surveys—imbecile, friendly, hardworking, left-side-of-the-path-runner, communist, fascist, hostile.

The Red Man was different. He was a tree in steady motion. Even when he looked at me, he didn't seem to see me. He was the only one I ever ran past that had the graciousness not to see me. The glare from his eye didn't penetrate. My assessments of him were all based on how he looked. I got no other impression of him. He had the physical dimensions of the General. Thoughts involving the red man had little to do with the man himself. It was a gift I gave to him quite naturally. I only looked at him directly a couple of times. The rest of the surveys were made from darting views, views from far away. He never said hello to me, he never waved at me, or nodded, and I returned the favor.

In the pursuit of clarity, the objectives are obvious. You have to move into the things surrounding you. You have to float, swish by people, run through the trees, swim underwater, move through the Earth, no more noticeable then a pigeon or a crow. Fly above the tree line. These were my objectives in running. The faster you run, the faster you move past people and the less they notice you. I ran with the wish to be the most unnoticed person I could be. It is foolish to demand of yourself less than the extent of your capabilities, but foolish too to make demands beyond that. Precision was everything in the warrior's preparation, and precision only came with practice.

I was jogging home in the middle of the road. On-coming traffic always moved to the correct side. A white van, parked on my left, facing me, moved to pull out but stopped at the sight of me. As I ran by it, the driver rolled down his window and yelled at me, "Why don't you get out of the road, you cocksucker!" I yelled back at him, "What road," and continued as I heard him drive off. I wanted to say plenty of other things like, "Why don't you shut up," or "Why don't I slash your tires" or "Why don't you blow your nose, you fascist!" I didn't have time to yell these other things. The situation required something quick, unexpected, something he'd struggle with, a flank. He'd wrestle with that question for half the day, "What kind of insult is that? What road? There's only one road. What does he mean by that?" And his struggle he'd assume all along was with my stupidity. But eventually it would hit him at a traffic light, in the middle of lunch, the struggle I had induced in him was like a small virus, passed casually. This was calculated, though. The stupidity he struggled with, which had raised his blood pressure, was his own. It was the stupidity behind the notion of engaging in the struggle at all. He'd suddenly hear the echo of my laughter in his ears though I would be miles away in space and time. In the engagement of battle, it is necessary to employ the most concentrated force with the least exertion of effort. That's how a knife cuts.

I got home and pealed off clothes down to my socks. The radio played more news. Israel had again agreed to hold its fire so as not to upset the Arab members of the Coalition. Officials of Syria, Egypt, and Saudi Arabia had indicated that if Israel retaliated against the Opposition because of another attack they would understand and not leave the Coalition. This was mighty good-spirited of Saudi Arabia considering the Coalition was the only thing protecting its ass from an Opposition ramrod. If anything, they knew that invasions in the Middle East were seldom polite. Out of the Opposition's capital came the statement that they were prepared to deal with the POW's on the basis of the Geneva Convention provided that this also applied to Palestinian people in the occupied territories. In my private conversation with the OL (Opposition Leader), I would have to say, "What are you talking about? What do the Palestinians have to do with you kicking the shit out of Kuwait?" He would only stare at me with beady eyes. Fever, aggressive behavior, and irrational thinking. I was beginning to think he had rabies. None of the experts speculated about that. The capital accused the Coalition of bombing religious sites and pledged to send suicide bombers to strike the

Allied forces. Echoes of Lebanon. They said that forty-one civilians had been killed along with ninety-one wounded. Allied officials again denied the religious-site charges. One of the oil field fires was very close to the border areas where Allied troops were massing for a ground offensive into the occupied country. The destruction of this oil field was the second threat of the OL to be realized. A Pentagon official said that attacking linear targets such as runways, railways, pipelines and communications links had been extremely difficult. "We know there are cases where we have bombed runways, they have repaired the runways and been back up operating within twenty-four hours," he said. The Opposition was not using its 650 fighter planes, said the official, but he had no reason to believe reports that the Opposition was sending aircraft to bases in Iran, which had pledged neutrality in the conflict. The President was accused by anonymous analysts of going beyond United Nations goals by threatening the leader of the Opposition with prosecution of war crimes. The analysts' analysis was confirmed by diplomats. Twenty-five Vietnam Veterans protested the war at the Vietnam memorial in town. They said the protests would continue and hopefully enlarge each Tuesday until the end of the war.

I pulled the darts from the board through the cool air clinging to me. I walked back to the line and began shooting. The floor boards creaked on the path. The bastards upstairs were making a terrific lot of noise. I told them they were jerks, unyielding jerks. They didn't hear me. I threw open my door and headed out into the hall, unarmed but for my anger. They obviously had no idea what they were doing to me, and I had to make it clear. They were just plain ignorant. I walked out my door and noticed, down the stairs, a newspaper lying at the doorstep of my new neighbors. Thinking for a moment, I figured that I could put up with the inconvenience of the noise for the convenience of this paper. There was a sense of risk being naked in the hall, but I dashed for the paper and went back to my room. From outside I heard Felix's voice.

"Georgia? Can you get this bag?"

"Yep," she said.

Looking out the window, I could see they had just been food shopping and were coming home to eat. I went back to the dart board and began to evaluate the darts. As weapons, they were concealable and easy to carry. They were reasonably accurate in a steady hand, although increasingly less accurate as distance from the target grew. Official distance is 7' 8 1/4". I imagined the scenario and escape. Sneaking up behind a guard in a dark corridor. The tips dipped in poison, I shoot bull's-eyes. I hit at least one out of a series of three. In my room, naked but for my socks, this is an acceptable ratio. I thought, however, that my life may depend, within the realm of all possible worlds, on one shot at the bull. What then would my bull ratio be? Walking over creaking boards, back and forth, pulling the darts and shooting each series, hitting one bull each time, this is what I considered. I hit ninety percent within the triples circle. Those were possible successes. If thrown hard enough into the back of a person, assuming I had a potent poison on the tip, these darts within that circle would probably achieve my objective. The ones outside that circle were killing me. Whoever I was throwing at would have just turned around and shot me. What would I think during that instant as I watched him turn? How would I receive that bullet? Would I be satisfied or content with my affiliations, commitments, declarations? Had I been self-defeating in considering this possibility? Would I tense up, try to anticipate the pain? Would I try to catch it with a particular part of my body? Would I not think at all but thrust forward in an effort to engage the enemy, hold his throat in my hands? Possibly. Perhaps I could render him combat-ineffective, without alerting his comrades. It seemed to be the only proper choice of action, and it was perhaps a good idea to have considered this before ever finding myself in the heat of it. The warrior never losses sight of the room for improvement. I read my horoscope out of the neighbor's paper: "Think about your future, your education. Having people be truthful will mean a lot. Others may need your financial assistance. Help if you can."

CHAPTER 12

▼

Will the real tactical expert please stand up?

There was water pressure this day, although occasionally the bathroom still shook like hell. I turned the water on as hot as I could stand it to warm up the bathroom. I shaved. I wondered whether they shaved every day during combat. You might want to meet your maker clean shaven. But I would have war paint on, and I'd be bound to look a horrible mess anyway. I got dressed in a hurry. My feet were cold. No news on the radio. I couldn't drive aggressively today. I felt a need to drive slowly today, to calm myself, assure myself I wasn't in a hurry.

On the way home from work, I drove the stick-shift using my left hand only again. Even in paying for the bridge toll I used my left hand only to get the change from the ashtray and roll down the window as I pulled up next to the automated toll booth. God bless good suspension. The toll collector hardly looked at me. He'd been reading a book. I said, "Thank you!" loudly. The skin around his eyes had thick wrinkles that burrowed under his beard and eyebrows. He made a smirk and nodded his head one quarter of an inch.

I drove down the main street and spotted the pub with the green awning. It seemed to be the only building on the street with light. I parked the car without really thinking about it. Time to hunker down with a pint. I walked in and saw all these people standing about with glasses in their hands, most talking to each other, some listening to others talk, some not listening or talking. Music was playing. Nobody looked at me as I walked to the bar near the door. There was a game of darts going on right there in the front. Then I said hello to the bartender calling him by name, but he didn't seem to recognize me. I asked him for a pint. John was a real bartender. He knew how to pour a pint. Only a real bartender can do that. It's a myth that just anyone can do it. The truth is he had a talent for it.

The first and foremost likable thing about this place, aside from John's skill with a tap and a glass, was that there was no attitude floating around. I stood at the bar for three quarters of my pint appreciating that fact. All too often you walk into a bar and some meathead with a flattop asks you for your identification, like some Nazi. They have to make sure you're old enough, by law I mean, to drink alcohol. It's not that I had anything against the Nazi son of a bitch that was proofing. That was the ranting, neo-fascist element engraved in the federal and state governments. No one can blame an establishment for abiding by the law. But it turns out that these guys, these doormen, assume this certain authority, this lummox attitude that seems to think my life depends on getting into whatever crummy bar they happened to be masturbating their ego in. They're usually these big muscle-bound guys that carry nude snapshots of themselves in their wallets. They act as if they made the law, as though they had the brainpower to even really understand it. The drinking-age law was inconsistent with military policy which allowed the induction of those under twenty-one into the armed services, entailing the issue of firearms and military apparatus with the express purpose of posing a threat to or actually taking human lives. Certainly, this random delegation of responsibilities had no more sound or moral reasoning behind it than a fixed poker game. But none of this pestilence lingered here in this bar. It was on the weekend that I'd been here last and the doorman barely looked at me when I came in. He didn't stand up; he didn't even have a flattop. A doberman pincer could see that I was over twenty-one. No attitude, that was the measure of a good bar.

I swished down the last of my pint and ran across the street to call Jake. I told him to come up to the bar and bring his darts. He said he was broke. That was okay. I had some money. He said "how much" and I told him "three rounds." I went into the Fried Chicken place to get a leg. "Just hand it to me," I told the guy. He put the container down and held out the tongs with the chicken in it. He didn't say anything as he rang me up and took my money. I ate as I crossed the street back toward the bar. I ordered two pints from John the bartender, and as he put them down, Jake walked in. I asked him whether he'd heard any news, and he said he hadn't. In fact I had to update him. He hadn't heard a word for two days. I signed us up for a game of darts. I don't know what darts did for Jake. It helped me focus.

The utility of playing darts in a bar is you can be social without having to talk to anyone. You stare at the board. You record your scores. It gave me the chance to synthesize work, all the things connected to each other, even though they seemed separate. I had had to go buy food at the Food Bank where I ran into a large man I knew as Brady. I had met Brady there months earlier, just before Desert Shield, and I'd also see him around the neighborhood now and then. Brady ran a homeless shelter, a place he'd started out as a patron. He was an ex-Marine who'd served in Vietnam, a fact of which he reminded me at each encounter by revealing his tattoos. He always wore sleeveless shirts, because his tattoos were on his huge upper arms, and he always took his coat off when he walked in from the cold. He was at least a head above me, and his barrel chest made him look taller than that.

"How's it going, Brady?"

"All right. You?"

"Good enough. How's business?"

"Up to my fucking eyeballs in business. This is the fucking season for it. Getting more fucking people every day. More God damn families. A few years ago you'd never see a family in that place. My God damn eyes bugged out the first time I saw one, cause, you know, that's a rough place. Now every day. How about you? You still working?"

"Yeah. Still going."

"It would be nice if the cash flow got increased when the people flow does. You know what I mean?"

"Yeah," I said. "I know."

"This is fucking bullshit. You see this load," he said gesturing to the cart he was pushing. "I'm paying for this shit with my own money cause we don't have it in the budget to pay for all the meals we serve. Now you got this fucking Gulf bullshit going on."

"You think it's bullshit, huh?"

"You're God damn right it's bullshit. Where did all that fucking money come from? I thought we were broke. I tell you it's a bunch of mobsters running this thing. I don't even give a shit that it's the oil. Look at the scale of this operation. Half a million troops. Do you know how much that costs…to feed half a fucking million people? I mean to feed them shit?"

"No. I don't," I said.

"You couldn't even dream that big. I gotta get going. We have to open up in half an hour." He started pushing the cart out the door. "Listen, do me a favor."

"What's that," I said.

"Try to keep your people from becoming my people. You know what I mean? I'm getting kids in there that think this is a way of life."

"I'll do my best," I said.

The Food Bank had a lot of ice cream and donuts which the shelter bought for twelve cents per pound. Occasionally, we got some frozen fish, which the kids would only eat breaded and fried. The other thing I did that day was make arrangements for a ski trip with the kids. This was something they mostly liked although they were surly about getting up early. Web, who had disappeared for a day, returned just as I was showing up from the Food Bank. I had been trying, as a professional duty, to get an understanding of the whole Lawrence thing. I really didn't want to know, but the reports that had to be filled out because of this thing fell on me somehow. Probably because I wasn't at the meeting. I was late that day so I got to do the report. I didn't think of it as punishment. If you're not there to speak for yourself, you get taken out, that's all. I had to spend the day with Web to try to get the information out of him. Lawrence was coming back to the shelter, and we needed to do all this and officially find him acceptable before the state would let us let him in. The fact was he was already there. I took him in because when they let him out of jail he had no money and nowhere to go, and I sure as hell was not going to take him home with me. I didn't want these kids knowing where I lived. I didn't particularly like them knowing the kind of car I owned, but there wasn't much of a way around that.

The Boss told me I was risking the program, but I told her to keep it to herself. We reported his spot as a vacancy, and no one from the state or anywhere else would give a damn as long as they couldn't get sued for it. And they couldn't. We had enough ice cream and gummy bears from the food shelter to feed him, so there was no question of resources. Lawrence knew we were doing him a serious favor and it was a pretty good chance that that meant something to him. No guns. We told him all about getting the overnight staff person if he didn't feel safe. If he didn't screw things up, we'd have approval in a couple days, and he would be there for another three weeks from then. "Practically a month at one address," I told him. "How does that grab you?" It seemed to appeal to him, but I couldn't help thinking that I sounded like a dick.

Web wanted to go see his father in the county jail, but I told him to forget it. I had one purpose, which I was sure he had guessed. He knew the system like a coat of arms. I needed to know exactly when, where, why, and how Lawrence got that gun. Since Web was the one who ratted him out, the system figured he knew a few things. I figured he did too. It wasn't like him not to know things, but he wasn't just going to give it up. I wouldn't say Lawrence and he were friends— what were friends to these people?— but he didn't want to make a full-fledged enemy for himself. I took him out to eat, and then I started in on him.

"So, what are your plans for the future, Web?"

"Yo, man, I wanna go see my pop."

"Your father?"

"Yeah."

"The one who is in jail? That father?"

"Yo don't be startin'. I wanna go see him. You gonna take me right?"

"No."

"Yo, I know you gonna take me."

"Go on your own. You don't need me."

"You're fuckin' with me now. You know that ain't so. You fuckin' with me. I know you don't like my mouth but it's true."

"Don't talk that trash to me."

"Well, don't be fuckin' with me."

I looked at him like I was taking aim. "You don't want a bed to sleep in tonight. Is that it? You get a free meal and you respond by talking trash. What else is it you wanted me to do for you?"

"Hey, I was just saying, aw right?"

"Well, then you learn how to say it. I don't fuck with you. You're just a little boy trying to look like a man; you're fucking with yourself too much already." He wanted to hit me then. I'd never been hit by any of these kids, though I'd come close a lot. The self-control was good for them. "What is it you wanted again? I forgot."

"You know what I asked."

"I said I forgot. What was it?"

"I want to go see my pop." He wasn't so cocky this time.

You had to look at him without blinking. "I don't like prisons, Web. I don't want to go."

"Yo, don't start that."

"Look, I don't like prisons…"

"He ain't in prison. He's in county."

"What's the difference? It's jail. It smells and everyone there is mean. It takes forever to get in and out every time we go. What can I say, it's a drag. What do you want to see him for anyway?"

"He's my pop."

"Does he owe you money?"

"He's my pop, man. That's it. He's my pop."

"How much? How's he gonna pay you?"

"He's my pop!"

"Yeah, whatever. We have to get back. This whole Lawrence thing makes us a little limited with our time."

"Oh, Lawrence. What Lawrence thing, man? The gun?"

"Yeah, the gun. Like it's no big deal? Yeah, the gun. We have to know how he got it in. We could be in big shit for this. There might not be a shelter if we can't figure this out, buddy. Let's go. I have work to do."

"All right look. I knew that's what it was. I got to get to my pop."

"Why?"

"Cause I got to, all right! I tell you what was up with Lawrence, but I get to see my pop tonight."

"I don't like prison, Web."

"But you wanna know what I know. Don't you?"

Apparently, the only reason Lawrence said anything at all to Web was to warn him against getting in the line of fire. Lawrence wanted to hit his target. The next morning, Web went off to school and never came back to the shelter.

All this was distracting me from my game. I wasn't focused, and we dropped the first game, because I couldn't hit sixteens. I started talking to a woman about fifteen years my senior. She had a younger look though. She was drinking Guinness. I don't remember how I started talking to her, because I didn't know her. She said something to me. Her voice was throaty. I thought it must have been sexy once, but she had a hard time saying long sentences. She spoke about the troops. They didn't have any alcohol or anything. She wasn't sure whether that was such a good idea. She knew guys that had been in Vietnam where they had a lot of drugs and alcohol, and she thought it served as a good release, a good escape from the pressures and terror of being there. She thought it would probably be a good idea to let them drink. I told her that if it were me over there that I would not want any distraction from my purpose. Just the physical deterioration that comes from intoxicants, no matter how slight, would be reason enough for me not to want any to be available. It wouldn't be enough for me just to choose not to drink. I wouldn't want the option. That way I wouldn't have to waste any of my attention or willpower addressing the question. That would be a complete waste of energy in a "none-to-spare" situation. It would be misguided. I said I wouldn't want anybody around me, fighting with me, to direct their attention to that either because that's still wasted asset to me. Given the option, I'd drink the beer. I wouldn't want the option. I told her the relief from tension would come from training, constant training. The more prepared for battle you feel you are, the more soberly you can approach it. Relief from the thought of an impending threat comes from the belief in a readiness to face it. If my commander offered me a beer, I'd shoot him in the foot. I didn't tell her that.

After a while the smoke from her cigarettes was chewing my eyes out. As I got up from her table to get another pint, I went back to darts and got into a game with this guy, Nick, a forty-six-year-old researcher for some chemical company. Nick was built like a soggy sack of bricks. He had a squinty frown cut deep into his face. His complexion was olive tan, smooth. He always had a cigarette hanging leisurely out of his mouth like an alley cat sitting on a fence. He always wore flannel shirts. His darts flew like spears from a gun. They called him "the graduate," short for graduate of the Zulu school for spear throwing. When I first met him I questioned him about chemistry and had to make up things, nonsense questions which he called me on without blinking. I might have been embarrassed but he didn't seem to care at all about talking to a moron. Each time I saw him subsequent to that I expected him to ask me why I had come up with nonsense questions. He never did. I began to think he must have figured me for an idiot. If so, he didn't seem to care. Nick didn't say much about the war. He said it was complete nonsense. He said we were going to destroy the Opposition without a contest. That's all he would say. For him, that exhausted the subject.

There was a guy playing named Al. He was in his forties. He had a flabby gut, a gray bowl-shaped haircut, and he wore glasses that got darker and lighter according to the light available. He was an average shooter. He would stomp his feet sometimes while his opponents were shooting. The pretense was that he was stomping to the music but he had no rhythm. If he were not stomping he might start singing, and he was even less capable of doing that. He was talking about the war. He said that if they used chemical weapons, "we're gonna go nuclear." He said it as if he'd just gotten the call from the General to confirm it. I pictured the General pounding Al on the head with his fist and driving him up to his neck into the ground. Al would moan and protest if somebody breathed or scratched an itch while he was shooting. He'd accuse them of trying to distract him. Darts is a game that requires sportsmanship, or you're just a pain in the ass. Only a real scumbag like Al will run up points, for example. The trick in playing Al was to maintain your own level of sportsmanship. If he runs points, you shoot his score plus one and move on to close out the other numbers. If he stomps his feet, you make it extra quiet while he shoots. The triumph is not letting a degenerate suck you down to his absurd vision. The icing is beating the bastard anyway, which is something we did regularly. Al was always trying to give scorekeepers a hard time just to rattle them. It took extra attention to defeat him, because for him it was combat. Before playing him, I always had to make the choice to engage in it. Was it worth the energy? Would the victory mean that much to me? I couldn't talk to people during these games because I couldn't get distracted. That was a consideration. A total assessment of cost and commitment is required before battle. One time during a game, Al was complaining about John putting a glass on the bar just as Al was to shoot. I was drunk, of course, but he'd been pulling this stuff all night. I yelled at him to stop his crying, that his diapers were soggy already. It was always a pleasure to beat Al. Always worth a little concentration, to remind him of his mediocrity. I asked him what his basis was for the nuclear comment. He just kept saying it: "I'm telling you if they use chemical weapons we'll go nuclear." I told him, "You should be on TV, Al. You're a God damn strategic genius."

Nick was standing next to me and he gave me a nudge with his elbow. "If you ask me, we got our balls on now. This is a good time to annex Puerto Rico as the fifty-first state," he said.

"They don't want to be annexed, Nick. They always vote against it."

"Doesn't matter." He turned his head away and blew smoke to the floor. Then he turned back. "We need them. We need fifty-one."

"Why?"

"Less divisible." He clinked my glass with his and stepped up to the throwing line.

We had one more game before closing time. I threw too hard and couldn't hit a thing. Sometimes it's good to be told that it's closing time. Even in my car it felt like the wind was blowing through me. When I got home, I put my heater on and left my coat on. I picked up my guitar which was out of tune. I didn't want it out of tune but I wasn't about to tune it. I played blues in E. In playing the blues in E one finds a commitment, once started on the progression, to finish it. And as the finish of this progression tentatively sets up the beginning again, one can find oneself traveling repeatedly through the progression without a way out. This hypnotic effect is more sustained in the midst of a few pints. I became entrapped in the progression, fatigued as I was. I had to go to the bathroom, painfully, but the blue hypnosis would not permit it. I was forced to play until my hand cramped or my fingertips refused to press on the strings from the pain, until I couldn't play. Then I could go to the bathroom. Then I could take my rest. The sour tones floated around and around me like smoke. Someday, I would learn blues in another key.

When I woke up, the radio was playing the press conference again. This automated sorcery was a real asset in the consumption of information and in waking up. I lay in bed with my eyes closed to facilitate the grasping of what was being said. The voice spoke. His tone was consistently matter-of-fact. The Voice didn't try to impress anybody one way or the other. The only reason he was talking at all was because he was told to. As if he were peeling potatoes. I listened through the entirety of what he had to say. Then the questions started. The questions never elicited new information. I had made note of this each day. The truth is that they began to bore me. I became frustrated at hearing some of them because I thought they were straight out stupid. Many could not be answered for tactical and security reasons. The voice had no way to confirm or deny the reports being asked about and would not dare to speculate. Questions that requested speculation were the most frustrating. The voice could not speculate. The business of the voice was uncompromising fact. Yet, the questions that got no answers came everyday. "Shut up," I would scream. "Can't you get it straight?" Every God damn day it was like this, making me angry. I put my heater on and got up to make the coffee. My bladder demanded relief. The noise from upstairs began. I would destroy those fuckers. This morning I stood in front of the coffeepot and watched it brew. Not because I thought it was interesting. It was an exercise in patience. Minute-by-minute expectation and desire, feeding each other. I needed to control these things to prevent a nervous breakdown. I remained even and temperate. The coffee didn't take all that long really, but sixty seconds is twice as long as one minute. I sucked down the first cup with deep satisfaction.

I went to my desk to digest the information. Opposition radio broadcast claims that Allied forces had destroyed a factory that manufactured infant formula. The voice confirmed that the factory had been hit and destroyed but that it was being used for the production of biological weapons. Massive fires continued at the oilfields on the border. Israel received more appeals to maintain its policy of restraint in the midst of Scud attacks. Officials said that Israel would remain restrained but reserved the right to attack at a time and with a force of its own choosing. The General had said that the Opposition's unwillingness to come out and fight was setting back the date of Allied victory. He said that if they had come out to fight, their air force would have been destroyed by now. It seemed the Dictator had some ability to reason after all. The Defense Secretary said that the Opposition had significant military capabilities and that the war was likely to run for a long period of time. He said there may well be surprises ahead. The President said the Allied Operation was right on schedule. He said that the Opposition Leader had sickened the world with his use of Scud missiles. He said no one in the world would weep for the Opposition Leader when he was brought to justice. BDA, Bomb Damage Assessment, was noted as having revealed that the Opposition's nuclear capabilities had been eliminated. An expert claimed that BDA was one of the more precise and scientific elements of warfare. The Chairman of the Joint Chiefs of Staff praised the Opposition's ability to quickly repair damaged equipment and to paint phony damage on to others. The Opposition threatened to respond strongly against Arab nations that were permitting attacks to be launched from their territory. They said that they were keeping a giant force for the real battle. The Opposition also requested a United Nations humanitarian mission to their capital to evaluate food and medical shortages. It claimed nearly 5,000 children and elderly had died because of shortages. It seemed to me that the Dictator was missing the correlation between the 5,000, and the action he had taken to initiate a war.

The threat, the scream, the Kiai, is a most powerful weapon. Sometimes it's the only weapon one needs, especially against inexperienced fighters. In preparation for combat, it is necessary to prepare for the Kiai. A good Kiai can make an opponent soil his pants. To handle the Kiai, one may return in kind. But this is effective only if your own Kiai is louder or otherwise more terrifying. If it is not more terrifying, the opponent has won a point in the battle. Another way is to ignore it. This requires great concentration and fortified will. The best way to develop a concerted defense against the Kiai is to expose oneself to it, perhaps find a good opera tenor to scream horrible threats. The Kiai is a show of spirit, a show of will to inflict harm. Even when it is not within an opponent's capability to inflict damage, it can be disrupting to hear of his willingness. The Kiai can be used by one whose opponent is physically superior. It can be used by one whose opponent is significantly inferior to inflict quick defeat. Often, though, the Kiai can indicate that one's opponent has great respect for your obvious strength, and is trying desperately to avoid annihilation by unleashing a most terrible and loud Kiai, digging deep into the most horrible torrents of humanity to evoke in you horrible images of your own demise; to engage those demons we deny yet that are present in us all. This denial is the weakness that will cause defeat if the tactic works. It is this evil strain in our humanity that warrants our hatred, and allows us to step on the evil barking Chihuahua with our might if we are able. I had come to these conclusions in my consideration of the President's response to the blood-soaked comments of the Opposition leader. The "Mother of all Battles" comment, the threat to make Israel a "Crematorium." What beyond hatred could these phrases evoke? Surely, the President hated his opponent. Persevering with the intense air campaign and projecting undaunted optimism showed the President to be ignoring the Kiai. He did not return threats with threats but merely stated his objectives which left the opponent barking like a rabid mutt. In that way he even mocked the opponent's Kiai. The opponent's threat to inflict damage and kill as many of our soldiers as possible was a realistic one. The most expert experts attributed that capability to him. But the President, now committed to the conflict, drew license from these threats, and he obviously knew that the more his opponent put up a fight, the more damage inflicted on Allied forces, the more freedom he had to crush the opponent. In effect, the opponent was gauging the degree to which he would be destroyed. This development, I thought, guaranteed that the end would be horrible for all.

I turned the radio station to the commercials. I was thinking about a Martial Arts class I'd taken. You learn moves in martial arts; you practice punching over and over again. You practice kicks. After a while you begin to wonder about the effectiveness of your strikes. How hard could or would you actually hit somebody? How much damage could a well-placed punch do to a person? How quickly could you annihilate the "average" opponent? How well could you avoid being struck? These thoughts are a natural development and can be used or wasted. If one sets out to satisfy his or her curiosity, the development is wasted. If one controls these thoughts, they become an exercise because mental control in the midst of this training invariably translates into physical control. The curiosity need never be satisfied because the power of a strike can always be greater, more accurate, more controlled. A more powerful opponent will always be available. I was sparring with another member of the class. He was an intense fighter. He had a particularly effective side kick that often caught me in the gut. In the midst of wondering how hard he could throw it, he often threw it harder than sparring calls for, and when he hit me I'd get angry. I was soon, though, able to notice his wondering and began to predict when he was going to throw it. This happened once during a match, and as he threw it, I grabbed his leg and pulled him forward. I was angry at that moment, furious that he'd done it again. I was positioned behind him and about to strike him in the ribs. It was an open opportunity, an opportunity to satisfy my curiosity of the power of my punch, to know what damage it could inflict, and to give an understanding of sparring etiquette. If I'd hit him half strength, he still would have been injured. In a split second I made the decision not to. I put my hand on his rib cage, pushed him forward, and we resumed the fight. One thing about wanting to be President—you have to be willing to kill people.

In the midst of the commercials there was a thirty-second war update. Israel had not issued gas masks to the Palestinians. Norway had said that they would supply them. There were more protests in Washington. There would be another update in an hour. The commercials again talked to me. They demanded I buy things, furniture, tickets, hamburgers, French fries, services, all kinds of services. Then they played music. Themes repeated of lost love, jilted love, a lot of songs about sex. These things streamed into my room, rhythm after rhythm. I played them myself on my own out-of-tune guitar. They were enjoyable themes that had so much and so little relevance. They engaged the loneliness of our everyday, drinking coffee, driving to work, eating breakfast, writing letters, doing all these things alone, being actively ignored even by your cat. The themes themselves became our companions. We walk around with them as our allies, introduce them to our friends who identify with them immediately. People whose loneliness has similar textures become friends, the best of friends, the kind of friends who apologize when they forget your birthday. And yet these themes bored me. They seemed redundant suddenly, without base, without import, complete nonsense, like trying to determine the IQ of a Saint Bernard. Loneliness suddenly seemed like a frivolous, luxurious ailment. "Oh, to be lonely," seemed like a reasonable plea. The warrior's preparation demanded solitude and viewed loneliness as a cushioned self-indulgence. There were no songs about solitude, the strength of solitude, the mental conditioning of it, the proper fortitude, the superior disposition, the perfect stride, the absence of the extraneous considerations and reflections. There were none of these themes to be heard. What kind of artistry was then being presented here? What kind of purpose? What kind of relevance? What was this woozy theme of loneliness and pathetic affection being accented and exclaimed on the air waves? The threat of death came from a threat of suicide in the wake of spurned love or lovesickness. Surely, death could be sung about, and it was obviously relevant. Surely, an allowance could be made to the loneliness fanatics who could take the "each person's death is their own" angle. None of those things were discussed, sung about, played in the sounds of the instruments. The songs sung your average, everyday loneliness, as palatable as over cooked gruel.

I turned back to the news station which by now was playing classical music. Vivaldi's <u>Four Seasons</u>. This was overwhelmingly relevant. Any reflection of nature, the natural forces, change, conflict; war was an intensification of the engagement between natural elements. The lessons of war are also the lessons of nature, and so any reflection on nature was welcome, in fact, necessary. I turned the radio to its top volume. I banged on the ceiling with a stick and yelled at those bastards to listen up. I called up the City Yard and put the mouthpiece next to the speaker. Natural selection, natural ability, natural strength, natural forces. No opponent was beyond the power of nature. No battle, no war was beyond the consideration of nature. Recognition of this fact, respect for it, this was a main ingredient of victory. Anyone disregarding the dictates of nature would find himself fertilizing it. I was filled with the consideration of nature. The music came upon me and presented this reflection that demonstrated victory in the midst of all conflict, even under impending defeat. Only the student of nature would turn defeat into victory. I reflected on my feelings that entry into the military would be suicide. No doubt it would, but what an opportunity to engage an understanding of conflict in nature. What an opportunity to realize the power of the warrior's preparation. I would never join up, but I could perhaps reconcile my entrance into the armed forces. I could perhaps accept the draft, accept the induction. I could perhaps welcome it. And to date it remained a clear possibility. I got dressed for the run and stretched out on the floor. I rocked my back to loosen the muscles surrounding my spinal column. I stretched my legs. I pulled on my muscles until they hurt. Today marked the eighth of the conflict. Today was an anniversary of sorts. Some people, those who fell victim to the plague of euphoria, had expected it all to be over by now. Even some experts. Still no proper candidate for a name. "The Gulf War" and "War in the Gulf" were the most common terms of reference. What kind of unimaginative trash had come up with that? How was anybody supposed to write that in a history book with any authority? How was anybody supposed to tell his grandchildren about the unleashing of awesome unnatural powers with an opening like "The Gulf War?" Perhaps we'd have to wait for the end of the war for a decent name. In many ways I had the same problem with the Vietnam War. It seemed though that even in other countries, people were well aware of what that open wound represented, what it referred to. Certainly, though, this was not true in Vietnam where war has been floating around for hundreds of years. Certainly "Vietnam War" was as ambiguous a term as "Vietnam flora." This was my concern with "The Gulf War." People there would invariably look and say, "Which one?" Not to say that titling it like a sporting event wouldn't be obscene. Yes, I recognized that. I didn't want a name like, "Mohammed Ali vs...." well, whoever. A good inclusive bloodstained name, that's what every war needs. I put on my sneakers and ran out the door.

The wind blew while the temperature stood around freezing. I was fully dressed, skullcap, socks on my hands. It was cloudy grey. Even tones throughout the sky. It didn't seem day or night. It didn't seem dusk or dawn either. I had no trouble getting across the roads to the Pond. Some parts of the Pond were frozen and made their own even tones. Some were still water and reflected the tones of the sky. There were ice patches on the trail with sand on them. Not many people were around. I ran with great intensity today. I ran against the wind, I growled at it, challenged it to come at me against the pain of my body, in my legs, in my hip, in my lungs. Again the Red Man was absent. I wondered if he was ill. But that sort of wondering was an intrusion, so I stopped it. I thought of Mohammed Ali. I thought of his training, his brilliance, his magnificent good looks. On the day I was born, Mohammed Ali knocked out Karl Muhlenberg. This was his first fight since being banned from fighting in the U.S. as a result of his refusal to be inducted into the army. His entire career was at stake, his livelihood, his life. He said no. And the greatest fighter of all time had his right to fight stripped away— it was thought. So, this fight on my birthday, aside from being personally signifi-cant to me and Ali, was politically significant. In those days, the story is told, fathers were forced to sit in a waiting room and received information as it became available through couriers, the final word coming from a doctor. There was com-plete removal of the father from the birth process. And so my father was directed to a seat in such a waiting room as my mother and I went into the delivery room. It suddenly struck my father that this historic fight was about to go on in Ger-many and be broadcast on American television, and as he wasn't doing anything anyway, he rushed home to watch it. After Ali knocked his opponent out, Dad rushed back to the hospital, and as he nestled again into the very same chair, the doctor came out and announced me. That's Americana. Many years later, after I'd learned to talk, I was told this story. A subsequent story, told by a friend of the family, noted that later that evening, around three or four in the morning, after a celebration of my birth (Ali didn't attend), Dad wound up the event out in the street in front of our house singing "God Bless America" at the top of his lungs. Ali was never made aware of any of this.

I ran long and hard. I nearly threw up after the finishing kick. Suppressing it was a matter of breath control. One needed the mental stamina to enact it but it was a simple thing to do; certainly better than throwing up. I used the run from the Pond to home as a warm down. I ran on the curbs that lined the streets. This was an exercise in balance, in control of erratic motion and impulses. I'd been doing it for months and had lately been able to increase my speed on the curb, jumping obstacles, like trashcans and such. In the midst of turmoil the key to sur-vival was balance. To disrupt an opponent's balance is the first step to defeating him.

I stripped down and took the hottest shower tolerable. The vermin upstairs disrupted my water pressure for intermittent moments. I got dressed and went to work. When I came home I started going through the bills on my desk. They were my credit-card bills. Who was the lunatic that had given me credit? I had no memory of things I'd charged anymore, nothing to show for them. Paying them felt the same as burning my money. Of course, actual money never was seen because I had charged whatever the purchase was, and I was paying the credit-card company with a check from my account, which was fed by an elec-tronic transfer of my paycheck. So, whatever it was I had earned that day at work was, in effect, electronically transferred to the credit-card company. My credit cards were now an exercise in control.

It was cold out but I was restless and went for a walk. I walked up to Centre Street. No people were around. It was past eleven. Up ahead of me I saw an attractive woman go into the pub. I thought that wouldn't be a bad idea. It was filled with smoke. John was bartending and he wasted no time in getting me a pint. I didn't recognize anyone playing darts. I wasn't sure what I should do. The woman was sitting with a group of people. They were all playing Irish music. She was playing a banjo. So I watched them play and listened. A man walked in. He wore a trench coat and a tie. He was Hispanic-looking with dark hair and a mustache, perhaps middle-aged. I'd seen him there before. He looked like a police detective, standing at the bar and drinking a Budweiser. I wanted to ask him whether he were a detective or an insurance salesman. Was he here for some reason? Was the bar under scrutiny, or perhaps he was on the take? Perhaps, he was just having some beer after work. Perhaps, he'd seen the woman as I had. I was not afraid to talk to him, but he seemed unapproachable, as though he did not want to talk to anyone. It seemed to me that he didn't even want to be noticed, so that I felt these questions I had of him were already an invasion. I thought to ask John the bartender, but didn't. The man was there, like a barstool—no, less than that, like a picture on the wall.

At work I'd seen a news clip of the Chairman of the Joint Chiefs of Staff on television. His appearance was tall, intelligent, firm. His movements and his speech were smooth. His voice was distinguished. He spoke with authority. I wondered all the same things of the Chairman that I wondered of the General. What was his understanding of battle and the warrior's preparation? Of course, the Chairman's role was quite different. He was not in the field. He wore his dress uniform daily, with medals. His activity was academic. How did he prepare for his role? Did he exercise a lot, did he play chess? He received data, studied it, made recommendations and adjustments in supplies, in troop apportionments, orders for ammunition. He made demands for information from the field; relayed information from the President; advised everyone around him; gave the General the green light or red. If in the field, I would never consider the Chairman. I would not be concerned with his leadership. That would be a distraction, because my task would be far from academic, and yet the magnitude of what depended on him was undeniable. In his dress uniform and charts and pointer and maps, he seemed so far from the conflict. He was in fact. As far, perhaps, as I myself.

C H A P T E R   13

▼

Fluorescent eyeliner.

U.S. submarines in the Mediterranean and Red Seas fired Tomahawk cruise missiles at targets inside Opposition territory. What a great name for a missile. Four members of a CBS news crew had been reported missing. U.S. bombers hit an Opposition oil tanker. An environmental authority had reported an oil spill that could have been a result of the hit. Somebody in the Air Force said the slick was refined oil, not crude, meaning the tanker was possibly empty and the tanker's engine was leaking. Baghdad radio reported the incident and the oil as coming from the tankers. An official at another agency said that there were two slicks, each about a mile wide, but that they were not major. Pentagon officials refused to rule out employment of chemical weapons if the enemy initiated their use. I acquired all this information in my sleep. Then I opened my eyes.

I sat up to talk about the press controversy. They were saying it went back to the Civil War. The question over access and censorship and who was going to say what about the boundaries. I knew for sure that the military was never going to release information that would compromise itself, certainly not in this war. A lot of this talk just wasn't relevant to the present. Maybe they were discussing possibilities, potential guidelines of future wars. The public was not into compromising the military. The truth wouldn't be found or told, good or bad, for years until the historians could have access to the facts, access they wouldn't have now under the best conditions, access to the people who were there caught up in it, the victims, soldiers, and high rollers all. Except the Opposition Leader. He'll be caught up in something for the rest of his life. He wouldn't tell anybody anything unless it could get him something, and his days were numbered anyway—if not in this war then the next.

Today was a no-work day. It took three hours, from the time I ended my run, pacing nude from the dart board to the firing line, listening to news reports, commercials and Rock 'n' Roll, before someone called me. Tasha was having dinner at her house for some friends. She wanted me to shop with her and stay for dinner. For the first time that day I thought I might be hungry. The Oreos had given out some days before. We went to a historic marketplace for the details. The marketplace was a tradition of the city carried on from a time when it served a vital role in the city's function. I had to admit that I liked it, but I also thought it was stupid. Overpriced vegetables and fish laden with a nostalgia tax? We had supermarkets for this stuff where it was half the price. I couldn't figure out who was making the money at this. All these trucks and people were taking up prime, downtown real estate. Sure the stuff cost a lot but what did all this cost to set it up down here? Normally, they'd be towed or arrested.

You could see everybody's breath. If the vendor coughed near your purchase, you'd know if he hit the target. I could smell cigarette smoke and truck exhaust and the scented steam that comes from cooking outside in the cold. The noise from the looming, elevated highway crept into the market space the way the vapors creep from dry ice and mixed with the sound of generators and shouting vendors. The canopies were dirty and everyone ignored the traffic of people crowding through the market like a crazy cousin on Easter Sunday. Vegetables, bright and over-flowing, never looked so good.

Tasha wanted pastries from the old ethnic part of town, so we had to walk under the highway. There were two men there among the pillars. One was playing a violin. I didn't know what he was playing. It was a classical piece that he was not playing well. He was frail and dirty. He had long hair, three or so days of beard, and he was under-clothed for the temperature. He held his instrument with some care, but at the same time it was clumsy. He looked at people as they passed but darted away from their eyes. There was some loose change in his case on the ground, a couple bills. The pillars holding the highway behind him were caked in pigeon shit, as was the ground all around him. The pigeons were hiding. They could hear his violin at the food stands, fresh vegetables, fruit, meat, and fish just fifty yards away. He was playing as best he could, but from the look on his face it was obvious there was something ever present on his mind, something damning.

The second man was sitting on a stone bench, an empty bottle at his feet. His hair was caked with dried blood. His face was red and swollen and with a shallow beard. He had on an olive green winter coat and black Converse high-top sneakers. His eyes were long closed. We could smell him from a short distance. He was leaning to one side. There was shit and grime all around him. I stopped with Tasha to listen to the violinist but watched the other man. He suddenly fell to the side he was leaning toward. I heard his face hit the bench. Nobody else noticed it.

Not even Tasha. Not even the violinist just thirty feet away. He didn't stir a bit, or twitch, perhaps he didn't even breathe. He could have been dead for all I knew. I tossed some change into the violin case.

The old section of town was quaint. We had ethnic things to eat. We went into churches. The walk around took about an hour or two. When we walked back towards the market, the scene under the highway was as we left it. The violinist played and shaded his eyes from us with his instrument. The other man lay exactly as he had been, face down on the bench, feet on the ground. I looked for streams of blood to appear. Perhaps he'd opened an old wound, or a new one. There was none. He looked to be in his thirties, that man, but certainly he had parents like everyone else marching around downtown. What had become of his people, his family and friends? What violence had they suffered to have stranded him? Or what had they done to force him to leave? What was the background of his doom? Surely, the conditions of a person's life were specific. Meetings, decisions, conflicts, wins, losses, abuses suffered, inflicted, indulged in, joys and sorrows, all are specific, and yet my culture is broken up into mounds of people, all within a particular mound doing, behaving, suffering, enjoying like things. Perhaps he never had any people. Who would ever know?

We walked back through the crowds at the market and on for a while to Tasha's apartment. I helped her prepare some of the vegetables, but she eventually sat me in front of the television with a beer in the other room while she finished. I watched Music Television. I watched videos. Images changed constantly. Things seemed to happen but nothing really did. There wasn't much being said. There was sex, lots of sex. Nothing seemed to be important but sex. These videos had nothing to do with the songs. I wondered whether the musicians were actually singing as they pumped each other. It was easy to forget there was music involved at all. All you could hear was a beat to which people moved their lips and genitals.

Tasha required you to call her "Tasha." If you called her anything for short, like "Tash," she would correct you, and on every such occasion thereafter until you got it right. She didn't think two syllables was asking much of anyone, so she demanded it. She was equally hostile toward adding syllables, as in "Tash-a-na-na." She must have thought I should have known that and wished only to remind me with a stiff shot to the groin. Her friends arrived, three or four of them. We'd met before, and they sat down around the room. They liked the videos. They'd seen many of them before and enjoyed them. They even rated them in an informal way. Dancing was a big hit and really good looking people. Animated humping was most favored. It was much like consuming the news all day and night, only much more abstract, or perhaps just far less encompassing. We didn't talk very much. They talked about videos and related topics. A woman named Francesca made the most significant comment, and she made it repeatedly; "Look at those tits! No one has tits like that! They have to be fake!" Dinner was excellent but hardly noticed by Tasha's friends, who hardly ate. Soon afterward, everybody decided we should go out to a club. I went along, although it was a little going to the dentist.

The club looked like a warehouse on the outside. On the inside it looked like a warehouse with a huge bar. There were very muscular guys that worked there. They were showing Music Television on large monitors but they were playing different music over a monstrous sound system. I sat at the bar. Tasha and her friends ran around dancing and hugging people like just released prisoners. They seemed to know a lot of people. I watched people for a long time. Nobody was offended, or so it seemed, that I was looking at them. There was a lot of staring-down going on there. I wasn't into the staring-down thing; I was just looking around, but I found people staring at me, and it was almost impossible not to stare back; to resist the face that was actually staring at you; the question of their thoughts—"What are you thinking about me? About this place? What brought you to this moment, looking as though to cut me open and swim inside without a touch? So safe to judge here, with no accountability, no need to be right; you have most of what you want, your judgments. No one asking for them will really give a damn." There was not a zit or a buck-tooth to be found, and their clothes were made to evoke the stare. I could only hear the beat, see the faces and bodies, and stare. It is an American art form after all. The question, the challenge, "Who is willing to die rather than blink." That's why Americans are slow to war. But when we commit, we commit to win. It is a matter of honor, or self-respect, of principle, or simply self interest. What my generation inherited as the Vietnam legacy was a blink, a shudder, a weeping defeat.

The most integral casualty in Vietnam was our attention and focus on what represented us as a nation, for it was replaced with apathetic chaos. Sense appeared, however modestly, despite the lunacy which rampaged Washington in the guise of public protests. "Withdrawal with Honor," became the saying in the mainstream. But the Washington policy in dealing with Vietnam was the equivalent of sticking one's limbs into a wood chipper in an effort to jam it. Hard to come away from an endeavor like that with your honor intact. The culture that endured ethnic, racial, and religious division from the most subtle to the most brutal, to the extent that we still could all have pride in our sense of being Americans. Added to that was the condition of a government divorced from its people.

At that time, apathy became an integral part of what the generation then being born would inherit. Those in the government had deafened themselves, had blended themselves, had deprived themselves of their own good sense, had run amuck, had detached themselves from the origin of their mandate, all in an effort to win a contest stacked pitifully against us. The influence of the coinciding war at home, the image war, so horrifically distorted all that war is, it rendered Vietnam an altogether forgettable war, as wars go.

From there, divided as we all were from one another, we began to stare each other down. The challenge—can you withstand my look upon you, through you if I can? Can you withstand rubbing your body against mine without becoming attached, without my becoming attached? Can you keep me interested enough in you to keep staring, keep dancing, keep fucking, without making me feel like you need me? This was the challenge of the staring in the disco. It lacked dignity, but more importantly it lacked humanity.

I sat alone for some time. Through it all I still felt unnoticed, which was perfectly comforting. A woman stepped up to the bar next to me. She was wearing fluorescent eyeliner. She asked me why I was sitting alone.

"Why not," I asked.

"Why should you?"

"Why not?"

"Don't you want to have a good time?"

"I am having a good time."

"Are you some kind of alien," she said.

"I am actually. Yes."

"What!" She seemed to work from a script.

"I'm an illegal alien."

"Get out. Really, are you from around here?"

"No."

"How about buying me a drink?"

"I can't. I'm on welfare."

"Where are you from?"

"I'm from Hollywood."

"What's your name?"

"Fredrick."

"Fredrick from Hollywood?"

"Right."

"That's a nice name. See you later." She walked into the crowd.

Tasha and her friends came up to the bar. I told them I had to leave. I told them I had to work in the morning and left. The car radio stung my fingers when I hit the controls. I searched for news, but none was being broadcast.

CHAPTER 14

▼

And so go miracles.

The next morning brought news that I would never have imagined. Not that I tried to anticipate events, the war, events of the war and so forth. I wished not to anticipate. This struck me though from far off into the stands, left of left field. The Opposition was dumping oil into the Gulf. They'd opened an underwater pipeline and let it rip. Speculation came that it could possibly hamper desalination plants on the Saudi coast. It was originally thought that the spill came from an Opposition tanker sunk by the Allies on Tuesday, when the slick was first spotted. Apparently, that was not the full explanation. They said it could soon be the biggest spill in the world. There was talk of delicate ecosystems, birds, fish, coral reefs, dying, dead, doomed. There was talk of the different kinds of oil it could be. Evaluations of the potential damage each could cause, the potential size of the spill, the potential daily output into the water in oil and in money. All the numbers in this war were in the millions. The lowest was a quarter of a million. The highest numbers were taken by money; which actually went into the billions, twenty-two billion, thirteen billion. The BBC (British Broadcasting Corporation) referred to billions as thousand millions. Patriot rockets cost one million dollars apiece. Aside from the desalination plants, nobody could figure out a tactical advantage to the spill. The desalination plants weren't really in immediate threat either. There were no immediate threats. It didn't threaten the naval vessels. It might possibly hamper an amphibious attack but there were apparently plenty of ways to get around it. The radio moved on. 2,707 sorties in the last twenty-four hours. This really blew the day for me. I hadn't even opened my eyes. It wasn't the upset-stomach blown day. It was the "...why should I bother..." day. It was the lost hope day. It was the day the Opposition denied completely a common bond of humanity. He held nothing in common with anyone. Not even Islam.

They called it Environmental Terrorism. I turned the radio off, and as I poured myself out of bed, stretched my eyelids up, and slurped down my first cup of coffee, I felt again the need to speak and be heard. Not that I could say anything. Not that I even had membership in any environmental organization, or anything whatever. My world had been attacked without provocation. I took out my typewriter.

25 January 1991

Dear Sir:

You offend. Your soul and demeanor are unkempt and without honor. In reference to my last letter, I cannot think of a clearer example of actions discordant with Tao. You are of no good purpose. A man who purposely misshapens himself provokes no sympathy, no ounce of understanding, merely disgust (If I am called upon to blow your head off, I will).

In your contempt for the common thread of humanity, your desire to deny the community of our race, you have accentuated it a hundredfold. You have provoked the evil that you represent, the desire to kill. You have stirred it in the souls of your enemies and the entire world. Make no mistake, they have set the sights of their hatred on you.

I addressed the letter as I had the other one. I made two copies and put one dollar postage on each, sending one "Care of the King of Jordan." Certainly, the Dictator was a raving lunatic.

I ran that day with anger and pain in my back and knees. I saw the Red Man. He was sweating heavily. I thought of the war. "The Gulf War," that name was sticking. My expectations of massive death and destruction were not being realized. The descriptions of battle I had gotten from movies and books and diaries had people getting it left and right. The experts and commentators all agreed. Casualties were close to nil considering the size of the force. Everybody made sure to preface such comments with assurance that any loss of life was a tragedy, but, to be sure, such little loss was a miracle. And so go miracles.

I paced naked for a while in my room. Without heat and wrapped in sweat, I felt the extreme cold. The pacing helped, though. The next important thing I had to do was eat. In front of that was showering and getting dressed. When the cold got to the point that I actively didn't like it, I wrapped up in a towel and went to the shower. I took it as hot as I could take it, to wash off the goose bumps and keep them away, so that the cold could feel good again. It's not so much the temperature of anything but how you manipulate your body's perception of it.

I got dressed in a hurry and went down to D's. This was a big smoky as hell bar, wallpapered with portraits of fighters. They served a good hearty lunch and in the dining section you could watch soap operas. The tables and chairs held up old women wading through boilermakers. The men sat at the bar. D's was a funny place. I couldn't understand how people could get tanked so early in the day on a regular basis and at their age. They must really be in lousy shape, I thought. The other thing about D's was the lousy as hell service. You basically had to run down and tackle your waitress just to get her attention, and you only had a fifty/fifty chance of her doing what you asked. It was on account of this that I was sick to death of the soap operas by the time I got my food. It was unnerving to think they'd taken the news off for soap operas. I couldn't see the point in assessing snot. I ate my stuff pretty quickly, and I shouted across the room for the check. The boilermakers didn't like that. I did it again.

I walked down to Jake's house, but he wasn't home. He told me he'd be home but he wasn't. I walked towards the train. There, a man stood outside the station, holding a dirty cat with big feet. The man looked transient, unkempt, and unclean. "Do you want a cat," he said. I told him no. Then he stepped toward me offering the cat, "Do you want a cat?" I told him no, why would I want his God damn cat? I was just getting on the train for Christ's sake. What suggested that I wanted a God damn cat? I didn't think just wanting to go on the train was crime enough to have a smelly cat shoved in my face. So, I didn't feel so bad about being snotty.

I took the train downtown and walked around the business section among all the well dressed people. There wasn't much to think about down there. I walked around and looked at things. I got some coffee and held it to warm my hands. That was all. Then I went home. I left the business district. I went to the non-business district. Actually that's not an accurate term. There was plenty of business going on in that part of town. But it was two-bit and illegal in a dirty way. I walked among the non-well-dressed people. I didn't buy anything in this part of town, although I did walk slowly, in my easy stride. This was not where you wanted to look too out of place or nervous, unused to a city street. But it wasn't so bad that you couldn't fake it. You never look around for street signs down here. That's a conspicuous action. If you discover you've made a wrong turn, you walk up to an empty doorway, take a leak, and turn around. If anybody's watching you or says anything, you ignore them but step in your own stream to show you're not ashamed. Nobody told me to take this tack. I'd reasoned it out and found it damned effective. It was a matter of taking clues from the environment, and I wasn't too bad at it. I just walked around. That was all.

I gave Jake a call from a pay phone. I thought he could meet me down there. I didn't want to be alone. I was thinking about the war. He wasn't home, and I got angry. I left a message on his machine. "Jake. I've been arrested in the South End. It's a big misunderstanding but they're beating the piss out of me down here. I need bail." I cut it off quickly. I didn't think he'd believe it for more than a minute or two, but he shouldn't say he was going to be there when he wasn't.

The next day the oil slick continued to spread in the gulf. Parts of it were said to be on fire. The idea of such a huge swath of oil in the ocean remained alien to me. There were no pictures telling enough. Plenty of reports though. Protests continued. Protests against protests. "Stop trading blood for oil." That was a protest. Governments around the world continued to pledge billions of dollars to the war effort. Our officials said that the Opposition continued to pump oil into the water. Birds and fish were dying. The President's administration sent a team of five environmental experts to help contain the damage. There were very many experts involved with the war.

The Buffalo Bills and the New York Giants (who resided in New Jersey) played the Super Bowl. The game was broadcast to the troops in the desert. A very famous singer lip-synched a pre-recorded "Star Spangled Banner." She had me fooled. If I were one to cry, I would have. The game was played in tribute to the troops. There was talk of postponing it but then someone said, "Let's do it for the troops." The entire country was watching. It was a one-point game. The stadium was full of yellow ribbons for the troops. The halftime show was a tribute to the troops. A ten-year-old boy with blond hair and blue eyes sang "Did You Ever Know That You're My Hero" for the troops. If someone wanted to attack the United States of America and hurt us, they would have attacked that stadium. But then again, that would have been suicide. The next day was a Monday. We had bombed the oil pumps to fight the spill. The spill was estimated at twelve times the size of the most recent largest oil spill in history, off the coast of Alaska months before. History was expanding at an alarming rate. The Secretary of Defense said that the Allies would be set to attack on land the next month, February. People were worried about sending in ground forces. There was talk of the half a million Opposition soldiers waiting for them. Talk of the variety of land mines, descriptions of them blowing the foot out of "foot-soldier." It was established that not much could occur on the ground forces issue because it was at least a month away; much could happen in that time, and any talk would require massive speculation. Speculation had been established as a waste of breath. While the Opposition's Scud missiles were bombing Israeli neighborhoods indiscriminately, the voice on the radio reported that 1.7 million Palestinians, conquered by the Israelis in 1967, had been quarantined in their homes for eleven days by the Israeli army. Crops were left to waste; jobs were not attended. To know that someone is firing missiles at you must be terrifying.

My horoscope read, "Venus in Pisces means a brighter picture in your love life. Public acceptance is also on the rise. Having friends you can trust is absolutely imperative for the time being."

Thirty-seven Opposition fighter jets flew north to an old but for now neutral Nemesis. Quite a bit of anger remained for the Old Nemesis, but they assured the world that any planes landing in their territory would remain there until the war was over. This was a good way for the Old Nemesis to keep its ass out of our sights. Speculation held that these planes were getting new paint jobs, and I knew that this war wouldn't see them again. Acquired Immune Deficiency Syndrome (AIDS) was at the center of a brawl between a minister and a secular public policy activist downtown. Specifically, the brawl was over whether we should distribute free and clean hypodermic needles. The minister was protesting outside the secular man's center of distribution for the needles. They engaged in a verbal exchange.

"Needles equals death."

"No, AIDS equals death."

Then, according to the minister, the secular man bit him on the nose, from where launched a scuffle. AIDS was yet another multibillion-dollar, life and death question to fathom, but not while war kept it off the table.

The next day, forty-one more jets fled to the Nemesis of old. The leader of the Opposition said that the war "…will spill lots of blood…." Speculation did not deem the fleeing jets as intimidating. This was Tuesday.

CHAPTER 15

▼

"…The cost of closing our eyes to aggression is beyond mankind's power to imagine."

The President

Our country was referred to in the printed press as "U.S.," which I read as an emphatic "us." From the dawn of our history, this country has been made up of "us and them." Us and them had been the struggle on which we were weaned. Now, it appeared, in one giant thin way, we were all us. Not even the war protesters were them. They were as much us as any Marine because they were doing what they thought was right; they were exercising their right to free speech, rights to public assembly and protest. They were demanding immaculate action. And most American of all, they were underdogs. If anything, Americanism is a religion formed on the principles of fortitude and the underdog. US made for a strange disquiet. We'd put off the summit with the Soviets. A Soviet official refrained from repeating recent criticisms of the effect of our massive bombing of the Opposition at the joint announcement.

The leader of the Opposition, whom I now regarded as moderately clever but otherwise devoid of anything complementary to the human character, asserted that he would use chemical weapons only as a last resort. It was reported that he said his country had already won "the admiration of the world" by maintaining "our balance" in the Gulf War by employing only conventional arms. "We pray that not a lot of blood will be shed from any nation." This was in contradiction to what was reported to have been said by him earlier. He was a mass of conflict. He said that there was not even a one in a million chance that his country would lose the war. He would not understand my letters to him. He lacked the intellect. He was a waste of my ink, and if I could have shipped a mailbox packed with gunpowder to him, I'd have sent it.

Vietnam was a nightmare to this country. Up to that point we had even won the war with ourselves. And even in the midst of the pullout we would not conceive the thought of our defeat. And we still could not. And after we prepared to defeat the other half of the world for forty years, after we accomplished major victories in that juncture without engagement in a primary military conflict, this little mustache in the desert shows up and thinks we don't stand a one in a million chance against him. If somebody walked up to me and begged me to punch him in the nose, I wouldn't want to, but the more he begged me, the more I'd be inclined to do it. The Opposition Leader looked as though he had been one of those chubby kids on the block that go around with orange soda stains on his cheeks, bossing all the other kids and sitting on top of them when he could catch them, shoving grass up their noses, or in his case sand. US hate that.

The morning newspaper featured a large photo on the front page of the President in the midst of his State of the Union address. He was making a fist with his left hand and holding it at chest level. Somebody behind him was drinking water. He looked earnest but respectable. He was making a delivery at the moment the shutter snapped. When a striped tie is tied, the stripes in the knot go in one direction and those on the tongue in the other.

The President said that the U.S. is "on course" in winning the war, the paper said. He warned that the Opposition Leader "is dead wrong" to believe that his tactics would succeed. The paper said that the President declared he was certain that the U.S. would "prevail." "We stand at a defining hour," the President said. "The winds of change are with us now." As the Opposition threatened doom at the onset of the inevitable ground war, the President said, without reference to these threats, that "Iraq's capacity to sustain war is being destroyed. Our investment, our training, our planning are all paying off. Time will not be Saddam's salvation," the paper said.

The paper highlighted a lack of attention to domestic issues in the President's speech. The word recession did not appear until the 38th paragraph, it said. The President quoted from a letter written to him by a woman from Massachusetts. "My heart is aching, and I think that you should know—your people out here are hurting badly." He said, "I understand. And I'm not unrealistic about the future. But there are reasons to be optimistic about our economy." The reasons he gave were three: no double-digit inflation, no big production debts due to a lack of inventory pileups, and steady flowing exports going at a record rate. I had no idea what those things indicated, but I was quick to agree that none of them sounded bad. The President called for a bipartisan study to help determine sound strategies to stimulate the economy. "Yes, the largest peacetime economic expansion in history had been temporarily interrupted. But our economy is still over twice as large as our closest competitor's." This statement made me feel very masculine.

The President said further about the war, "Each of us will measure, within our-selves, the value of this great struggle. Any cost in lives is beyond our power to measure. But the cost of closing our eyes to aggression is beyond mankind's power to imagine."

That last statement of the President's was brilliant. It seemed to reach out and say something profound, guiding. The public would look at it twice with admira-tion. It was the kind of sentence made for scrutiny in verse, and yet the sound of the sentence was effective, too. This was the mark of brilliance. The Secretary of State said of the Opposition's statement, that we had not a one in a million chance of winning, that it was "whistling past the graveyard." How was it that one acquired the persona of victory?

Germany was moving their troops into Turkey. This provoked more refer-ences to World War II. They'd sent arms to Israel and $5.5 billion to the U.S. This was a world effort after all. I assessed the similarities: Global involvement, war crimes, the Opposition had been accused of playing the role of Hitler, now Germany was involved. A damn fascinating Global Event. It was a tremendous thing happening. And I was a consumer, one of hundreds of millions. Perhaps more than that, but I can't think that high. My concern with a participation in the conflict came from that same feeling I get when I stand on high ledges. It's the nervousness I get. But it isn't nervousness from fear that I'll fall. I know I won't. I'm not an idiot. I have the clarity and physical grace to keep from top-pling over a ledge, taking a step I most sincerely don't intend to. The nervousness comes because I am aware of my attraction to the void beyond the ledge, the attraction to take that step. Unable to take it back. Feel the terror of the plum-met. That the attraction exists makes me nervous. That if I didn't have constant and oppressive control over it, that it would take me. That I take it with me, in its cage to look over the ledge. That I watch it stare and salivate. That the foam drips down on the back of my neck. Hanging over a ledge, I don't feel nervous over the precarious elements, but over my own precarious, American nature. A desire for action. A denial of abstention.

CHAPTER 16

▼

"So far, the war's heroes aren't human."

The Germans themselves were wary of their own involvement in any hostility. German citizens were split on the initiative to send troops to Turkey. The Opposition had threatened Turkey for allowing the Allies use of Turkish air bases. If an attack occurred, Germany would be in it. Young people were fearful of the legacy of Germany's involvement in the two big wars. Turgat Ozal, President of Turkey, accused Germany on German television of being an unreliable ally and losing its fighting spirit. It seemed he was missing something. It had been a German policy not to send any arms to regions of conflict since the mid 1960s, it was said. Figures published recently, it was further said, revealed the number of German companies that had sold products to Iraq which assisted the buildup of that country's chemical arsenal and Scud missile technology as 100. With the recent arms shipment to Israel, this had Germany supplying both sides. Something was obviously significant about all this. In the words maybe. Not so much in the action. Just remarkable business sense.

I didn't mind the payoffs from other countries. I was confidant that the American military could do it right, whatever it was we needed to do. Communication was the primary tool in a command, and coordinating foreign armies would lead the whole operation into wasted effort, supplies, and lives. There is no bigger waste than putting a bullet in someone on your own side. Militarily, that kind of thing is a proclamation of suicidal discombobulating. The payoffs were, first, a way for us to assure and assert the commitment of other countries to our cause without suffering the befuddlement of coordinating their somewhat less competent militaries, and, second, a way to take away the bite this conflict could potentially have here at home. A stroke of luck might even bring us a profit. On the radio I heard the English broadcasters refer to the $5.5 billion as five thousand million dollars. "Those bastards better catch up," I thought.

A Palestinian refugee camp was shelled by Israeli gunboats in retaliation for a rocket attack on Israel's self-declared security zone in Lebanon. Our manifest destiny would bring us into this conflict in one way or another, it was clear. Jordan continued to receive the refugees pouring in from the Land of the Opposition. The Opposition was said to have said that an Allied pilot being used as a human shield was killed in the Allied bombing. I believe this constituted a war crime. Ten of their jets flew north to Iran. Unidentified officials were reported as saying that oil had stopped flowing from a loading terminal off the Kuwaiti coast and a fire had been put out. The French Defense Minister resigned because he disagreed with the Allied bombardment. "Day 14," they called it.

The headline read, "So far, the war's heroes aren't human." Neither were its victims, really.

I went downtown on the subway in the afternoon. There were three large men on the subway and some other people. The three large men spoke about prison in loud voices which were intentional, I thought. They seemed not to notice that there were other people around them. That what they were saying, and the language they chose to say it, was offensive. That there were children around. They didn't seem to notice. Or if they did, maybe they just said to themselves, "So what." Nobody looked directly at them. Looks of disgust were tossed back and forth. The men never looked directly at anyone either. They looked around a lot. All three of them. Amidst their loud voices and animation they looked the train car over a thousand times before I realized they were doing it. I remember one sentence distinctly. "Bullshit, man, I told him, I been to the joint, I got nothing to fear. Now you better hand that shit over." That would have been enough for me. Prison is a thing that goes as far as I care to imagine. Prison seems to push the strength of a person's motivations beyond even the power of desperation. I was afraid to consult desperation. Beyond it was the unthinkable.

I couldn't get in touch with anyone so I was walking around town hoping to run into somebody I knew. There were stores to go into. I went to the pubs. I skipped the disco. I skipped the sports bar. The sports bar talked about the war with no understanding. In the pubs there were no televisions. People drank beer and danced to the music in the aisles. I danced a little bit myself, but I liked the beer far more. People were friendly and talkative. People talked about anything. I was taking a leak when some guy took the urinal next to me and started telling jokes. "What do you call the useless flesh around a pussy? A woman." He was a big guy so I waited until I got to the door to say, "So, in a way your mouth and a pussy are pretty much the same thing." That kind of thing is the hazard of the men's room. That and all the piss you have to wade through.

There were some women there. A group of them together. They were drinking beer and shots of tequila, a preference of mine. I was up front talking with them about some kind of nonsense. They were very happy and had lots of jokes together. They bought me a shot of Gold, a liqueur with flecks of pyrite. A man came in the door. He was dirty. His hair messed up. His clothes looked like he had been hit by a car. He was talking rapidly in a normal tone of voice. I couldn't make out what he was saying. He walked around the pub, through the crowd of people, very quickly. He was talking the whole time. People ignored him when he came near them and stared at him the rest of the time. He was coming toward me. Talking out loud. He was looking at me. I stepped toward him. "What," I said. He got to where I could hear him, as if we were conversing. He was speaking nonsense. Not even forming particular words. Not of any language. He said a couple of times, "I don't know," and, "You know what I mean, man." I said, "What?" and "I'm sorry. I can't understand what you're saying." He kept talking, and he darted away and out the door in mid-sentence.

The bartender looked at me and made a waving motion with his left hand as if to dismiss the man.

"He's crazy. That guy's out of his mind."

"What do you mean?"

"He's totally schizophrenic. Good for him he's not violent."

"What do you mean?"

"If he were violent he'd be in fucking jail or something."

"Where does he live now?"

"I don't know? In the street I guess."

"What kind of fortune is that?"

"Who's to judge," he said and shrugged. It was at that moment that I saw Jake barrel through the door. He was holding a pint of beer close to his chest, which didn't spill as he came in, and he was smoking a cigarette down to the butt. I was surprised to see him but more surprised to see Felix and Georgia come in behind him. Apparently, he knew Georgia from school. I found out that she was very generous when buying drinks, and that Felix didn't feel comfortable displaying his affection publicly. Otherwise, it was difficult to communicate as the swelling crowd and the noise began to crush us. Jake had been incoherent from the beginning.

I was loaded when I got on the train and very concerned about getting mugged. There was a definite loneliness sitting on the last train, just myself and strangers, drunk. The whole time thinking of violence. Ready to fight. A little frustrated with all that anticipation. I had to piss. Maintaining my seat without wetting it was painful. It kept me awake. If somebody tried to mug me, and I had to fight them, I would probably wind up peeing in my pants. The pain was almost disabling. On the walk to my house, that man asked whether I wanted to buy his cat.

"I don't want your damn cat!"

I dreamt I was in the front lines. I dreamt there was a little desert community set up. That there were two chain-link fences, on either side of a highway built right on the border. The Opposition forces figured that they would drive out in Cadillacs, station wagons, jeeps, and tanks up and down the main drag. Strutting their stuff. They figured we wouldn't bomb them because they were so close to us. So all of these people drove out in their station wagons and such, none of them in uniform, and we drove forces through them to cut their rear ranks off from the Republican Guard, which was up front. Then we bombed the shit out of the Guard. I woke up to the pain of my enlarged bladder. It was a pain to get to the bathroom. It was cold tiled floor on my bare feet.

I slipped on some shoes and walked downstairs. I grabbed the neighbors' paper. The coffee was brewed by the time I got back to the kitchen, and I took it to my room. I put the radio on and laid the paper out on my desk. "12 U.S. Marines Dead in Fighting." My God. They're dying. The Marines are dead.

Growing up, we had next-door neighbors that my family knew all of my life. When we moved, we kept in touch. Harvey was the eldest son of that family. Five years my senior. As he grew up, his intelligence inspired his peers to beat the piss out of him. I was young. I remember it all very well. He was due to visit us in our new house. I was fourteen. He was due on this one particular morning. I'd come home after my parents had gone to bed. It was a Saturday morning. The night before, I had come in and watched a music video show. I went into the dining room and lay down in my clothes with my head on my arms and went to sleep. I awoke at 7:30 in the morning. It was one of the most restful sleeps I'd ever had. The kind of sleep that leaves your body feeling unburdened. I stood up and walked from the dark dining room into the hall. I rubbed some crust from my eye. My mother appeared, coming down the stairs.

"There you are," she said.

"Yes. I slept down here."

"Why did you sleep down here?"

"I just did."

"Go upstairs. Your father wants to talk to you."

"Why?"

"Because you have to know." She went into the kitchen.

I was confused. She said those words without much inflection.

I wondered what it could be. I was sure she had made more of it than it was. My mother always did that, made little things seem so dense.

I walked upstairs to find my dad sitting in my room.

"Mom said you wanted to talk to me."

He stood up and faced me, a few inches taller.

"Last night, Harvey was out drinking with his friend. They were driving. They got into an accident and the car went off the road." He stepped forward and embraced me. He rested his head heavily on my shoulder. This was an action remarkable in itself.

I was waiting for the rest of the story. I had no idea what to say. Confronted by the silence, the unusual embrace, I said, "What hospital is he in?" Tears in his voice, my father said, "I'm afraid he was killed." This was the first time I realized my father could cry, that a man was capable. But never did I fully realize, not through the funeral, nor at any other time, Harvey's death, and not even to this day. And though each member of his family cried their tears on my four-teen-year-old shoulder, his death never fully occurred for me—hardly more than my own.

Sitting down looking at the article, sipping my coffee, I felt Harvey slip into my room, slip over my shoulder. "Twelve Marines are dead," he said in a low tone. "They're dead."

He said, "You live your life as impeccably as you want, and you're never guaranteed life. Life insurance, you see, is actually death insurance. Gambling the cost of your policy each year that you're going to die. You get the present moment. After that is a gift, a surplus. You don't have any guarantees beyond that of the present moment."

I said to him, "Oh, come on, Harvey! Why not just live it up then? What's the purpose? Should my one moment be something or nothing? Productive or destructive? Does it even matter? What are you coming here to tell me?"

Harvey said, "Look at me. I didn't expect to die, and then I was dead. The Marines were warriors; trained to fight, to survive, mentally trained. Then they were dead. You see it, don't you—the foolishness—by acting without purpose, you add to the everyday conditions that threaten your life. Invincibility is a fool's game. I should know."

All the training. All the effort. The education. All the things I've ever done. Thinking about the people I would become. The striving for an impeccable life-style. To come to death. To Twelve Dead Marines. Then what do we all work for together? What is it that we do, that we strive for? The tremendous conflict over the ends. All the talk of Armageddon. The air raid drills. Crawling under our desks together in grade school. Filing out in the hall with hands laced behind our necks, heads bowed, our elbows braced against the wall. For what purpose, anyway? I couldn't have felt safer anywhere in the world than in my grade school. One more absurd requirement with no good purpose but to make me do something I didn't want to do. And to make me do it for a good long time. The drills were boring. A lot of waiting in line. Breathing the hair of the kid in front of you. I didn't wash much; I didn't mind. At least it was a break. Rotating boredom.

"Armageddon," said Harvey. I was getting another cup of coffee, and he was talking all the while. "Your one death is Armageddon? In dying, everybody thinks you've died while you think everyone else has." He paused. "It's all pretty fucking grim," he said.

"It's just the way it is," I said. It was cold. I put on my heater.

He continued. "You think of your own death, the end of everything you know. And then your community. Aren't we born with investments in community? Whatever "making something out of yourself" means, don't we do that only by virtue of the fact that we live in community? Armageddon is just another kind of death."

I whispered to him with my coffee breath. "I see what you mean, Harvey. Especially now. All you and I and our peers have known is not more than that we are capable of destroying the world. We don't have to entertain religious fantasy. Religious considerations have been pre-empted since before we were born. Twelve Marines are dead. I've never expected anything less of war than Armageddon. But since I never could fathom my own death, I always envision myself as the one left alone."

Harvey jumped in, "And isn't that remarkable? All the stories have one man left. Or a little community. It's an interesting parody really, because on one hand it suggests we don't believe in ourselves, and on the other hand we can't stop. I always liked the idea that you could eat canned food for the rest of your life and read books. All the time to do everything. But actually, a person alone on this earth would be totally deprived of all that. Without life, without people, without the interaction, art becomes a vehicle of decay. It represents past dead things. Art becomes a daily exercise in gouging one's eyes out only to have them grow back every day. The scene, you see, is a lone man chained to the Earth by his life, surrounded by art. The art becomes his sickness because it represents his relationships, the normal human feelings humans have in community. Now, without that community, the art slaps him in the face with the sickness that sits out in a devastated plain and awaits him. The relationships he will have, the sickness, with rocks, with buildings, mannequins, his own reflection, his own right hand. Couldn't you see a man cutting off his hand to spite the sickness? Like an animal gnawing off its foot in a trap. What kind of an idea is that for a world anyway?"

As many as 4,000 Opposition soldiers and 160 tanks rolled across a fifty-mile front. They drove south with turrets pointing north. When they got into position, they rotated the turrets and opened fire. They killed twelve Marines. They took an abandoned town called Khafji. Their government made a big deal of it. As if they'd gotten something from their effort. Our government said that enemy troops in Khafji were pinned down by Saudi troops who surrounded the city. The government said that the enemy lost as much as a quarter of the armor involved in the attack. How many of their soldiers were killed though? What was the score?

The radio talked about one of the dead Marines who was from Salt Lake City, a lance corporal. The Marine's father told his Congressman to tell the President that he supported the war effort.

CHAPTER 17

▼

There's always one way out.

I wheeled my chair over to the window. There was a man throwing dirt on the street, my neighbor. I'd often thought I'd like to cripple that son of a bitch. He was obnoxious, always ranting if anyone parked in front of his house. A private way is a free-for-all as far as parking goes, I explained. He finally put these big granite rocks down in what he claimed as his spot. He drove a truck, and no car had enough clearance to go over them. He was doing our little community a favor down there, making his contribution. I realized that even though all the houses were nearly built on the same foundation, I knew only a couple of people by sight. Everyone probably knew that whining crud. I saw him in the post office once and he was whining then too, suggesting that someone there had stolen his package.

I watched the dirt hit the ice and disperse. He was probably killing my chances of winning a lawsuit. I was cold. Harvey was gone. The radio was playing very loud, but I don't remember what. I had clear plastic on my windows for insulation. I heard the dirt as he threw it. I heard the wind. I was trying to imagine dead Marines, trying to imagine the impact, but could not. What was the role of death in all of this, and why had I no understanding of the death of a countryman? How many times had I seen people butchered on-screen? Didn't I see for myself over and over again, how death, violent death, would appear to occur? Yes, I had. These were men of my land, but I noticed no difference without them. Soon there would be pictures everywhere of family members in grieving agony. Of course there would, that was the usual thing. This was the start. The American death toll would begin to rise, and this feature in the news of the families would disappear. It was the usual thing. I would never see their faces again, not hear their names, nor hear their sobbing. Dependents of the men would receive checks from the government for the rest of their lives, and not even on each

November 11, while running around in some park enjoying the holiday, would I hear of it again for the rest of mine.

I had never been on foreign soil. As I watched my neighbor with the dirt, I began to think of it for the first time. I didn't think of England. Maybe because I speak English and have seen English TV. When I thought foreign, I thought of France. I thought sunshine, and the South of France came before me. My coffee was cold. I saw the beach. All those distractions. All the pleasant noise around there to fill you up and pack your nerves in tightly. No jumping around. I'm not a beach person, but I could sit on the beach, under an umbrella, on the Riviera. I could drink margaritas all day long, all week long. Of course, no picture would be complete without the woman. Some miscellaneous woman, some incomplete. I knew all the ingredients of a margarita, but the woman? I'd work on it anyway. Pick a face from a magazine. Or someone walking down the beach. That one. What would she be like?

CHAPTER 18

▼

Finally, Honest Warfare

Apparently, the bipartisan congressional standing ovation evoked by the President during his State of the Union address won tears from members of the military serving in the Gulf. The open, warm, enthusiastic show of support, like a father's for his son, was a demonstration in the face of the Vietnam legacy. Troops would not be sent without a declaration of purpose, nor would they be politically undermined once committed. It was a display for Americans to see and digest, to make it part of ourselves, the way one would a surgically rejoined limb. It was a display for the world, to understand the meaning of "American Military Presence." We had checkmated the Soviet Union across the board into submission. Now there was no chess game. Only honest warfare.

The paper reported a consensus of a number of Middle Eastern political figures, all of them hotshots. It was expressed that the Arab people were always looking for a strong leader to lead them against the major players and that the enemy may, to some, be that man. The one-man-against-the-world image intrigued many Arabs, it was quoted. They speculated on the birth of the enemy's legend describing its appeal to the Arab people in the same way one might describe the appeal of Robin Hood to the poor. They said he was reviving the conflict between Islam and the West, a conflict going back to the bloodletting days of the Crusades. But those were the days of religion, when men went to kill with the excuse of God—Saint Louis IX of France mustering the seventh and eighth, dying on the latter in 1270, just twelve years after the Mongols took Baghdad. The Mongol Horde, that was a godless group. They followed a lackluster shamanism. Presumably their lifestyle hardly gave them the time to ramble on about it. By this time the Mongols had adopted the practice of leaving as many of the conquered population alive as possible (as a means of generating more wealth) and always had a firm policy of religious tolerance, eventually even embracing the variety of religions encountered (which was their doom).

As imperialists, the West laid down the banner of the Crusades long ago. And religious tolerance? The U.S. had at least this in common with the Mongols when it came to motivations for war. We were indifferent. Was it with Islam then that we were in conflict? If there was any aspect of Islam in conflict with the rest of the world, it was due only to the fact they were the last holdouts for world domination based on theistic principles. If it were the Mongols in Operation Desert Storm rather than the Americans, the battle would have certainly ensued and been over by now, with the land of the Opposition becoming the fifty-first state. The puny neighbor they had assaulted would become the fifty-second.

About the enemy, the Middle Eastern hotshots said that it would be better to leave him alive and clearly diminished, for his death would serve only to prop him up as martyr, his propaganda turning to belief and in turn to reality. In many Arab countries, the popularity of the enemy was deprived of a voice by the leadership of the respective governments. Syria for example, enforced Hafez Assad's anti-Iraq policy by the use of their secret police. The enemy's appeal to pan-Arab sentiments, anti-imperialism and Islamic fundamentalism was certainly clever, considering the fact that he had invaded and proceeded to rape his Arab/ Islamic neighbor.

In further news, the paper reported a questioning by appropriate officials of whether or not the country will be prepared to meet the needs of Gulf War veterans with an already overburdened relief system. Military and private hospitals were predicted to be overrun. Also, minoxidil was touted in an advertisement, dressed as a news article, to work on ninety percent of patients undergoing hair-loss therapy.

My mind was all over the place on this, day fifteen of the war. On the run I thought of no one, noticed no one. As I walked up the stairs to my door, Georgia called to me from her door. I turned to her, still out of breath. She wanted to know if I'd seen her paper around.

"Where did you leave it," I said. She explained that she hadn't left it anywhere, nor had she even seen it.

"How do you know it exists," I asked. She got irritated (I was surprised this was possible).

"What?" she said. I apologized.

"I'm a little light-headed," I explained. She told me the delivery service insisted it was being delivered but she hadn't been getting it for the past few weeks.

"What color is it," I asked her.

"Black and white," she said.

"And read all over?"

"Not by me," she said. "You don't know anything about it then?"

"No."

"Thanks." She closed her door. I suppose right then would have been a good time to start feeling guilty about stealing the papers, especially those of a neighbor, and then lying about it. Perhaps, I should have even considered stopping the practice. But practice it was and it was practice I needed. It took a certain bravado to waltz downstairs in full view of even the rock wacko and swipe that paper day after day. A day here, a day there, who would notice? But every day, including Sunday when the booty weighed you down? That was beyond practice. It was training. As far as guilt, no question I was guilty. But, the feeling of guilt is only an impediment to the practice of war. That's why the Mongols were such good warriors. They felt no remorse.

Georgia and Felix were having a party that evening to which I had been invited. I would, of course, have to go, for the walls being as thin as sheets, I would experience it one way or the other. Georgia was the director of a local arts organization and made almost as little salary as I. I never did determine her own interest in the arts, whether it was as an artist or as a connoisseur. She was apparently very well connected. The guests at the party consisted of a range from the guy who had offered me the cat by the subway to a member of the city's Board of Education.

I began preparing for the party right away, as I had nothing else to fill my time. It was a mere eight hours until I was expected. I began with a damn hot shower. I wondered about Georgia, wondered about intercourse with her as one often does at these times. Felix did not seem to be a hateable guy, kind of a hippie guy. There was a lot of disdain for hippies around the country. The President and his Predecessor had been a part of that movement by creating the "Great Liberal Scare." The President's campaign had made the word "liberal" a dirty one. He was so effective that some liberals shunned the label. Knee-jerk liberal. After the election that term ran a chill up your spine. Of course, hippies were far left of knee-jerk liberals.

But that was not the whole of it. That was not why the driving force of the American scene, the nation's young people, hated liberals. Those of my generation hated liberals because many of our parents had been hippies, and had since made money hand over fist giving us all that we wanted while selling their souls. They then tried to regain the nostalgia without the ideals, inundating us with movies, television, and radio stations up and down the dial that were totally devoted to their generation. How many movies and television shows about the

Vietnam War and about the 'sixties and what a great time it was, and what a crummy time it was, and how the whole thing was to be open with yourself, giving, and if you weren't honest to fake it. And the God damn radio stations playing the same God damn music they'd been playing for years, since the day I was born. And worse, many of them refused to play anything new unless it was by an old artist. And the reason all this went on was because in the 'eighties, all these baby boomer bastards came into power. Often, I'd hear one of the old sellouts say, "We really thought that we were going to change the world…make it a better place…there was a real sense of that." I'd often think, "Then why did you stop?" Sure, most of the political leaders of the movement were assassinated, but leaders aren't movements; they are still just people. I often wonder what became of the legacy I was supposed to receive from them. Suddenly it was just fashion with which we were being bombarded. And the values? The values were gone.

Aside from the hallelujah rhetoric about their generation, I had nothing against the hippies of old, though I had far more respect for people who had fulfilled their ideals. Those were few and far between, and these days they could be found leading antiwar protests again. The new hippies, most of them, were just people who didn't buy into the rampant meism we were fed as children and teenagers. I didn't have anything against Felix.

I decided to go to Jake's house. He was hung over, and there I spent the day watching television, the boon of popular culture. It was my first all-day affair with the thing in years. The programming consisted of advertisements for Lawyers, Psychics, Trade Schools, and Insurance Companies. Daytime television, it seemed, was a seminar on how to deal with feelings of loneliness, incompetence, obscurity, victimization, vulnerability, and boredom. Daytime television was directed at the adulterated cauldron of misery which was unemployed America. The network of 900 numbers, some of which cost five dollars a minute. Lawyer's television included the most asked question, "Have you, or someone you love, been in an accident?" Insurance television asked, "Are you or someone you love, over fifty-five?" Another popular insurance theme was, "Attention veterans of the armed forces discharged after 1929 or currently serving, and members of their families…This special plan is only available to veterans discharged after 1929 and members of their families." Trade-school television created technical places like the "New England School of Office Procedure and Refrigerator Repair." Truck-driving school promised an opportunity to "step up into some steady work and have a chance to make something of yourself." It promised "On the road, I'm my own boss." It was like I had invited the violin drunk from downtown to my living room. Like he was sawing the bow and singing, "Staring at the TV, reflects the you in me," over and over again to some blind and groping tune. At the end of each commercial, he'd laugh his soggy head off. I wanted to call up the psychics and scream, "How stupid do you think I am?" But that wasn't worth five bucks.

Jake and I got to the party about an hour early. I asked Georgia whether she'd found anything out about the newspapers. No, she hadn't. I was talking with Felix much of the time and the guy with the cat. He didn't recognize me. The guy with the cat was a "this and that." That's what he answered when I asked him what he did for a living. He told me he was in a band, but that they hadn't played any gigs yet. When I asked him what kind of band he said, "Rock band." He was the singer. Felix was an electrician. He always smiled when he spoke to strangers like me, seemingly to assure them that what they said was interesting. He had the habit of nodding his head a lot. He only spoke about himself when asked directly. He made flat statements to answer questions. "I am an electrician," he said baring his teeth. He didn't want to appear to be hiding anything, but he wasn't real helpful in driving the conversation. The apartment was clean and decorated with post-college bohemian crap, tapestries, candles, unusual art prints. A step up from cheap with a mark of maturity and style. There was an old banjo hanging in the widow. The rugs were vacuumed. The bathroom was clean. It made me feel cheated to think that my place was in the same building as this one. While I was talking to Felix, I kept looking at this huge spider web in the corner of the ceiling. He saw me looking at it but refused to acknowledge my doing so. I was going to say something, but it felt a little like asking a librarian how she got "that black eye." So, I didn't.

Felix had a friend named Robin, an engineer who had been working for the state constructing public housing. She had been laid off for some time. She was the kind you'd have in a worthwhile conversation, and just as she or you were about to say something, she'd see someone she knew and nearly bolt over you to say hello to them. But in fifteen minutes she'd swing around the room, and I'd find myself in the same conversation as though we hadn't missed a beat. She did that to me three times. Jake spent most of his time hitting on the woman from the Board of Education, who, he later told me, was secretly a clairvoyant. "I just know it," he said.

I got into a conversation with one woman who was some kind of kamikaze skier. She told me about jumping out of helicopters onto mountaintops, telling me it was the rush of a lifetime. It was better than sex. I wondered whether that was meant as a challenge to me. She was talking about the local ski scene mostly because she hadn't yet raised enough cash for the bonsai extravaganza she was planning. She was hoping to get television coverage for it, but with the war and all, that had been difficult even to talk about.

"Around here I just ski without poles, but the slopes suck. I mean I have to drink Cutty Sark all day just to make it the least itty bit challenging but even then it's not much around here." She laughed and looked around as if to see whether anyone was listening. "Then this friend of mine, you know—he's a madman, he's crazy, he strapped a ski to his head once and went all the way down some mountain out there in Colorado—well, he told me to rub lemon juice in my eyes. That does somethin' for the excitement, cause you can't see, you know, you gotta worry 'bout other skiers, you really got it on the line then, lawsuits and everything, injuring somebody in all kinds a ways you can't imagine. Gives me shivers just thinkin' 'bout it. But the lemon juice stings. You can only really do it one run out of the day. I did it twice once but that was a son of a bitch. You can't wear goggles or nothin' cause your eyes are tearin' too much. But then you get the wind. These mountains suck around here. It's better than nothing I guess. We do have fun. On that second run, boy," she laughed, "I had a couple close calls. But it was so painful. That was the real bitch 'bout it, the pain. Some people have fun when they're in pain, but I can't get that into it." She laughed. "So, do you ski?"

"No. I don't really have time, you know, with the job and all."

"What do you do?"

"I'm an exterminator for the Internal Revenue Service." She laughed. "I'm very serious," I said. "I am. I just started though a couple months ago."

"Well, what do you have to do to get a job like that?"

"Nothing really. There's a special trade school in Wisconsin. I specialized in "Low Impact Methods of Extermination."

"What do you mean 'extermination'?"

"I exterminate people who are heavily in debt to the government. Mostly tax dodgers. Some people who have welched on favors they've been granted, but that's strictly freelance. The government finds it's easier to collect on estates of the deceased than from live people. It avoids a hell of a lot of paperwork and saves the taxpayers a tremendous amount of money."

"You're joking."

"No. Dodgers cost a lot of money. Court costs, government attorneys, agents tracking them down. Usually, in collecting from an estate, there's no protest. The agency identifies people who are heavily into the government and show no promise of remitting payment. There's a whole department that determines the net worth of the subject, possibility of collecting on the estate, and if it all looks good the specs get sent to my department, and my supervisor assigns cases from the list. It's very interesting work."

"You're telling me that the IRS trains and assigns assassins to kill people that owe the government money?"

"Well, assassin is a strong word, but essentially, yes, if, and it's a big if, there's a good possibility of collecting the money. There are many people in prison, for example, who are penniless. That's why they're in prison."

"That's ridiculous."

"No. It's very true."

"Why would you be telling me this?"

"Well, it's perfectly legitimate. You know. It's legal. My agency was voted into law on New Year's Eve, 1988, as part of the funding for Head Start. I fill out a W-2 form, and I'm registered as an exterminator."

"What do you have to do with Head Start?"

"Nothing. It's just that Head Start never would have been funded without my department. It's the way they play the game down there. Anyway, here I am."

"If this were true, there's no way you'd be able to tell me this. You're joking."

"Well, you don't owe any money on your taxes do you?"

"No…"

"Then we have no professional relationship. Why shouldn't I tell you? You're a taxpayer. Besides, no one told me to keep it a secret. It's a trade school in Wisconsin. An 800 number on television. I just called them up. Wisconsin is damn cold but it was a small price to pay for a one-way ticket to an exciting career. I get to travel all over the country. I eat well. There's tremendous planning involved. It's kind of like hunting. I have to know the subject's environment. I have to conform the extermination to specific orders. It's very detail oriented. Virtually no margin for error. Sometimes I get to ski. But I'm not very good."

"That's crazy."

I leaned over to her. "Look, rubbing lemon juice in your eyes is crazy. I'm just making a living."

CHAPTER 19

---▼---

We're all in this together.

The next morning I awoke under a cold blanket with a roaring headache. It was brutality. The phone rang, and I let it ring a few times. It was like staring into a hail storm, naked.

"What is it," I said.

"How are you doing?" It was Jake.

"I'm shit. What do you want?"

"I was mugged last night."

I didn't get too excited right off. I didn't have the energy, but I also figured he wouldn't be calling me on the phone if it were too bad. "Are you all right?" I asked.

"They beat me up. I got a big black eye."

"Did they break anything on you?"

"No. I didn't have any money. That's why they beat me up. My eye's like a softball."

"Do you have a headache?"

"Yeah. I think a concussion. I've been waking up every two hours."

In the midst of taking it in, I closed my eyes and nearly slipped back to sleep. "Where did it happen?" I asked.

"Right down the block on the way home from the bar."

"What were you doing alone?"

"You know how it is. My friends wanted to go home for hours, but I kept running into cool people to talk to and I wanted to talk to them. So I did. I guess they got tired of waiting so they left."

"Okay. I'm coming down. I just have to get my ass in gear. I'll see you in an hour…wait! Do you have a paper?"

"No."

"Okay. I'll be down."

I dropped the phone and closed my eyes as if for the last time. My head felt as though my brain were expanding against the confines of my skull, as though my eyeballs were being pushed out from the inside. My stomach was rolling into itself like a tourniquet. I rolled out of bed and onto the floor. I opened my eyes as if for the last time, quick and wide. The world on that floor was hard and cold and shocked me to my feet. It seemed like ages before I got washed, and I dressed myself with deliberate motions, like a fighter getting ready for the ring.

As I walked out the door, I bent over and swiped Georgia's paper, snickering to myself. It was sunny and cold. When I got to his apartment, I found Jake as he had described. He had a wicked headache, probably worse than mine. His eye was puffed so that he couldn't open it. He hadn't been to the hospital and didn't want to go. It looked to me as if they hit him a few times on that one eye. I was surprised he hadn't been knocked out. I got some crushed ice in a towel for him, some ibuprofen, and some whiskey. I didn't let him sleep the rest of the day. The headache was making him feel nauseated, so I mixed the whiskey with water. I thought I was going to puke as I handed it to him. The ice bag was painful to him but after a bit the eye was numb, and then of course the whiskey did its part. Jake decided he didn't like drinking alone and coaxed me into taking some whiskey with him. I poured the drink and sipped it as if it were my last. It was my first. The demon assaulting my eyeballs took his rest, and the rest of my ailments began to pass away with each sip.

Jake told me there were two guys who had attacked him. Would he call the police? No. He didn't get a look at them at all. It was dark, really dark. When he pulled his pockets out, showing them he had no money, they grabbed him by the hair on top of his head and punched him in the face. When he fell on the ground, he heard one of them spit, but he didn't think it hit him. They walked away. He did not know in which direction. He said he had no way of identifying them. He had not looked at them when they confronted him. He looked past them trying to see whether anyone else was around. After they had started hitting him, he just collapsed on the ground. He said they probably would have killed him if he'd resisted. Perhaps so.

After a while I asked, "How do you feel, Jake?"

"I'm feeling better." The swelling of his eye had gone down a bit. I poured him more whiskey.

"How do you feel about the attack, though?"

"I wish it didn't happen."

"But how do you feel?"

"How do you want me to feel? I got beat up. It happens. It's not the best neighborhood. I don't think I'll be walking home from the bar anymore."

"What are you going to do?"

"Drive."

"If I were you, Jake, I'd be deranged with anger right now. The fact that these assholes just walked up to you and demanded money from you, victimizing you, feeling justified. They probably didn't think twice about it before or afterwards."

"Probably not, no."

"But then they strike you down because you don't have anything for them to steal. Hitting you just because they felt like it, because they could. What's behind that? Nothing. Not even savagery. They walked away, you said?"

"Yes."

"That disgusts me. Probably didn't even need the money. Just saw you walking there and decided to mug you, like deciding to pick up a quarter on the ground as you're walking down the street. Those fucking bastards, we ought to cruise the fucking streets with a shotgun."

"I wouldn't be able to recognize them."

"Fuck that! You would, Jake. I don't suppose we'd have to kill them, unless they were in a group or something. No sense in taking unnecessary chances. You should at least report it."

"There's no reason to. I wouldn't be able to identify them anyway."

"The fucking cops probably know the bastards by name, too."

"Don't take it so personally."

"How can you not take it personally?"

"It happens all the time; those guys didn't know who I was. I was scared. I'm happy it wasn't any worse."

"Yeah, well you're the one sitting there with the God damn black eye. I don't see how you can't take it personally. It was an attack on you. They were going to take your money. They punched you. I don't even think it matters why they did it. The fact is, they did. If you had a gun would you have shot them?"

"I wouldn't have let them hurt me, but no, I wouldn't have shot them. But I was drunk. The way they came at me took me by surprise. That's why carrying a gun or anything is stupid. Because if somebody attacks you, they'll probably take whatever it is and use it on you."

"Bullshit! I'd have blown their fucking heads off. That's why I don't like this neighborhood. There's no sense of fucking community. If I were walking at night by myself, or even with someone, with a gun, that thing would be in my hand just under the flap of my coat. God damn it, Jake! Those fuckers should be caught and flayed! Why don't they have a God damn life? What are they doing walking around at two in the morning preying on members of their own God damn community? Don't they have any respect for themselves? There's a God damn war on and we have our own beating us up. That's sickening."

"It's a fact of life," said Jake. "We live in a city. People get beaten up every day."

"I know they do, Jake, but for Christ's sake what are they thinking about. We're at war, the economy is in the shithole, and we have our own people attacking us. We need contribution, restoration. People like that attack without purpose, make no contribution, they're liabilities. For Christ's sake, if you're not going to do anything productive you don't have to make it worse for everyone else. Those bastards are going to force you to drive home from that bar from now on. Now, you could kill someone that way, but what's your option? Getting killed yourself on the walk home. That's a hell of a choice to have."

Jake said, "What are you talking about? People get attacked in cities; they get murdered for no reason. It happens everywhere. It's no big surprise that I got mugged. I knew it was risky to leave the bar so late. You ever hear of people sticking their hands under lawn mowers while the damn thing's still going? They don't have to believe the warning. They lose their fingers just the same."

"I know all that shit, Jake, I know it. But where's the sense of community? Your neighbors shouldn't be beating the crap out of you."

"You don't know if they were my neighbors. They could have been from anywhere. Besides, I wouldn't know my neighbors if I was looking them in the face."

We were both feeling a lot better physically, though Jake still looked like a pile of guts. This whole thing had gotten me agitated. I was thinking about the pizza guy getting shot in the head. What crime could a pizza man possibly commit to deserve that? I picked up the paper. Khafji had been retaken "after fierce fight." The paper said that forty-two enemy tanks had been destroyed and 160 prisoners taken. It said the Leader though might still consider the defeat a worthwhile effort. It said the enemy had achieved tactical surprise, managed to lead some of their forces out of a town the Allies had sealed off, had held the town for a day and a half and showed that "the agenda is not necessarily set by him who wields the biggest club." The paper said that while the General said that the Khafji incident was militarily insignificant, the leader could claim at least a propaganda success. This was a feature of "News Analysis." I felt a little undermined by it. You stand before your foe rippling with muscle, squashing his spongy head, and when your enemy reaches out to slap a pimple on your biceps they say you've been embarrassed. The General's assessment was the proper one of course. "No military significance." The enemy loses forty-two tanks, 160 soldiers captured, they never mentioned Opposition casualties but I would have bet plenty, all for nothing, and they say it's our embarrassment. Whose side was that son of a bitch on?

I read a story about the dead Marines. It was confirmed through family members that at least eleven of the twelve firmly believed that they were fighting for a just cause. The leader of the Opposition was referred to as a madman in the article. Of course, it didn't matter what the soldiers believed. I was thinking that if they spent any time out there on the field wondering about that, they had wasted time, energy, and concentration. On the field, there is no room for a consideration of the justness of the fight. The fight is before you. Fight. They were young, all of them. Maybe they just didn't know.

London announced that U.S. B-52 bombers would be allowed to fly missions from British air bases. Damn gracious of them, I thought. The paper further stated that few details of the battle over Khafji were available. Journalists who had visited the front told of street fighting; Marines firing machine guns into enemy positions, the enemy responding with rocket and artillery fire. Word was that Saudi and Qatari troops sustained heavy casualties. The Old Nemesis, to the east of the enemy, was reported to have said that they couldn't get a straight story from the pilots of the renegade Opposition aircraft.

Sometimes, when you know you're going to destroy an opponent, when it's obvious to the naked eye, and yet the mustached little shit stands before you jeering, intensifying the fight, you have to wonder, "…is he just that God damn stupid, or does he know something I don't?" The nuclear capability, the chemical weapons: he was holding two wild cards. "Weapons of mass destruction," a trashy, convoluted term. The question was, "Does he have them or did we knock out his capability?" One day we'd hear a huge percentage of his capabilities had been knocked out by air strikes and the next we'd hear of rumors that we hadn't knocked out as much as we had thought. Whenever I saw or heard this kind of thing, I'd say aloud, "Well, which is it, fellas? God damn it!" You'd think with all the military technology they had over there, bombs that could find a pimple on my ass if they wanted them to, and all the press over there, those CNN renegades in Baghdad especially, they could find that one damn thing out. Does he have those fucking weapons or doesn't he? And why the fuck are you telling me you've knocked them out when you haven't? All that jerking around seemed almost deliberate.

The truth of the matter was—and I hadn't heard a word said about it by all those commentators and analysts because it seemed none of them had balls enough to fill their jockey shorts—that the line had been drawn on the sixth of

August, 1945. If the enemy intended to step up to that line, it would be the last step he ever took. His decision would wipe Baghdad off the face of the Earth. Justification of the use of nuclear weapons on the part of the United States would be obvious. An immediate and waste-laying strike would be the only cure for a cannon loose with nuclear and chemical warheads. The enemy thought he was terrifying. Like the historical Dracula, Vlad, who had a greater thirst for blood than his fictional counterpart, who lined the front wall of his castle with hundreds of his own subjects impaled on tall stakes to repel an attacker, our enemy thought he could display the terror within him, and that with that he would defeat the world. But the U.S. was a country whose forces historically proved an understanding of terror; when we faced it, and when we used it. Our relationship with terror was not an emotional one, our experience was not a psychological indulgence. Terror was a tool to us when we used it, and when we faced it. The only supernatural force we believed in was that of our own will. Even in Vietnam, the war we lost, we left the mark—craters, the carnage, the crowds of incinerated flesh—of the terror with which we were equipped. What this desert rat thought he could accomplish became more and more clouded. The lives he had poured into the war with his Old Nemesis, our Old Nemesis, the gassing of thousands of his own people, extermination, the commitment of his people to yet another already devastating war, the dumping of oil into the Gulf, the Holy War proclamations, the "Mother of all Battles" bullshit seemingly copped from the forty-second street doomsayers in New York City, this was his terror. Strategically, none of it touched us, or even represented a threat. I began to understand that as long as we had our guns on him, whether he had the weapons or didn't made no difference. Those who have an emotional relationship with terror are terrified of losing their own skin. They wouldn't risk it or sacrifice it for anyone or anything. When in power they will frequently kill the people closest to them out of paranoia. If he had them, he wouldn't use them. That would play into our hands.

"Jake! Wake up God damn it! You trying to kill yourself?" I poured him another whiskey. "Drink this."

"I want some coffee," he said.

I went into the kitchen to get him some more ice. The right side of his face was numb; he was drooling out of it. "There's no coffee," I said. He took the whiskey.

"Did you hear about this drug thing, Jake?"

"No."

"The courts ruled it was okay for the military to require troops serving in the Gulf to take unapproved drugs to protect against biological and germ warfare. The military is refusing to specify the types of germs for which the antidotes are being provided."

"Why would a court have anything to say about that?"

"Somebody brought suit against the military. They say it's using the soldiers as guinea pigs. They're saying the soldiers should be told about the side effects and have the opportunity to refuse. That's not militarily feasible."

"How do you mean?"

"The last thing you want the infantry thinking about is getting gassed and whether or not they should risk this or that and take the drugs or take their chances and possibly choke to death on the battlefield. You get them thinking about that and you'll have guys soiling their pants at the sight of dust. It's the responsibility of the leadership to weigh the risks and make decisions like that. That's the nature of any military structure. You can't have an infantryman worrying about that stuff. He gives up that task when he joins up."

"I wouldn't want to be taking drugs that no one knew anything about."

"They know something about them or they wouldn't be giving them as antidotes."

"Yeah. But you think about things like Agent Orange. The government still doesn't take responsibility. People that were exposed to that stuff are dropping like flies because they were using something they knew nothing about."

"Those people are victims of war but that's definitely a glitch in the system. Okay, after the war the military leaders should be held accountable for things like that. They exercised poor judgment. The leadership of that war should have been crucified right from the top. But during war, decisions have to be made and actions taken immediately. There's no room for democracy in a military structure." He was asleep. "Jake, wake up!"

"I'm tired man."

"I don't think you should sleep, not yet. How's your head?"

I can't really feel it."

"You look okay. Are you dizzy?"

"A little."

"Let's go for a walk."

"I don't feel like it."

"It'll be good for you. Then you can sleep." I didn't know whether this was true, but I had to get out of there, and I couldn't leave him alone.

Jake showered and tried to straighten himself out. The newspaper had more on eleven of the Marines killed in action. All kinds of family and friend comments. War pages were titled "War in the Middle East." There had been 105 non-combat deaths since the war had begun. Seven were Missing in Action. Eight had been taken Prisoners of War. The Federal Bureau of Investigation (FBI) was interviewing Arab-Americans and Opposition nationals.

The President urged an eleven percent hike in federal spending on the drug war. The emphasis of the drug war was on supply reduction through law enforcement at home and abroad with somewhat less emphasis on demand reduction through education and treatment, the paper said. The President noted that occasional cocaine use was down twenty-nine percent and frequent use of cocaine was down by twenty-three percent. Glutathione had been found to suppress the spread of the AIDS virus, a researcher reported, the paper said. Glutathione was a molecule vital to cells in the body that played an important though unknown role in the immune system, not unlike the CIA in the war effort. Victims of the smoking fashion of the fifties and sixties were beginning to die in significant numbers. During a meeting of Yugoslavia's top officials, the leaders of the Republic of Croatia walked out. Russian President Boris Yeltsin urged the Soviet President, Mikhail S. Gorbachev, to refrain from allowing troops to patrol the city streets. The Soviet Union was going to hell.

Jake wore sunglasses because the sun hurt his eyes. He didn't seem any dizzier than I was. We walked around that day with no direction. We paused occasionally to catch our breath, or our balance, or to buy a small thing to eat. We stopped at D's for a whiskey to warm up but shortly went back into the cold. I was turning the corner of the building when someone ran into me and knocked me down. He started cursing at me at first, and then he realized it was me. It was Web.

"Oh shit, man, I'm sorry. I didn't know it was you."

"Why don't you watch what you're doing, for Christ's sake?"

"I'm sorry man."

"Well, what are you cursing at me like that for?"

"I didn't know it was you. I thought it was some old cracker, see."

"You ought to watch yourself, man. You don't just run people down and then start cursing them out."

"I told you, I didn't know it was you, man. Who you, man?" He was talking to Jake.

"This is a friend of mine," I said.

"Yo, he ain't got no tongue in his head? What happened to you, man? What you get hit with?"

"He got mugged last night. Right around here."

"Oh, shit, man," said Web.

"That's right, oh shit. Do you know who did it?" I knew that Web knew everyone in this neighborhood that was capable of beating up innocent people. The more I thought about it the more I thought he could even have done it himself. He seemed to be laughing about it the more he looked at Jake. "I want to know what you think is so funny, Web."

"Nothing, man."

"Nothing, huh. Where have you been lately? How come I haven't seen you?"

"I been busy man, like I'm busy now. Yo, I gotta go, pops."

"What do you mean you gotta go?"

"I gotta go, man." He smiled at me as he walked backwards across the street. He smiled at Jake and pointed to him, "Yo, one eye, I'll check you later." He turned around and ran away.

It was that kind of bullshit that always pissed me off about those kids. They always acted like they knew something, and they would never talk to you about anything. We talked a bit about Web as we turned back to our walk. Because it was a shit neighborhood we lived in, we talked about poverty. We were never in need of a place to stay, or of something to eat, or a drink. It was all around us, though, people in need. We walked through sections of town that day that looked like pictures I'd seen of Beirut, sections that looked as though they were from a Third World country. You get a little nervous walking around that kind of dilapidation. You begin to expect animals, human animals, transformed by some holocaust, to come out and infect you with a bite, to make you one of their own, condemn you to their fate. Did it horrify those that had to live here? Or, did they get used to it? I wondered if getting used to it made it any less horrific. There were abandoned cars. A dog roamed. We saw a burned mattress in a vacant lot. Did someone sleep on that? Jake could open his eye now. The sun began to drop. It was getting colder. We launched into a path toward home.

CHAPTER 20

▼

It's better to know when to quit.

The next day was a Saturday. I woke up early. As I grabbed the paper and turned to head back up to my apartment, Georgia's door flew open and she yelled at me.

"What the hell are you doing?"

I was stunned. I hadn't even had a cup of coffee. I was moving out of habit, didn't even realize that I should take care. Taking Georgia's paper had become as natural to me as flipping on the radio.

"What are you doing?" she repeated. I was impressed that she could be this angry. She had seemed so pleasant, not the kind to ever get angry. She must have been waiting there for hours for me to take the bait, and now she had me by the neck, and with the taste of my blood on the tip of her tongue she whispered in my ear, "Just try to get out of this."

"You're stealing my paper," she said.

It was as though the Supreme Consciousness threw the universe into orbit around me in that hallway just for the sake of emphasis. I looked sharply, as though my eyes were my being, through Georgia's glasses, diving into her eyes. Her long dark hair looked as though she'd just gotten up. I saw her image before me as—I suddenly realized—I had held it with me and run my thoughts over it day by day; her slender shoulders, her wistful hands, her thighs in black just heavy in a way which complimented her. How did I know the subtleties of her grace so well? How many times had I watched her from my window walking down the street? How closely had I watched? With what distance, that only now was I realizing what I'd taken in?

"I'm sorry, Georgia. I have been taking your paper and that was wrong of me. The fact is I've been doing it because I often sit in my room imagining conversations with you. I hardly know you, yet I feel a closeness to you, more than the distance between us would make it appear. When you walk up the porch steps to the front door, you swing your arms like you're stepping up into the air. I watched you push your car off this street to the hill by yourself. I watched you jump in and pop the clutch. I watched you the other night, talking to people, gesturing as you spoke, giving everyone your elixir smile, listening to morons and making a conversation with them. I noticed you never put your hands in your pockets unless to retrieve something; that you always wear at least four colors. I take the papers because they are my only palpable connection to you. I read this paper as if I am speaking to you. Sometimes, I imagine you're eating while we chat, that you gesture with your fork. I've often thought of approaching you, but I didn't want to cause any problems. Felix seems like a decent guy. You seem attached to him. I didn't want to cause either of you any trouble by trying to take you from him. I thought maybe if I talked to you more, maybe sway you to me subtly. But knowing there was nothing subtle in what I felt for you, I was always stunned upon seeing you by the task of holding back all that was within me, by the fear that the droplets released in "Hello. How are you?" would lead to an onslaught such as this. But this isn't an onslaught really. It's just my telling you the way things are, explaining myself. In the absence of a real touch, I stole your newspapers, feeling in a way your presence in my house. I know it's odd what I've been doing. But I don't do it out of oddness or obscenity. Please don't think of me as obscene! I don't have sex with the paper or anything. I merely read it to feel your presence. I won't say I love you. I know my feelings are just based on impressions. I don't expect you to someday come running into my arms either. I know that all I really have is imagined, and my expectations don't go beyond that." She tried to say something but I jumped on her words. "Please don't think I'm too peculiar. I'm not saying all this because I expect something of you. I'm just saying it. Confessing, I guess."

I didn't take my eyes from hers for a moment, nor did she shy away, but looked directly back. Her expression had not changed, strained but focused.

"May I have the paper?" she said.

"Certainly." As I handed it to her, I caught the headline. The state unemployment rate had achieved a new high. She took the paper as she turned around, walked back into her apartment, and closed the door.

I was a little baffled by all I'd just said. I had felt a sincere focus on the present during my declaration to her. That was gone. I got dressed in my room and went to the store. There were buses and traffic on the main street. It was pretty warm for a winter's day, a lot of exhaust in the air. I got a paper from an automatic box. Walking back to my apartment with the paper tucked under my arm, I noticed a feeling of surging irritation. I was trying to figure out what I'd been doing that day and couldn't think of a thing, beyond reading the paper. I glanced at Georgia's door as I walked upstairs.

Joblessness had hit the highest level since 1982. Reports noted enemy casualties at sixty with 500 being taken prisoner. U.S. military officials denied the reports of enemy massing at the front. A story related that the all-volunteer force in the Gulf did not reflect the make-up of our society, that blacks contributed more than twice their proportional share. There was a report that U.S. Marines dug in at the front were bombed by two Allied fighter-bombers dropping four cluster bombs apiece. For the fourth day, Israeli forces traded artillery and rocket fire with Palestinian guerrillas. Journalists in Baghdad reported Tomahawk missiles had struck the city. France gave permission for U.S. B-52 bombers from Britain to fly over its territory. We all remembered that Libyan incident. Israel was said to be giving Palestinians gas masks. Iran said it would join the enemy if Israel stepped into the Persian Gulf War. Iranians placed the number of enemy planes which had fled to Iran at eighty-nine, while U.S. officials reported the number at ninety-eight. U.S. officials reported that oil leaking from an enemy loading platform had created a slick of twenty square miles. An investigation was reported to be under way of the deaths of eleven of the Marines killed at Khafji to determine whether they had been killed by Allied fire. A spokesman for the Pentagon said, "It's possible we will never know exactly what happened." Enemy radio had reported that Allied planes had been firing on large numbers of women, children, and old people in cold blood. The radio said further that captured Allied pilots should be treated as war criminals and that the enemy would hunt down and punish our President, as well as the leaders of France, Britain, and Saudi Arabia. U.S. officials asserted that every effort has been made to avoid hurting civilians. There was no guarantee, it was said, against collateral damage. Soviet military sources were said to have estimated the number of Opposition dead at 1,500 during the battle of Khafji. Vidar Kleppe, a Norwegian legislator of the right-wing Party of Progress, nominated the President for the Nobel Peace Prize. Mr. Kleppe was said to have said that the President stepped into the front line in the fight against oppression, torture, and totalitarian acts against human dignity, by leading Allied forces against Iraq.

And so, another reporting had been leveled at my head by the nobodies. I put the paper down and stared at the phone as if expecting it to ring. This was my participation in the conflict. I hadn't even broken a sweat or stained my fingers with newsprint. I hadn't even taken a shower. I had no charge, no leader, no role. What was I? The war went on, the soldiers had their part, the press had their part, and who was I? I consumed the reports. I was the consumer.

It was a rage I felt. I looked at a picture of the President in the newspaper. "Tell me what to do!" I screamed at him. I thought of how I might do something. Join the service? No way. They didn't need me yet. I decided I might go on a trip. Maybe hitch my way to Buffalo or something. It was too cold for hitching though. I'd drive. I needed to drive. I called my boss. "Boss. I need a couple of weeks off, maybe a month, something like that."

"Is this a joke," she said.

"No. No joke."

"What's wrong?"

"I'd rather not discuss it."

"Well, how do you think I'm going to get coverage for you? You're supposed to supervise a ski trip in two days."

"Call the office. They've got plenty of morons down there that can fill in."

"Call the office? What are you trying to do to me?"

"I know I'm putting you in a spot. I know I am, but I need the time. I'll call you in a week."

"Are you crazy? You're just going to leave like that?"

"I have to. I'm sorry. I'll be back, I swear. I'll call you."

"This isn't good."

"I know. It's lousy. I know it is. I wouldn't do it if I could help it. I have to go. Goodbye." I hung up. I got a map out. Buffalo. That was way out there. Niagara Falls. Big stuff. I considered driving at least to Syracuse that night. I'd been to Syracuse before. I would have eaten at the Blue Moon diner on the east side of town. Last time I'd been there I met a couple, an older couple. Never asked where they were from. He was a carpet salesman and he chewed my ear about the different kinds of carpets there were. He didn't even have any to sell; he just liked talking about them.

"Tell me something," I said. "All those carpets that are stain resistant, fire-proof, and all that other stuff; how are they made?"

"Well," he said looking at his wife and then back at me, "I don't really know exactly. It's all done by machines, of course."

"Of course," I said.

It took me an hour of looking at Buffalo to decide I didn't want to go there. Buffalo wasn't Buffalo. It was Niagara Falls. And that was for honeymoons, and I certainly wasn't going on any honeymoon. I wasn't going to Syracuse either. I made no decisions at all that night. There was only west to go, or north, or south, because the ocean was east. I wanted to go east. That's where the action was. Without inspiration, I went nowhere.

CHAPTER 21

▼

A type of diplomacy in dealing with neighbors.

At the crack of dawn, I ran around the Pond. It was cold and glorious. The water was flat and clear, the breezes whispering. I kept thinking that this would be so even without my presence. On the way home I ran to a newsstand that had not yet opened and took a paper from the bundle lying at the door. There was nothing in it. Two U.S. planes lost to ground fire. More talk of the enemy digging in at the front. The Old Nemesis was said to be emerging as a key player. Nobody liked those bastards. Allied officials declined to estimate the total enemy deaths thus far, but the newspaper accounted the number at more than thirty. What word was there from the President? Stay the course. "Yes," I thought, "I shall do so."

There was a lot of talk on the radio about the press lockout. All this information I'd been getting had been reported by journalists with U.S. troops working under military escort and submitting their reports to military censors. I supposed this was interesting in its own little way, but all the God damn conferences going on about it? Analysts and experts all getting into the act? Debates on Capitol Hill? Everybody had their jobs. The President had his, the Army had theirs, and the press had theirs. And if they were willing to take the Army's word for everything, then they had no complaining to do. Doesn't matter where you get the story, as long as you get it, and get it right. And if you get the story wrong, it doesn't matter where you got it, you can go to hell. That's the way I felt about it anyway.

I had visions of going to the Rocky Mountains. I would go there and practice my shouting from a mountaintop. I would cultivate power and store it all in my voice, so I could hurl my words at those below me, towering as they fell, like the thrust of an avalanche. I might observe an avalanche to acquire technique. A lack of technique is a lack of sophistication. And then, after months of practice, I would go to the enemy's land. I would climb up into the mountains and bombard him with the power of my voice and my words. I would crush him to dust the way the Berlin Wall was crushed.

I was in a bar the day the Berlin Wall came down. I'd just arrived in this city as the economy had taken its nosedive. I was working some pissant temporary job, and I was out for a beer with a guy from work, ex-Navy. We were both looking for a job, something to make us feel worthwhile. I was standing in front of the bar when I looked up at the television and saw the rubble, people sitting on it. "What is that," I said to the bartender. "That's the Berlin Wall."

"Impossible," I thought. Not in my lifetime had I even imagined I'd see that wall come down. And then it all began, the Velvet Revolution, Poland, and finally the Soviet Union began to crack to the point where we now hardly considered them in undertaking the Desert conflict. Before, consideration of the Soviets was involved in nearly every breath we took. I could breathe freely for the first time in my life without the threat of a fight looming over my head. I was out of a steady job and living hand to mouth. My personal outlook was a view of the shit-yard. Yet, I began to experience an easy hope for the country, for our people, for the world. It was an experience I'd never had. I felt that now we wouldn't have the distractions. Now, we could turn our resources on the country's needs and clean it up. Scrape all those people off the streets, make them productive, make them citizens again, make sure I wouldn't be joining them there. I began to see a chip in the mental block of modern history. Then came Desert Shield, and with it the notion that we were heading right back into it…three steps forward, two steps back…that kind of routine. One thing was clear; oil was becoming a chain around our necks.

After a quick shower, I was in my car heading north. I was driving up the coast to Maine, just a place with a different name. When I got to Maine I felt uneasy. I didn't know why. I was listening for a call from somewhere and heard none. I turned left toward New Hampshire. It was green wilderness through New Hampshire. The towns all had their yellow ribbons out for the troops, all the way to Vermont. I stopped in a town there with one crossroad. I stopped to eat. There were farmers in the diner, truck drivers, others who lived there. The children were all in school. There was snow around that town, just as it should have been. The trees bare. I remember yellow ribbons on the street lights. A yellow ribbon seemed to say, "No matter what else comes out of my mouth, I support the troops. My heart is with them and may God bring each of them home safely." I got a warmth from this town that made me think I could sleep on the sidewalk and never feel the cold. It seemed a town that wasn't going anywhere, had no ambitions to be this or that, one that cut itself a decent living from the rhythm of the world, a solid honest rhythm beaten on maple trees and barn doors. A rhythm that the people stepped into without a desire to molest.

My own rhythm being what it was, I pulled out, heading south. I passed through Massachusetts and hit the Yankee Doodle Dandy State of Connecticut. Connecticut always reminded me of Ichabod Crane, gawky and innocuous. Heading east again having not made the decision to go anywhere, I realized that I'd been driving the whole day without the radio. I turned it on but could only get music. I tried a bit of the talk radio thing but couldn't stomach it. I felt like a gerbil in one of those clear plastic balls that lets them run around without getting shit all over the house, without letting them disappear until you find them weeks later at the bottom of the Wheaties box.

After eleven hours of driving around the Northeast, I found myself late that night in Rhode Island, a state founded by outcast Protestants who, in turn, had cast out some themselves. I pulled into a Mobil station on the highway that was lit though it seemed deserted. Nobody came out when I pulled up. The fuel gauge was on empty. Finally, a man did come out of nowhere and walked up to my window.

"Hello," I said. He nodded. "Can I have some gas?"

"Well," he said, "Do you have any money?" He was serious.

"I have a Mobil card. How will that do?"

"Oh. Well, that's okay."

It was as if he asked me, "Do you have anything to put it in?" I was thinking to myself, "No, I'm not from this planet, Wilbur."

As he was pumping the gas, I realized I hadn't really talked to anyone all day. I'd been driving. When the guy came up to my window to get paid I said to him, "Did I say I had a credit card...well, you see, that's just it, I had a credit card, a Mobil card, but you know how things are, I a...Well they took it on me...But let me see...," I started looking around the car, "...Um...well, what's the use in this? I did have some money in here but, uh...well...I don't like to say this in public, you know...but seeing as no one's around...well, I spent it...I spent it on crack-cocaine."

The guy looked at me blankly through his thick glasses as if going through the files for the correct response.

"Relax," I told him whipping out the card, "I'm just kidding." He took the card and ran the transaction without skipping a beat. Maybe it was because I had been thinking about serious things, and I just had not said it funny.

"I was just kidding," I told him.

"Okay. Bye."

I started driving again and without flexing a muscle one way or the other found myself making the turn into the private way. The way was lined with cars on either side except for the stoned space in front of my neighbor's house. I realized I could tuck the car neatly into the spot by propping the left side wheels up onto the stones, parking the car and pissing that worm off to China at the same time. So it was done.

It was late when I got back, around midnight. I'd been driving winding New England roads all day; my back was killing me. I took aspirin and whiskey and went to bed. I wanted to dream that night. I lay down with that ambition. I'm not sure when it was because I never looked at the time, but I was awakened by the blast of a car horn just outside my window; a continuous deliberate horn. I looked out the window to see that pustulation standing next to his truck causing the racket. I threw on my pants and went to the window in the hall.

I yelled down at him, "What the fuck are you doing down there!"

"Somebody took my spot!"

"That's not your spot."

"It is too! It's in front of my house. I put these rocks here to mark it."

"The parking on this street is a free-for-all. How come everyone else who lives here knows that except for you?"

"The way I see it…"

"You're too God damned dimwitted to see anything. Now shut the hell up, or I'm calling the cops."

"This is your car isn't it? If you don't come down here and move it out of my spot, I'm taking a baseball bat to it!"

I roared up to the other houses surrounding us, "Did you hear that friends? He said he was going to beat my car up with his baseball bat. We can throw a big party on that very spot with the settlement from the law suit. I'll try not to inconvenience too many of you for testimony. And if his truck gets stripped and burned out by one of you while he's in prison, well, I never look out my window anyway. Then again," I aimed my words back at him, "maybe I should break out my camcorder. If you're going to sue the underwear off someone, you may as well do it right!"

"You better watch yourself pal! I'll come up there and kick your ass."

"I'll leave you some plastic explosives in my will you dirty fuck. Now that's twice you've threatened me. If you don't quiet down I'm calling the cops!" With that I shut the window and went back to my room. He stood down there shaking his head for a few minutes, looking from my car to the place I had been in the window. He was a shady bastard that was for sure. I wouldn't put it past him to slit my tires some night, or scratch it up sometime, break a window. But he had the ounce of brain stuffed up the crack of his ass which told him I could retaliate anytime. He lived right in front of me, his truck was always there. He'd probably just devise another scheme to prevent my car from being able to park there. That I didn't mind so much. It was something about him that I hated, as if everything that had ever bothered me was funneled into a hate for him. I fantasized about waiting for him some night hidden behind a tree, up ahead along his path. Waiting quiet and poised and swinging with a baseball bat just at the knees. But that was no way for a good citizen to behave. He finally got back in his truck and backed out to look for a space elsewhere.

It became Monday without my noticing. I woke up to the sound of construction above me. One small explosive device to blow those fuckers up, that's all I wanted. How could they live with it up there? It never stopped. I got out of bed and got ready to go somewhere, pushed by a feeling that I had somewhere to go; I did not. I looked through the cloudy plastic that covered the window. I did some pushups. I swept the kitchen floor. I washed it. I did each of these things with a notion that I'd be heading out as soon as I was done. I also began to feel I was forgetting to call someone yet I couldn't think of anyone to call. I pissed away half the day this way. I told somebody I was going somewhere, my boss, but I was going nowhere. I finally put my shoes on and shuffled on down to the subway. Walking through that station made me feel as though I were walking into a movie. The station was big with expansive concrete walls. The tracks were not covered, so beyond the platform in the direction of downtown, as if the track led right to its base, you could see the ugliest building ever built standing downtown as if it had just landed there, like a spaceship, and was waiting for you to take off again.

I got off downtown and walked into the library. That was a novelty. I'd never heard of anybody just walking into a library because they had nothing to do. Usually, it was television that answered the call of nothing to do. The Mongols never had television. I wasn't sure what I would do there. Usually people went to the library because they wanted something from it. I suppose I wanted something too, but I didn't go there wanting it. I wound up sitting down with some poetry. Poetry wasn't my thing, and perhaps that was why I took a seat with it. You had to know a thing to put it down with any meaning.

It was interesting to note that in a preface to one of his poems, Percy Shelley put forth his view that the Greek war for independence from the Turks prognosticated the final overthrow of tyranny. He must have been a real joker, I thought, saying something like that. The twentieth century must have been howling laughter in his dead ears.

> "A power from the unknown God,
>   A Promethan Conqueror came
> Like a triumphal path he trod
> The thorns of death and shame
> A mortal shape to him."

I wondered what the Freudian would say about that.

I found myself looking for a good war poem. I thought I might send it to one of the soldiers. You could send mail addressed to "anonymous soldier," meaning anyone who needed it would get it. It would probably even get passed around. But all the war poems were depressing. I wanted to give them something uplifting. I didn't want to write a hokey letter, "I think you guys are swell." I wanted something short with correct meaning and power. I borrowed a piece of paper and a pen from an elderly woman studying sheets of music. In the midst of my search I paused to hear the poem I needed. A poem I knew by heart.

> Oh, say can you see
> By the dawn's early light
> What so proudly we hailed
> At the twilight's last gleaming
>
> Whose broad stripes and bright stars
> Through the perilous fight
> O'er the Ramparts we watched
> Were so gallantly streaming
>
> And the Rockets' red glare
> The bombs bursting in air
> Gave proof through the night
> That our flag was still there.
>
> O, say does that Star
> Spangled Banner yet wave

For the Land of the Free
And the Home of the Brave.

I wrote these words on the piece of paper. So much shrouded by the sounds of cannons and fireworks, by the awaiting game of baseball, by the blurring feedback and echoes of stadiums, I hadn't ever looked to understand those words. If words could fire young blood, these were the words. Ours was a country founded on wiry idealism, and these words turned that idealism to granite in the heart. Probably the only poem I knew by heart, it was complete in my head somewhere, though I was hardly aware of its presence. Complete, too, in my heart. Francis Scott Key, the poem's author, wrote it after witnessing the bombardment of Fort McHenry in Baltimore Harbor. He was a graduate of St. John's College, the same school from which my father would graduate approximately 150 years later. The guard came around to kick us all out. It was closing time, but I still had nowhere to go.

The next day as I was coming out of my apartment, I saw Georgia and Felix walking out the front door at the bottom of the stairs. I said hello to them cheerily. Felix bowed his head and nearly broke into a trot trying to get away from me. He might have heard all the yelling from the other night and thought I was a little crazy. Georgia glanced up at me, giving a curt greeting as she walked after him.

"Hey Georgia," I called.

"What," she didn't pause a step in her gait.

"Do you have yesterday's paper lying around?"

"What?" She stopped.

"I mean if you're done with it. I didn't get a look at a paper yesterday. I just wondered whether you were done with yours. If you have it around, I mean, I'd like to read it."

She turned again and started walking, "I don't have it."

"What did you do with it?"

"I burned it!"

I didn't expect that. "That's not good for the environment, you know."

"Go screw yourself!"

I checked my mail as they pulled out. I kept getting bills and sweepstakes entries. As I walked to my car, the cretin came out onto his porch and called to me, "Hey. You're making friends all over this neighborhood, ain't you?"

"Go screw yourself!" I told him.

As I started the car, I half expected it to blow up in my face because that's just the kind of unclean swine he was. I pictured him making pipe bombs in his living room from an old family recipe as he watched The Evangelist go on about the Scriptures foretelling of a war in the Middle East prefacing Armageddon. The Evangelist had been a candidate for the presidency in the last election. He owned his own television network and was an inspiring leader of his kind, like the Pharisees in olden days.

By Thursday, I still had gone nowhere and done nothing. I was considering a return to work, but I felt as though I'd made a stink of it to get off, and if I were to show up it would damage my credibility. My neighbor had dug four-foot metal spikes three feet into the ground around the stones. I expected something like that. I had spent the last two days doing push-ups, eating rice, and reading a history of the Modern World. I was assessing the changing purpose of war and might.

As I was going for a run, I saw the cretin getting out of his truck.

"Hey," I called to him in a congenial way, "your mother was just by here looking for you. She asked me to tell you something."

"Oh, yeah. What'd she say?"

"She said you suck!"

CHAPTER 22

▼

A new world order.

The next morning I began to feel anxious about work. Perhaps, I thought, it would be best to go back, having failed to determine a true course. My boss may feel better about it anyway. As I was taking out the garbage, I noticed yesterday's paper lying in a pile. I took it. I felt a bit more secure.

Danny Thomas had died on Wednesday. U.S. warplanes shot down two enemy fighters fleeing to the Old Nemesis. King Hussein of Jordan called for an immediate cease-fire, saying that the Opposition was being destroyed. "So what's your point," I thought. The enemy claimed that an Allied raid on the city of Nassariyah killed about 150 civilians. The President said, "I feel very confident that this matter is going to resolve itself, and it's not going to take that long and it is going to be total and complete," the paper said. Later in the day, he was reported to have said, "…The road to peace will be difficult, long, and tough."

A U.S. Marine amphibious force which had been practicing strikes Tuesday at an undisclosed position in the Gulf had reportedly moved into an attack position. The Secretary of State had said that the Allied Coalition should assist in the rebuilding of Iraq after the war, as he did not believe that the country should be scorned for the criminal ambitions of a dictator.

Partners of the Coalition had pledged $9.7 billion for 1990 to partially cover the expenses of Operation Desert Shield (the prewar excursion), leaving the U.S. share at $2 billion. $6.5 billion of that pledged had already been received. Since the war began, our partners had pledged more than $42 billion, and the Secretary of State said that some of those pledges were already being paid, the paper said. It was reported that hospitals in Kuwait had been raided by enemy troops. A Boston-based group, Physicians for Human Rights, said that health-care workers had been removed and tortured. Here I referred back to the quoted comments of the King of Jordan. He said that the Allied operation was "a war against all Arabs and Muslims." What was going through his mind? I thought. In a report based on thirty-four eyewitness accounts, primarily Kuwaiti and Egyptian medical personnel who had worked in Kuwait before the invasion, occupying soldiers were killing doctors and other hospital personnel, raping nurses, terrorizing patients and looting medical equipment. The report was also said to contain reports of restrictions on doctors against treating Kuwaitis even in their homes, and access to hospitals during the initial occupation was completely cut off to Kuwaitis. This included the removal of large numbers of infants from incubators, it was said. Again I read the comments of the King, and wondered what was going through his head. The U.S. was said to be pressuring the Saudis to reopen the oil pipeline to Jordan. Apparently, the Saudis were a little pissed about Jordan's public support of the enemy and were prepared to watch that country sweat.

The Old Nemesis with its Peace Plan was getting some attention. According to the London based Kuwaiti exile newspaper Sawt al-Kuwait, the plan would be initiated by an appeal from Iran's Spiritual leader, Ayatollah Ali Khamenei, for a cease-fire by all belligerents. The enemy would withdraw its troops, and then we would simultaneously back off from the region. The armies were supposed to pretend that Khameini was Moses. The plan was said to call further for an Islamic peace force to be sent to Kuwait as a buffer, and an Islamic committee would then study the territorial disputes. It was an interesting little card game going on there. A side bet. The Iranians were setting themselves up as peacemakers, but it gave a lot of power to the fundamentalists. The initial step of the call to peace by the Ayatollah would be a stage show but have profound implications. They wanted the most powerful nation on earth to wait for the Ayatollah to give us the word and then withdraw on his command. What kind of wet dream was that to be floating as a peace plan? No one with an ounce of power in the region would give the go-ahead to a plan like that, yet with the world watching, everyone, even the most hated enemy, had to give a visible nod to the Old Nemesis in the arena of the public show. The Old Nemesis had balls.

An American soldier who had refused to participate in the operations of Desert Shield and who was subsequently sentenced and jailed for his actions had been adopted as a prisoner of conscience by an international human-rights watch group. Haiti's first democratically elected president, Jean-Bertrand Aristide, had been inaugurated.

I went into work that day. The world must go on with that attitude. I was told that the cost of living adjustment had been suspended again. Raises, of course, were still hardly conceivable. Cuts in the human service budget were wiping programs out all over the state. Yeah, whatever. My boss didn't pursue me for explanation, glad to see me back. She had had to work double shifts. It was warm for a winter's night on the drive home. My thoughts turned to Armageddon.

The religion gigolos were spouting Scripture to the masses. The enemy was the messenger of the Antichrist if not **the** Antichrist. How many times had he been served to us as the historical son of Hitler? That sounded like something out of Hollywood. Someone had saved Hitler's testicles in his freezer and bred him a son, the Butcher of Baghdad. Nobody was going poor making these analogies. Here it was again, from the Goths to the Mongols we've had people assuring the populace that their judgment was coming. This kind of message, if heeded at all, gave the messenger a certain power reminiscent of the social power of witch doctors. Funny, I thought, that we in the Western society, the modern world, should stand on our golden pedestal of science and calculation, while our own little witch doctors, receiving privately funded wealth, run around its base undermining it. It was primarily the Armageddon sorcery that fueled the blood of at least a few Crusades, the boiling and the taste for it. "I will have God if I have to cut your throat for it," it seemed to say. Chingis Kahn, scoffed at by conquered Islam as a barbarian, returned the favor, saying, "Why do you make the pilgrimage to Mecca? Don't you know that God is everywhere?" It astounded me, the propositions of these preachers that God would exist "only within our borders and only within the iron gates of our hearts."

There was always, of course, the keen play of racism in a war. The cultivation of hatred is, so far, more effective when there is a physical manifestation to distinguish the hated. Indeed, with the most drastic dullard it is required. In the old days fighting was a good way to take your mind off your crummy life, and for the illiterate masses it was a good way to make them think they were doing something useful for themselves. Hatred being an asexual, self-generating disease, it was easy to fill the empty cups with hatred, and so it still is today. To the warrior's thinking, though, hatred is cancer. Like the hunter who must enter the mind of his prey, the warrior must know his enemy. The greatest warriors are those who can evaluate the enemy and know him intimately on sight. For the warrior, hatred veils reality.

Our country was one that depended upon the Old Country for its values. We had been growing and re-shaping ourselves for all of our two hundred and fifteen years. We separated the native culture from our society, wiping the slate of tradition clean. It has been put to us to mix the value of the old, now foreign traditions, and extirpate the hypocrisy, cauterizing the wounds of that separation with our fervor. This call for a New World Order, this redefining of the world, would require yet another revision of the sense of our purpose, our being, our meaning.

Within that new order, the proportion of what we were on this soil, as opposed to what we were on the old, now foreign soil, becomes predominant.

The next day, as I was running back from the Pond, some kids in the street were taunting me, for what reason I do not know. I remember that I could not understand what some of them were saying, as though it was another language, though it was not. Why were they attacking me? I'd never seen them before.

As I ran up to my door, I heard Georgia's door close. I knocked on it, but no one answered. I called Jake to be sure he was breathing. He was. I ate some toast. I cashed in some pennies for gas money.

CHAPTER 23

▼

"Hear me, O Lord,…for you have power to listen the whole world round to a man hard pressed as I!

Iliad; Book XVI; 481-3; Glaukos to Apollo

That was a Saturday night, and I had an extraordinary dream. I dreamed I was a seed in the desert, though I had not yet grown. I dreamed I was cool, though it was hot all around. The tanks came. They had planted mines across the spectrum but without spoiling me. During this dream, I discovered I had power, that I need not wait to grow but could grow by my will. As mines became the land and the planes became my sky, I discovered I could shape the world around me, manipulate it in a sluggish way as though it were all a cumbersome gel, pressure here causing a swell there. I began by brushing sand but soon graduated to exploding mines far off in the distance. I never saw my stalk but knew only that when I willed to grow higher, I did. I could hear men in bunkers, whispering, talking, crying, and screaming. To start a panic, I need only set off a mine, or push sand down a hole. I saw smoke in the distance, smelled it and felt its residue. I grew further to see its origins, but could not. I grew higher, and the men in the barracks paid no attention. Then I heard explosions in the distance; then up close. It was my spot being shelled, and I was wavering just as I began to see the burning pumps. The blast from the explosions and the shaking of the ground knocked me over, pulling my roots up and forcing me face down in the sand. That's all I saw, though I heard the bombs coming from behind me. My malleable reality had gone, and the dream was done.

It was a beautiful day, sunny and warm. On the way home from the run, I was forced to purchase a newspaper. The weather had brought out all the Sunday strollers staggering across my path, and this called to my attention my recent lack of discipline and purpose. It seemed that my sense of purpose was degenerating from the lack of threat. I bought the paper out of duty. Sunday's paper at $1.50

contained a lot of crap I didn't want, so I left the crap on the counter. "What am I gonna do with it?" the guy said to me. "Ask your therapist," I said.

The Land War. Speculators commented on what a blood-fest it was going to be. The paper reported on Day 25. It was reported by the military that the first reconnaissance mission into Kuwait had taken place on Thursday night. The Opposition had severed diplomatic ties with the United States. Yawn. The high-way from Jordan to Baghdad was reported by correspondents to have been turned into a death trap by relentless bombing, the paper said. Allied losses included thirty killed in action. Enemy losses as reported by the Allies read as seventy-nine soldiers killed, though officials refused to estimate total Iraqi deaths; 936 or more of the enemy taken prisoner.

It was reported that a German construction firm had broken the U.N. embargo against the enemy seventy times. Jewish servicemen and woman in Saudi Arabia were to receive traditional provisions to celebrate Passover on March 30. Lithuania had voted overwhelmingly for independence from the Soviet Union. There were some articles containing chatter with the troops-mostly reporters trying to act as if they could tell a story rather than report it.

As I was leaving the little dirt road, Georgia drove up. I walked up and called to her as she got out of her car. She was cold in her response.

"Georgia. I'm sorry about this newspaper thing. I've been under a lot of pressure lately, not getting sleep. I just wasn't thinking about what I was doing. Look, I'm sorry. Really."

She continued to walk to her door. She said, "Okay. Never mind then. We'll forget it."

"You're angry. I don't want you to be angry."

"Listen, I don't really know you, so I don't see what it matters. I don't know what you do up there in that little room or why you say the things you do. They're just a little weird, that's all. So, let's just forget about it…"

"Did I say something to offend you? Did what I say the other day offend you? I didn't mean anything by it."

"No. It didn't offend me. But you don't just come out with something like that. We're almost total strangers. What a bizarre thing to come up with. And stealing my papers, what possessed you to do that? How much does a paper cost? If you had asked me, I would have given it to you when I was done. Why would you steal it? And then lie to me like that, and then keep on stealing it?" She waited for me to say something. "And that crap about being in love with me…what would make you say that? Just stay away from the papers, okay?"

"I will Georgia. I'm sorry…"

"Okay. Goodbye." She closed the door.

Some people take everything so God damn seriously. I could swear at times I was living in a menagerie. I was heading down to D's for a bite to eat. Something about being in the same room with the old lady boilermakers made me feel better about myself. It wasn't a long walk from my house but still the commotion was the commotion of strangers. It made me feel distant and strong at the same time. I wondered how long these streets had looked this way, or if when coming back, sometime years later, I would find them the same.

Walking into D's gave me reassurance. Enough cigar smoke to choke on, soap operas on the television, and soap operas in the bar among the less fictitious (not so pretty) boilermakers; the pictures of boxers; the brawl of sandpaper voices among the ladies off in the corner. I didn't often sit at the bar because I never felt welcome, but I saw Brady standing there and took a spot next to him. With a roast beef sandwich in his mouth, he nodded to me as I sat.

"How's it going, Brady?"

"All right. You?"

"Good enough. How's business?"

"You know as well as I do," he said.

I ordered a beer and a roast beef sandwich. Brady ordered coffee. He took a bite of his pickle and as he held it up he said, "This is my only God damn pleasure in my life. Most of the time I just eat the crap at the shelter. I been eating it so long I don't even notice what it's suppose to be sometimes, it all tastes the same. I can't even have a beer like you're doing now."

"Why not?"

"Nam gave me a fix for the fucking bottle. I told you I was in Nam," motioning to his tattoo.

"Yeah," I said. "I know."

"When I came back I was drinking a quart a day of whatever I could grab. I didn't give a crap. Waking up in some shithole like the shelter or someplace every fucking day."

"You seem okay to me." He was shaking his head and grinning. "Where were you in Vietnam," I asked.

"Oh, who the fuck knows. I was a God damn piece of carrot in the biggest fucking meat stew you ever seen. I was every fucking place getting my ass kicked. I don't remember most of it. It was all bullshit to me. Plus my memory is gone from all that cheap shit booze; plus getting cracked in the head so many fucking times." He waved his hand. "All that shit's over for me."

"How'd you get cracked in the skull?" I sipped my beer.

"Oh, the fucking cops see a guy my size it don't take much for them to swing those fucking sticks, man. I'm surprised I didn't get shot. I used to get arrested a lot in this town, you know. You got no place to sleep, you don't eat and you're drinking leftover shit booze, you just fall down someplace. A couple times I just passed out in the street," he was shaking his head. "I hated going into jail, even in that condition. It was just fucking, uh, it was degrading, is what it was. I always gave the cop a hard time, you know, just yelling and shit, but because I'm so big they'd just crack me. Sometimes the one guy would be talking to me, and his partner would just walk up behind me and bang! You know? I had a fucking headache for fifteen years. I was so fucking punchy from all that shit I fell for it every fucking time. I got a hard fucking head, but it still got bust five or six fucking times."

"You're cleaned up now, though," I said.

"You going to eat that pickle?"

"No, go ahead."

"Yeah. I still smell like shit and I'm still eating the mess. But I give some of those motherfuckers a shot, anyhow."

"You don't smell that bad, Brady."

"That's cause I ain't been to work yet. You think you and me do the same thing? We're in a different line of work, you and me. You got kids, right?" I nodded. "Well, a kid can straighten himself out a whole lot better than some bum who's been on the skids for ten, fifteen years. You ought to ride the van sometime at night."

"What's the van?"

"We got to, uh, ride around town in the van and pick these mother-fuckers up so they don't fucking freeze to death. Just find them sleeping in alleys. I know where they all go to sleep now. If you were just driving around, you'd never find them all."

"Why don't they just go to the shelter?"

"Can't make it. Too burned out. Most of them don't mind dying, you know. There's at least a few guys a month that I know by sight that fucking kill themselves. Oh, but the smell of that fucking van. None of those people bathe."

"Why not?"

"It's a pain in the ass. Plus your shit gets stolen while you're in the shower. Why the fuck would you? Nobody wants to talk to you anyway. Some just got the normal body smell. But a lot of these people are sick all the time. They have diarrhea, throwing up. They don't always have a toilet available to them, if you know what I mean. When you're that fucking fucked up, messing yourself ain't that big a deal. I never got that bad myself. Being a Marine and all, keeping your ass clean was like a fucking instinct. I didn't get sick so much except from the booze. With that I remember throwing my fucking intestines up a few times. You're a fucking clean kid though, man. See you don't even know this shit and you're in the business."

"There's an awful lot of shit to know in this world. Isn't there, Brady?"

"You got that right, man. Hey, could you loan me a couple bucks? I want to get another sandwich while I'm here. I'm going to be at work for the next three fucking days."

"Yeah, Brady. I'll buy you a sandwich." I ordered him a sandwich and myself some fries and a beer. I was thinking to get full on this meal.

"All these fucking budget cuts now. I have to work one day a week for nothing now. We have no fucking relief, the pay is shit already, nobody wants the fucking jobs to begin with and now we get cut back."

"Why do you do it, Brady? I mean your whole life now is doing that."

"I do it for those scum-sucking, dirtbag motherfuckers. I don't do it for anyone else. That governor, cutting everything back like we're all living on the fucking high hog at the fucking shelter. All I want is fucking five bucks an hour so I can buy a fucking sandwich and not have to hit you up for money. But these fucking guys, I mean, I know what it's like to be freezing your balls off, lying on fucking concrete, so God damn sick you think your own guts have turned on you, all you want is for someone to stop and pick you up or put a bullet in your head. You need someone to take you someplace warm even if it does smell like a sewer, even if you know you're going to wake up just another piece of shit in a pile. I remember getting picked up by a van a couple times. It's like having fucking God come down. It ain't no fucking God, though, man. You know that when you wake up. Ah, it's all fucking bullshit. I've been chewed up all my life at the bottom of this big fucking machine, the God damn government. Now I'm stuck. Now that I survived it, it would kill me to go anywhere else. What about you? You must be getting hit with all this shit?"

"Yeah," I said. "We're getting cut to the bare bones. But we're protected by the courts. We've got no relief. Positions have been cut. We'll survive."

"Yeah, I guess you and I will survive anyway," he said. Just then the ladies in the corner began cackling over something. "That's a fucking life, huh, sitting in a fucking bar all day drinking fucking boilermakers. God forbid they should do something fucking positive." He motioned his head to the television. "That's fucking pretty, huh. They can pay all those worms to weep and moan and fuck each other on TV, giving these sows something to do, and the whole time they watch the fucking homeless pile up in the street." Brady was shaking his head, not quite smiling. The fries came, and he asked for more coffee. Somebody propped the door open and a saber of light cut the darkness. Glare came off the faces of the boxers. I ate my fries. "And I'll tell you something, that fucking Gulf War has still got me pissed off. What's the difference from being in the street to being over there? Every day you're on the street you're risking your life. People cruise the streets and just beat the homeless up; they just pound a guy for the sake of doing it; to see how it feels. You get guys being lit on fire. They get their stuff stolen by their best friends. They eat shit. They don't sleep. It's the same in the field. Three hours of sleep a night. No food. Scared shitless of the wind blowing. Never knowing who the fuck is gonna turn on you." He stuffed another quarter of the sandwich in his mouth. "I'm telling you I could mobilize those fuckers down at the shelter to start doing shit around this city. They could fucking clean the parks or the streets or something. I'd get them to do some fucking thing with just a little bit more money to do it. Half those fuckers have been in the Army or Marines, or something. Everybody just wants them all to die. I know what that's like, too, having everyone want you fucking dead. They ought to make a God damn movie out of this life in the street or in the shelter."

"Who the fuck would want to go to a movie about homelessness?" I said. "There's no heroism in that life, Brady."

"Heroism? What the fuck is heroism? I'm talking about people's lives and you're talking about heroism. Why don't you talk about fucking Santa Claus?"

"You need heroism to make a movie."

"Fuck that. I'll be the fucking hero. You know how many lives I've saved?"

"Yeah, but they're lives that nobody cares about." I was eating my fries.

"Well somebody should do something. That's fucked up. All the fucking preaching motherfuckers. All that Baker shit, Tammy Faye, that bitch! People laugh at that shit! It ain't fucking funny! God damn Wonder bread motherfuckers giving money to a car salesman. What the fuck is he doing selling God? They wouldn't drop a fucking nickel to a guy lying in the street, but they'll give their life fucking savings to a guy running around in a Rolls Royce."

"Well," I was finishing up my sandwich and took a long drink of beer. "I see what you're saying, Brady. But how are you going to change people's outlook? People send money to a guy like that because he claims to be righteous. They hand over their money so that their faith is committed and not running wild all over creation. I think they believe they're doing right by God, but their money doesn't just represent their faith, it is their faith. If they give their faith to Baker, they can see it week after week dancing around in a nice suit offering them assurance about things they fear they have no control over-immortality, heaven, purgatory, Armageddon. The spiritual life in this country is all about wandering around half convinced of nothing at all. People hand over money as a declaration of faith so they can witness the transaction of their investment."

"What the fuck are you talking about?" said Brady.

"What do they get if they give one of your guys anything? They get to watch some smelly, dirty, foul eunuch roll around in the dirt. I mean you give them a buck and what do they do? They don't buy food."

"Some of them do," said Brady.

"Well, maybe some, but most of them go get liquored; that's what everybody sees anyway. I mean those guys could be standing on the cliff above a hundred foot drop, and they still wouldn't know which way to step. Why should I give my money to a guy who's just going to use it to perpetuate his miserable fucking life?"

"Look man," said Brady, "if a dog shits on the rug, you teach him to go outside or on the paper. You don't beat the fuck out of him for going on the rug without showing him another place to go. If you don't show him what's right, where is he? He's got to go, but he knows you're going to kick his ass. At first he holds it until he can't, and then he shits all over the fucking place; you kick the crap out of him, and soon enough he just gets used to it. He's got no choice. So every day he shits the rug, and you kick his head in. That's a nice little life for both of you. I mean, come on, there's no Einsteins running around out there; you're not going to find the prince of Siam. A lot of these people are just depressed. You lose your job, your life starts going to shit, you got no supports and boom, you're out on the street. There's a guy down there that used to be a fucking physics professor at MIT. Where is he now? Let me tell you something. There ain't much fucking difference between you and them. If everybody were so God damn fucking smart, they'd see that. That distance ain't so much. We all walk the same fucking streets, you know. I'm telling you this country is fucking bankrupt. But you know that."

"Yeah. I guess I do. You want these fries, Brady?"

"Yeah. Thanks."

"Let me ask you something, though. Do you give money to every person that asks for it?"

"No. But I know most of them. If I gave a nickel away they'd be all over me in a second."

"Well, if I gave a quarter to everyone who asks me for a dollar, I'd be broke in a heartbeat. And all the bullshit you get from some of these people. Even if you know they're destitute, I don't like to get scammed," I said.

"A lot of them will tell you any fucking thing, that's for sure." Brady spoke as if he were reminiscing. "They don't mind lying. I been doing some reading though, I tell you. Not that I'm a Jesus freak, but you know the shelter is part of the church and you got services there. I was reading the New Testament and in one of the books there Jesus says something like, 'When you look upon the face of the downtrodden, the poor, the crippled, you look upon my face. And when you turn away, you turn away from me.' Now I understand that, all right, because I do what I do, and I do it cause the people in church in this country don't know what the fuck that means. They take care of nobody but themselves and only some of them take care of their own. Half these fucking places wouldn't let Jesus Christ in the door if he showed up looking the way he looked. You get these fucking volunteers coming in from those church groups, which is great, we need them. But some of these people come in once, say, in two months…you know…save it. They waste my time showing them around the place, and then they never show up again. I mean, what is that? That's shit on a stick!"

Brady and I sat silent for a while. The sunlight, when I looked over toward it, was blinding. The women in the corner had begun to grow bored of each other. The two sitting on the ends of the aisle had turned themselves outward, while the other two drew in their cigarettes and stared at the walls. They all wore glasses, and the light reflected off them. I was leaning back on the bar stool, just glancing at people as they walked in or out. Brady was standing up and had his elbows leaning on the bar.

"Did you ever box?" I asked Brady.

"Yeah, a little. In the service. I got shipped off quick though, so there wasn't much time for it."

Through the doorway I could see Georgia across the street. "Uh-oh," I said.

"What? You know her?" She walked by the bar but didn't come in.

"Yeah," I said. "She's my neighbor. I sort of pissed her off." Brady started laughing.

"You pissed her off?" he said.

"Yeah. Why is that funny?"

"That chick knows Voo Doo, man. She's like the queen of Voo Doo." He was laughing.

"What Voo Doo?"

"She's going to hex you, man. You pissed her off?" He was shaking his head.

"How do you know that?"

"She told me. She helps me bring food down to the shelter. She knows a lot of big shots and she's helped me with a couple things, mostly getting food and clothes. She makes those weird fucking charms for me sometimes. But she's into it man."

"She's not into, like…killing chickens or anything like that, is she?"

"I don't know. I guess you'll be finding out."

"Oh, God. That's all I need. What is she going to do?"

"I don't know. She'll probably get some fucking spirit to fuck you up."

"Fuck me up. I didn't do anything to her. I just pissed her off."

"What's the difference to a ghost, man? Ghosts are like fucking gangsters; they're above the law. Sometimes they go a little overboard."

"She seems so normal."

"Yeah, she's normal. She's just into Voo Doo," said Brady. He asked the bartender to turn the television to the twenty-four hour news network. The ladies in the corner stirred for moment as if a fly had landed on them. The boxers on the wall glared.

"Where do you learn Voo Doo, for Christ's sake? I mean is there a school for that kind of thing," I said.

"I wouldn't be surprised. There are places in this country you can go to learn to be a fucking mercenary."

"Are you kidding?"

"Nope. It makes you fucking crazy running around the world fighting in wars all your life, but there's some good money in it. There's a couple guys at the shelter used to be mercenaries. But they're useless now. Lost their nerve. Scared of shadows on the wall now. They picked the wrong God damn curtain, that's for sure. Dialing for dollars with the Devil. You see it in their eyes. Used to scare me just to look at them. You ever been scared like that, scared to fucking breathe?"

"Yeah. Once when I was a kid. I was in the woods, and I saw this snake, you know, it just went across my path, didn't stop to look at me. But it scared the shit out of me, and I thought I was going to be eaten alive any second."

Brady let out a big sigh. "That's what it's like walking through a mine field. One day I'm out on patrol, with eight or ten other guys, some of them new. We were doing a sweep, you know. All of a sudden, big explosion, guy gets blown to fucking shit. So, obviously we're heading into a fucking mine field." He began to chuckle a bit. "Two of these fucking new guys hit the fucking deck and if I wasn't shitting in my pants I would have laughed my fucking head off. So, when you find you're heading into a fucking mine field, you know you backtrack. And I mean you step in your tracks exactly because, I mean, there could be a fucking centimeter between you and you in a lot of pieces. So we get about thirty yards back figuring, you know, we couldn't have got out that far without tripping something and we were about to fucking regroup and figure out our shit when another guy gets blown. Holy Christ! You talk about fucking losing your shit. I mean, you just walked backwards for thirty yards and for all you know, you're still in the middle of the fucking field. The FNG's," he laughed, "are crying. They're standing there with their M-16's balling like babies." He laughed again. "Like that's gonna help."

"How did you get out of that?"

"I think we backtracked for another hundred yards or so, holding our balls the whole way."

"Why were you holding your balls," I asked.

"Well, it keeps you sober. If you squeeze them hard enough the pain keeps you from freaking out. Besides, if you step on a mine and you live, most guys would rather live without their hands than without their balls."

I let out a big sigh. "I don't envy you that experience, Brady. I sure as hell don't. You came out of it though. You're helping people. That's really awesome."

"Yeah, I'm doing good now. Still a loser's battle but, fuck it, nobody's trying to kill me."

"Well, I hope we get this fucking thing over with," I said gesturing to the television. "That's no way to see the world."

"Don't worry about it, man. Half a million troops. They won't need half that number to win this fucking thing. The TV talks about this thing and Vietnam. It's fucking bullshit. They shouldn't waste their breath. I was in Vietnam. None of this shit is familiar to me. This thing here is like fucking Disney night at the movies. I mean, everybody get your fucking popcorn and see the laser show you've been paying for these last twenty years. And let me tell you something; the fucking scars don't just come from seeing your buddies get their balls blown off. It's walking over dead bodies, inspecting what you did to those fucks on the other side. I had to go through towns, you know, that were bombed out. And, there's fucking bodies hanging from the trees, guts, fucking intestines, arms and legs, heads rolling all over the place, dogs running around eating this shit, the maggots. Those fucking bombers up there never see what they're doing. They go out, drop some bombs, and come back. And then they come back home and get some fucking job in a corporation or something. You're not a fucking person after they send you off to a real war."

"You're not bitter, are you Brady?"

"No. I'm not bitter. But it's my fucking life, you know. It shaped my whole God damn life. I can't remember a time when Vietnam didn't exist. When I think back to when I was a kid, I think of it like, you know, fifteen years before Vietnam I had my fifth birthday. And I can't escape that. That's it. I got to live with it. Just because I say it was bad doesn't mean I'm bitter. It was fucking bad, and I wouldn't wish it on anybody."

"Do you think it's going to be bad for those guys coming home?"

"Fuck no. They'll get a hero's fucking welcome. All that Super Bowl shit. There's your fucking movie."

"I mean as far as the combat?"

"It depends on the ground war. The reconnaissance that's being told to us is fucked up. They got land they got to take, they got air support. The fucking Iraqis have no air support, no radar, they're pinned down, their supplies are cut off. I think they're going to crush them. How long could it last? A month? A month of combat won't do to you what a whole fucking year will, even if it is the whole God damn war. It's a funny thing about this one. Because of Nam, everyone is fucking crying about casualties. There's no tolerance for it because no one wants the country to lose its shit again. Oh fuck it! I don't make fucking policy. It's always this way. Those fuckers don't understand the fucking power they have. I mean they fucking sneeze and somebody down here gets his fucking balls cut off. I'm telling you this thing is fucked up. Nobody has the fucking mind that can cover all this. Everybody's running their own God damned show, you see, and nobody's running *the* show. You know what I'm saying?"

"I know what you're saying, Brady."

He took his coffee down and called out to the bartenders. He and the bartender laughed about something, I didn't understand. Brady's voice got gruff when he raised it, and it boomed. His hair was long and kind of wild. He looked like Moses for a second, all those things he'd been saying. I laughed to myself. He gave me all the money he had and I told him I'd carry the rest. He was going to work. I noticed as he handed me the money he had adhesive bandages on almost all his fingers, as well as cuts and scratches on his arms. Before he put on his coat, he combed his hair out and tied it back, tucking the tail into his shirt. He grabbed my shoulder and jostled me, and then he said goodbye and that he'd see me around. As he walked out he filled the doorframe. I sat at the bar for another beer, but as more people came in and the boilermakers started to leave, I no longer felt comfortable and went home.

The next day I went to work early to finish up paperwork that had been around for months. I was very serious that day, intending to get things done. I began to review procedures I had ignored, guidelines, policies and regulations. I needed to know them, not to adhere to them, but to know how to manipulate them. I disdained these things because for all their intent they lacked humanity. They were the body of the spirit of bureaucracy.

The next several days were a period of adjustment and revitalization. I wasn't sure why. I did my run. I threw a game of darts, shivering naked in the cold. I took scalding showers. I did pushups. I went to work. In that time I caught up on paperwork, as though I were cleaning house, preparing camp. In those next few days, I avoided the war and this relationship I'd developed with it. I felt I had fallen out of step or had lost my bearings and that I needed somehow to align myself or I would simply be a deficit, that my frustration was a deficit. Frustration was an emotional activity, I understood that. In the field, if you're told to stand next to a tree for three days you do it; without thinking why, without wondering. I, of course, would never possess that kind of discipline. I had been shaped to where I couldn't subject myself to that kind of authority. I began to realize this while I studied the bureaucracy. At times I had felt that the experience I was having was peculiar to me, that the war had been put on a platter before me in this special way, through the media, for my own purposes, or perhaps rather to show me whether I had any.

I began to wonder about my duties as a citizen. I figured the cost of all the newspapers I had stolen from Georgia and left the money in an envelope under her door. I didn't have much of a desire to speak with her after what Brady had said of the Voo Doo. In the back of my mind, I thought of dead chickens when I walked by her door. I spoke kindly to the bastard across the street. I called up the City Yard and complimented them on the fine condition of the city roads. They hung up; but that was no reflection on me. Sometimes when walking to my car, I looked up and imagined bombers there, flying over. Sometimes while running I would break into a sprint as if being chased. When I got the sensation that I was about to throw up, I learned to suppress it. I was very happy about that.

CHAPTER 24

▼

The People must be heard.

On Tuesday I was told at work that I was the new Community Relations Officer for the facility. "It'll look good on your resume," said the Boss. Well, maybe I didn't want it on my resume. "I left a note in the log for anyone not interested to write in their name and yours was the only name not there. I suggest you start reading the log."

The reason we suddenly needed to fill the Community Relations position was that there had been a series of break-ins around the neighborhood, and, of course, the neighbors looked to the only youth shelter on the block for possible suspects. My duties consisted of walking around the neighborhood, becoming friendly with the neighbors, "educating" them (as the Boss put it) on the shelter, and trying to convince them of the extreme unlikelihood of anyone sneaking out to commit robbery. The neighbors were, of course, as open to me as a rich man is to a communist in the dark. I kept hearing how property values had fallen, and how this one or that one had voted against the shelter being in the neighborhood, but there it was anyway. "Well," I thought behind a bullshit smile and an understanding nod, "next time they break in just fucking shoot them. It'll make both our lives a lot easier."

There was a house about a half mile down the block, on the same side of the street as the shelter. It was a small grey house with green shutters. Immediately after I rang the bell, the door swung open, and I was greeted by a man in his forties, with brown hair, thick dark-rimmed glasses, smoking a cigar and wearing shorts and an undershirt; the tank top kind, the kind my father used to wear. He greeted and invited me in before I could say a word to him. As I stepped inside, he said, "Oh, sweet Jesus, is it winter already?"

There were stacks of newspapers and magazines all over the house, yellowing, piled high and leaning. It was extremely warm inside. The man offered me some water which I took and we sat down on two chairs in the middle of the living room. These were the only clear surfaces I could see. The man had moles scattered all over his arms and shoulders. As I introduced myself and started to tell him why I was there, he interrupted me and asked me to start over again. He asked me whether I was with a religious group.

"No," I said. "I work in a shelter."

"Oh, that must be very interesting, yes. Did we talk about this already?"

"Excuse me?"

"What I meant to say is, well, what can I do for you?" He spoke very quickly.

As I began to explain myself, he interrupted me again saying he hadn't gotten my name. When I gave it to him again, he asked me whether there was anything wrong, whether I'd broken down or something.

"You see," he said, "what I'm trying to do is figure out why you are here, why you have landed on my doorstep. I should tell you something because I can tell by the look on your face that I have gone through this with you already. You see, I used to be a chemistry teacher in the high school here but now I have some kind of imbalance where I don't have any short-term memory. Just woke up one day and started losing it, you know. It's a chemical imbalance in the brain. That's all they can tell me about it. They don't really know; but I can't remember anything beyond fifteen or so seconds. That's why I make lists about everything, everything I do every day so I'm not doing things over and over again. And you can see I keep all my newspapers and things so I can reread them all the time until they get committed to my long-term memory. My long-term memory is very good you see. But I used to be the chemistry teacher at the high school for fifteen years. Now, I'm living on this disability thing. So, I suppose I'm telling you this because I've asked you this before, what are you doing here?" He took a puff of his cigar.

I told him my name and explained to him that I worked in a shelter in the neighborhood. I explained that I was the Community Relations Officer.

"Do you have any pamphlets?" he said. "Did I explain about the imbalance?"

"Yes."

"Oh, I did. Good. Do you have any pamphlets I could read? Because if you did, I could read them, and they'd be around and I wouldn't forget them. Otherwise you see, I'm going to forget you were even here tonight as soon as you leave. Unless I have the pamphlets you see. That's why I keep the newspapers." He glanced down to a newspaper on the floor. "Oh, sweet Jesus!" He picked up the paper. "What's the date today?"

"February 12," I said checking my watch. "1992."

"Did you know we were in a war?"

"Yes."

"What war is it?"

"It's the Gulf War."

"The Gulf War? Never heard of it. It's a new one," he said half questioning.

"Yes. It's new."

"Oh, thank goodness. I thought I was having a flashback. I don't think I've had any flashbacks. Wow. If I start getting flashbacks I won't know where to hang my hat. My name is George. Did I introduce myself?"

"Yes. It was a pleasure meeting you, sir."

"Did you tell me your name?" He puffed his cigar.

"Yes, and I better be going. It was nice talking to you George." I had unzipped my coat but still had sweat on my forehead.

He asked me whether there was anything wrong. I told him no, and that I'd be back to say hello sometime. I told him I was sorry I couldn't stay longer.

"Oh, not at all," he said as we got to the door. "Did you leave me any pamphlets?"

"Yes," I said, "you put them on the kitchen table. Have a nice evening."

"You too," he opened the door. "Jesus, it's getting cold. Well, winter's coming. Bundle up."

It was cold and dark outside, so I headed back to the shelter thinking about George's absurd disease; to be in constant want of information and constantly receiving it, constantly inundated with ever growing and repetitious material, completely unable to retain any of it. What if we all were like that? I wondered about the constant mood swings, about reading the horrible things over and over again, being freshly horrified at each turn. Was that a fate worse than death? Here was a man, a teacher, now a mole in a house of newsprint. I could imagine him puzzling as he read the paper, "What's going on now? What's going on now?" Checking the date at each paragraph. I wondered how he kept track of time. All he had in a newspaper was a declaration of events printed on a particular date. To him, last year's news would seem the same as the present, resting like a snapshot in print. Eating news but never digesting it, as though his esophagus had been detached from his stomach. "Did you know there was a war going on?" he'd said. I did seem to know that, yes.

George's house had a smell like cooked pork that seemed to stick in my clothes. As I walked the streets it made me keep thinking of pork and rice. You only needed a little bit of pork to flavor up a whole plate of rice, as long as they are fried together. I heard all the Freudians screaming about cholesterol. "Why are you trying to kill yourself?" they moaned. I wondered why pigs, being so full of cholesterol, didn't all die of heart attacks. Why didn't their arteries just clog up and cause them to explode? What a mess! Maybe we were just saving the carcass by cutting their throats and letting them bleed to death. And trichinosis? I had a dream that night. I walked into a steam room. There were pigs all sitting around in bath towels. They were smoking cigarettes and drinking vodka while they played cards. Every so often there was an explosion which threw bits of carcass all over the place. None of them stirred from their card games. One would say, "There goes another one."

The next day was the same. Pushups, one, two, three, four…running. Work. After work I went to an all-night diner in the cruddy part of the city. I'd completely forgotten to eat that day. Brady was there, and he asked me to sit down with him. He was sitting with another guy I'd never seen before, a guy named Frank, almost as big as Brady. I felt like a dwarf sitting there with the two of them. Frank was a loud-mouth. He took his size for granted. I noticed Brady blinked a lot while Frank talked. I was immediately sorry I'd walked in there, but because I liked Brady, I stayed. I acquired a piece of the definition of myself. It began with the radio.

Frank had a comment about everything playing on the radio. What a cunt that one was, or what a piece of ass. The men on the radio were all faggots. He went on for about half an hour about Johnny Mathis. Frank was hate. He manufactured hate. Because he talked so loud and so constantly, I had the peculiar sensation that he was making sense at times. Brady, being sensitive to loud noise, would only occasionally utter, "Oh, fuck you." With that Frank would get louder and more exaggerated, waving his arms, so tall that when he leaned forward it seemed he was hovering over my plate. He had the social grace of a mule with dysentery. Then it came as I finished my eggs, the war update on the radio. He sneezed, exaggerating the noise and wiping his nose on his sleeve as it finished. Then it went into regular news. More protests about the war, insensitivity to Martin Luther King Day, condoms into the schools.

"Those little desert monkeys are lucky they got oil over there, boy. What the fuck! If it weren't for us, they'd be fucking killing each other and, what the fuck, there's less of them coming over here. Dirty fucks running around with sheets on their heads. If it weren't for the fucking oil, we'd have nuked the little shitstains."

"Oh fuck you," said Brady.

"Fuck you?" Frank was leaning. "We fucking showed those greasy motherfuckers what the fuck was up over there. They'd still be sitting around with their thumbs up their assholes. Fuck them. Fuck them all. They're all fucking niggers. I don't give a fuck. Every fucking one of them. The fucking spades over here. They fucking shit all over the place. Everywhere. Fuck them. That fucking Martin Luther fucking King fuck. Fuck him. That guy was a fucking pervert. The FBI's got pictures of that guy fucking with every fucking thing under the sun. I seen them. Fucking pictures of what a pervert he was. I seen them. That's the fuck responsible for the condition of this country. Fucking things were under control, and he fucked it all up. Now look at the fucking place. We're fucking overrun with queers and niggers. Martin Luther King. Why don't we have fucking Hitler day while we're at it?"

As he spoke, I sat across from him with a wrenching stomach. I looked at him, trying to look into him to know him a little bit more. I went over his gestures. He held his fork with his right hand, the way you would if you were going to stab yourself in the chest. He took big bites and talked with his mouth full. He put his left elbow on the table and flailed his greasy hand around as he spoke. I could tell he paid attention to his hair, because it was stiff, like it had gel in it. The skin on his face was pocked, and the teeth in the back of his mouth looked rotten. As I looked at him, I was overwhelmed with the feeling that I was staring at my enemy. My countryman, my enemy. How American! To see him in the flesh before me, without even having looked for him; it was a gift. I let him talk without speaking myself. He was exposing himself.

I was the kind to tolerate anyone, the most rank and disgusting. I would sit in their company, speak to them too, but mostly listen. I listened intently, watched while they spoke. I watched them breathe and smoke, smile, pick their teeth. I was bleeding them in a way. My passivity seemed to give them confidence, though most of them wouldn't have the self-respect to cover the lesions on their character. I wanted to know about people, everyone, and this meant listening to those who were distasteful to me; they were in fact, in a way, the most valuable. It was through that process that I was able to identify not only what I didn't like about them, but also exactly why; and if there were indeed threads of meaning in them that seemed redeeming, just what those threads were, and whether those threads were in conflict with what disgusted me, or whether they somehow co-existed easily in the same host. The lack of thought in a person, of introspection, tended at the very least to irritate if not infuriate me, especially in those who were disdainful of others for no purpose but pure hatred. I drew from the world in this way. It was my way, but I identified in myself in that moment the compulsion to tell those who evoked a strong feeling in me, those who deserved it, exactly what I thought of them, exactly how I found them, because, if for no other reason, I had every God damned right to.

When he paused, I looked him in the eye and broke in. I enunciated so he could hear the difference between us. "Let me get this straight. You were looking at pictures taken of a man having sexual relations in the privacy of his own home while he was unaware of being photographed, and your conclusion is that *he* is a pervert? Is that it? You know, the truth is, that the deficit of this country is no-talent, garbage-mouthed, mental pygmies like you. If we were serious about making this country better, we'd corral all you losers, lock you in a yard, and watch you eat and fuck each other to death."

All the years of drawing from the world then began to surge within me. I was full enough of it that I didn't feel obliged to listen silently to those I despised. During all this time, from my earliest years, I saw myself in a predicament I was unable to escape (surely, I would have if I'd had the strength), and I often thought that someday I would regret all the time I had wasted; that by refusing to publicly deny these things I had failed to construct my own character. It came though that I was more sure of myself in that moment than of anything in the world. And though it wouldn't take much for a prick like Frank to break my back, that fact didn't make me any less right. Sometimes that point has to be made clearly.

He looked at Brady with a smirk, but Brady was as surprised as he was. He looked back at me.

"Hey, what the fuck you saying?...All that mental shit..."

"I'm saying that you have plenty of energy to cry about the problems of this country, and point fingers and call people names and lay blame on people about whom you have not got a clue, but you're too God damn stupid to realize that it's you and your hatred that brings all of us down. You're a twerp!"

"Hey," he said, "I don't like that. Who the fuck do you think you are? I'll take you out in the fucking parking lot and show you how fucking stupid I am. You want me to kick your fucking ass; you don't have to go to all that trouble."

"Well, that's the truth. If you don't like it, kicking my ass won't make it any better for you."

He pointed his finger in my face. "Hey! You're starting to piss me off." As he leaned forward he pinned me in the booth with the table. "You fucking cocksucker. You don't have any right to be talking to me like that."

Brady was sitting next to me and started to intercede here. He was as pinned in the booth as I was. Frank was standing now. Brady stood up on the chair and stepped over me. The corner of the table was digging into my chest so I was relieved to see Brady taking some action, though I wondered, since I hardly knew him, how much he would do to intercede. Fortunately, Brady had instinctive loyalty. He was not afraid of getting hit, and he was used to his life being in danger. He was also good at defusing people and managed to get Frank sitting down again. He had Frank by the arm and reminded him that he had to get back on the dock. Frank was, in fact, supposed to have been working this whole time. He put some money on the table for his part of the bill.

"You ought to say you're sorry."

"Why? Did I offend you?"

"Yeah. You offended me, you fucking asshole."

"Well, you offended me first. I mean, your whole God damn existence offends me."

With that he reached across the table and slapped me with his open hand. It was enough to spin my head and knock me to the floor. I had no doubt he was going to kill me. It was obvious he had a lot of respect for Brady because Brady got him out with relative ease. Maybe he didn't intend to kill me, just then. My mouth was bleeding, I was dizzy for a few minutes, and my ear was ringing. Brady came back in after a long while and sat with me.

"He was one fresh fucking daisy," I said to him.

Brady looked at me in a concerned way and said, "I don't think you should come in here for a couple years."

War requires a strange, committed, obscene eccentricity. It came, this thing, in pages, videotape, and words as great as any nation. Time, immediacy, exhaustion, saturated stupor, these were the elements of my war. The media were my gargoyle friends, in my room, that spoke to me in the privacy of the darkness there. Though I could not speak back, they would relate that they had heard me by quoting other commoners, that is, non-public-eye personnel, a tactic the President himself began to mimic. The message came that everything was occurring, that I should stay tuned. It all occurred without my saying so, but I should remain in tune.

The next morning rushed over me when I woke up. I hadn't listened to the news at the diner, distracted as I was by the Asshole. I had a need to know. A need reminiscent of the anxiety I'd felt at the restaurant the night Israel had first been bombed. I got out of bed still in my clothes, put my shoes on, and scurried down to the news/luncheonette/laundry place with the bloated guy wearing rubber gloves. The front page was about the war. "Good," I thought. But I didn't want little pieces of it flying at me while I was paying for it and walking home. I wanted the whole thing. I wanted to sit at the table with a knife and fork and eat the news of the war in a civilized way. It was windy and raining, which helped me on the run home. It helped me discover a hole in my shoe.

The pictures on the front page were taken from a television set. It was Valentine's Day. The headline told that a U.S. raid had "reportedly" killed hundreds.

The story was that hundreds had been killed when U.S. fighters bombed what U.S. officials maintained was a military-command bunker, and what the Opposition labeled a "civilian bomb shelter." The U.S. officials said that the Opposition had placed civilians in what was clearly a military target. The CNN renegades had filmed the bodies of women and children being taken out of the rubble while people wept and gnashed their teeth. The renegades said they saw no signs of any communications equipment or any military stuff after having been allowed by Opposition officials to roam the wreckage. One of the fascinating aspects of the story was that at about four in the morning, still under dark skies, the stealth fighter dropped two laser-guided bombs onto his target. The bombs fell through the roof and exploded. A school across the street, a mosque 300 feet down the road, and houses all around the target were untouched by the blast. With precision like that, the issue, it seemed, was that those civilians would have been far safer from bombing in their own houses. One reporter who had inspected the area noted that there was a sign outside that identified the building as a bomb shelter in both Arabic and English.

In the capital, Washington D.C., the Secretary of Defense said that the Opposition had a history of parking military equipment among cultural and civilian sites. He gave as examples two MIG fighters stationed next to a Sumerian pyramid near Ur, the birthplace of Abraham. Yeah, yeah, yeah.

The paper also noted that no air-raid alarms were sounded as the stealth bomber flew over the city, and that the roof had only recently been painted camouflage in the residential neighborhood. The military briefer in Riyadh had been asked by the press if the civilian losses had been staged for the purpose of propaganda. He said, "Quite plausibly."

Jake called from the train station. He wanted me to pick him up. "Okay," I said. "I'll be right down." I sat back in my chair after pouring more coffee. This thing had caught my eye about the shakeup of the jittery Alliance. I was constantly amazed that such an alliance existed. It was said that the Arab countries didn't like aligning themselves with Westerners. It was clear they didn't want to be left at the hands of the enemy. Peace in the area was in everybody's best interest. By the standards of any other war, the number of civilian casualties was light. "Any loss of life is a tragedy," that old hymn was getting bantered around. Were they making a demonstration of their humane fiber or reminding us of the fact? Civilians were getting killed. That happens in war when one people make war on another. That's sort of the point. But we were fighting one man, not a people, one man with an army of people. The people were like wandering elk in the desert, their radios and televisions burrowed into their skulls telling them what to

think and how to behave. To kill such prey you need only send the leader running off a cliff. So, if that's the only way to kill the leader, well…

The other Arab natives reportedly did not see the docile desert folk as their
enemies, and they did not want to be perceived, especially by their own people, as
funding the means of their deaths. The talk turned to rushing the Ground War,
which was promised by some to be a bloodbath, in order to finish the war before
the alliance had the chance to deteriorate. Again, it was said that the enemy had
gained a propaganda advantage. Here, history was being made. The media were
not only relating the war, but had become players, a third party. The media could
have instantaneous effects on the most unprecedented alliance in world history.
Dissenting members in the United Nations were making waves on the diplomatic
front. Dissenters were made up in part of longtime troublemakers, communists,
and dictators. The enemy was making a concerted effort to form a New Islamic
Front, the paper said. At a news conference in Jordan, the enemy's Deputy Prime
Minister, Saddoun Hammadi, defined their enemies as disbelievers, the imperialists, Zionists, and colonialists. It was reported he said, "The war is going to be a
long war. The aggressors will pay the price for their aggression." (Aggressor?
How'd you like a fat lip?) Hammadi wanted to separate the fate of his people
from that of the rest of humanity. Were his people Arab or Muslim? He was
more comfortable with Muslims killing Muslims it seemed, as his country had
proved relentlessly and would prove yet again. "This war is illegitimate," said
Abdalla Saleh Ashtal, Yemen's U. N. Ambassador. Was it really? The King of Jordan said that his week-old comments supporting the enemy had been misunder-
stood and that his country would maintain its neutrality. Foreign journalists
inspecting the site were permitted by Opposition officials to file their reports for
the first time without censorship after inspecting the wreckage, the paper said.

I thought of Chingis Khan buried on his forgotten mountainside. What made
him the conqueror of conquerors was his power to mobilize armies and revise and
utilize systems of organization and warfare. Once he had conquered the surrounding steppe tribes in the early stages of his career, he suppressed the conditions that had divided and impoverished his people for so long: cattle theft,
kidnapping, and the owning by Mongols of Mongol slaves. But life on the
steppes, which required almost constant time in the saddle and expert handling
of weaponry, made those people ideal soldiers, unequaled in endurance of pain
and discomfort, callous and totally lacking in sympathy. He was almost always
outnumbered and, therefore, became expert in obtaining objectives with the min-
imum amount of force. Mobility, firepower, and communication were the principles upon which his armies existed and conquered.

One of his tactics was to send spies in to encourage dissidents that the invaders were sympathetic to their cause. This lessened the enemy's ability to defend himself and got a sympathetic indigenous population to help rule the conquered territory, if help were needed. In the taking of a city, for example, the Mongols would sometimes separate the dissidents and slaughter the rest of the population. The greater the resistance encountered, the greater the fury they leveled at the population. On other occasions, Chingis Khan simply slaughtered everyone—to strike fear in nearby princes, to prevent any future resistance, or because he had no use for them at all. This, of course, avoided the concept of "victory in defeat" or "propaganda success."

In some of the commentaries on the radio it was stated that the possibility of a nuclear strike against the Opposition "had not been ruled out." The Armageddonists must have been drooling. The ingredients were all there, and they were making the cake. Perhaps this was a ploy on the media, perhaps not. The devastation of a nuclear blast lacked precision as far as the radioactive fallout, which was only as predictable as wind patterns. The blast could easily enough be equaled with our store of conventional weaponry. Somehow "nuclear warheads" was more horrifying than "12,600 pounds of explosives." The home-front propaganda objective of the Administration was to assure the People of the United States of America of a finite limit on the number of those among them who would die, and a picture of a nuclear missile with a smile was certainly effective insurance. If war requires the loss of life, it is best when the enemy puts in your share. As for Chingis Khan, he would not have considered the nuclear option. He had a definite concept of God, whom he regarded as being everywhere, and aside from seeing no purpose in wasting the energy to conquer a land you can't exploit, he'd have not opted to create an unnatural wasteland.

I saw a thing in the paper talking about the Soviet Peace Initiative. Tariq Aziz was in Moscow to meet Mikhail S. Gorbachev. Their discussions were reportedly focused on how to stop the war. It was repeatedly pointed out by the Press Secretary that to stop the war the Opposition need only drop their weapons and head north. The Soviets were said to be concerned about the strong American military presence. As if we wanted anything from them except for them to get their act together. An official from the Soviet government was quoted as saying that they were against the war and that they wanted it stopped. Frankly, I didn't give a fuck what the Russkies wanted. After the Lithuania thing they were in less of a position to moralize than The Evangelist. Chatting with the enemy, what grotesque little creatures the Russkies had become.

I saw an article on an out-of-work plumber. He had moved out of his father's house to a tent in the lot next door to his father's house and had only been in the house for three showers in eleven days. He said a medical condition had prevented him from signing up and that he'd been turned away from a recruiting station. He was selling war paraphernalia—T-shirts and things—to raise money for American children orphaned by the war. He had a big sign with an American flag that covered the side of his father's house. There was obviously something missing in this guy's life, something he was sentimental about. I wondered whether he shouldn't be out volunteering his unemployed plumbing ass to a family or an organization that could easily find use for money saved. Wouldn't that be just as patriotic? Wouldn't that be a real investment in America? But that wouldn't have gotten his picture in the newspaper.

A German official stated that Syria had revealed to him through their Foreign Minister, Farouk Sharaa, that Syria would be willing to recognize Israel's right to exist, the paper said. The Syrian leaders, however, quickly made statements confirming that they remained committed to a 1973 U. N. Security Council resolution, though the paper failed to specify the substance of that resolution. Syria advocated for support of an international peace conference on the Middle East, and called for Israel to withdraw from occupied Arab territories. Israel expressed enthusiasm for discussing peace with the Syrians, the paper said, but was not confident that the Syrians would agree to such a meeting. Israel's officials also said they had not heard from Syria.

Comments were made regarding the accuracy of the bombing of the bunker, that it had not damaged surrounding buildings. It being apparent that this was not enough to prevent civilian casualties, attention was drawn to the intelligence that had determined that the bunker was a military target. I remember an article on the subject said that one of the satellites used could differentiate people in military uniform from those in civilian dress and could see a license plate, though not close enough to make it out. "That's outrageous," I thought. Here I was designing bombs with mailboxes, and they had things like that; and those were the things they were willing to tell us about. The Dictator had nothing like that, I was sure. It was noted in the article that there was a satellite over the area once every couple of hours and that this might explain why intelligence was unaware of a civilian presence. The General pointed out that though Allied forces had not targeted military centers in civilian areas, they were permitted to do so under the Geneva Convention. In my estimation, we were their enemy and everyone the world over should expect us to behave as such. As for the Geneva Convention, everyone was holding it up as a flag of righteousness, but in practicality it was an afterthought. I was surprised the General had time for such things.

Terrorist attacks on U.S. targets were reported around the globe by the State Department at one hundred. They did not seem to be part of a concerted effort by Enemy-based groups, but rather locals, the paper said.

In other news, the President had issued his transportation plan. The plan, the paper said, gave emphasis to roads, including privately financed highways, over initiatives for mass transit. I wondered whether our military, there in oil-land, was getting all its fuel for free. I thought, "We must be hooked right up to the fucking well."

The next several days were covered by banter about the bunker thing. "What the hell do I care," I kept saying. "What am I going to do about it? What do you want me to do about it you jerks? Write my fucking Congressman?" I laughed when I said that. "The people have to be heard," Harvey said. What people? The Press Secretary said, "Well, we weren't looking for civilians." And why the fuck should we? By my estimation they should stay the fuck out of the way. That Enemy fuck was responsible for putting civilians in a God damn military bunker. What the hell was he trying to do with that? He wasn't trying to protect them. The General said that American pilots were risking their lives trying to avoid civilian casualties. That's as much folly as I was willing to endure. We shouldn't be at risk in the least. No blood for oil. Fuck you. These types of alliances have been going on for thousands of years. And there never has been such a Boy Scout do-gooder operation as the U.S. military, ever. Risking our lives to avoid civilian casualties? Fine. I was willing to accept that. We were kicking the crap out of them. The radio voice said, "We are not fighting the Iraqi people..." We're fighting one big mean ugly guy. Well, we're fighting whoever the fuck gets in our way. What are we supposed to do, apologize for being so good at it!

CHAPTER 25

▼

The War of Immaculate Conception

Reports related the letdown felt by Allied forces. Up to day twenty-nine they had led a "clean war." It was proposed that, "there are limits to a clean war." The morning on day thirty-one, pushups…one, two, three…running. I saw the Red Man…the voice from Riyadh.

"We are doing everything we can to avoid civilian casualties. If we wanted to cause civilian casualties, they would be in the hundreds of thousands. Collateral damage will occur but no doubt the most surgical weapons ever used in warfare are being used to avoid them."

Oilfields in the occupied country were being set on fire by the enemy. Oil pumped into the gulf was washing up onto the beaches of Saudi Arabia, disturbing the operation. I did more pushups…One, two…three…

When news came that the enemy had offered to pull out of the occupied country I was shooting pool in a hall that smelled like a rat's ass. I refused to play for money, which infuriated the men around me because I was no good. I wasn't very rich either. The word was that the enemy had offered to adhere to U. N. Resolution 660, issued August 2, which called for the unconditional withdrawal of Iraqi troops from Kuwait, on conditions including Israel pulling out of the occupied territories, Syrian troops leaving Lebanon, a cease-fire and withdrawal of Allied forces, payment by the Coalition for the rebuilding of Iraq, and a replacement of the government of Kuwait by a choice of the people. A dictator demanding democracy in a neighboring state? Who was writing this stuff? The President called the proposal a cruel hoax on the world and particularly the Iraqi people, who reportedly were dancing in the streets when the announcement was made. I must admit that I nearly broke into small feelings of euphoria at the beginning of the announcement. All this tension had been taking its toll on me. I wasn't sleeping as well as I could. Of course, I was getting in shape but not eating well. This absurd proposal had come just two days after the return from Iraq of

Yevgeny Primakov, one of the Soviet President's men, who had been trying to negotiate a solution to the war. Well, Yevgeny, nice try anyway. I decided to write another letter.

16 February 1991

Dear Sir:

If it were me marching into Baghdad, I would humiliate you first. I'd tie your testicles to your feet with short fishing line, and I'd make you walk the 100 miles back to your little home town of Tikrit. Then I'd stick the barrel of a .22 caliber pistol up your nose and shoot you dead. A bullet that small would bounce off and around your skull and carve the meat to ribbons. We'd steam your head, chop off the top, and dine on the soup inside. I am sure that sentiment intrigues you. Well, sir, you need only invite me in.

Always,

Your Enemy

After sealing and addressing the envelope, I thought, "Perhaps I ought not indulge in this kind of fantasizing. It might not be healthy." But then to second guess an attack often proves fatal. I addressed and sealed the envelope, knowing truly he'd never set eyes on it. But that was no reflection on me. Expressions needed to be made. It wouldn't be my fault if he never received it. It was the only attack I, my person, could make; and when I dropped the letter in the mailbox, it was made.

Towards the rear of the paper, a paragraph reported the fire-bombing of what the attackers and the media called an abortion clinic located in a building owned by Planned Parenthood of Central Ohio. No one had claimed responsibility for the bombing. Terrorism within our borders. Yes. Dissenters. A different paragraph related that sixteen federal judges had been "issued assassination threats in letters prepared with the same typewriter used to label bombs that killed a federal judge and a civil rights lawyer…" Way in the rear I saw this. A lack of unity. An attack coming from within. A terrorism far more despicable than anything our foreign enemy could launch. Why had this no prominence?

We would have to turn to these enemies after the war. We would have to cut out the cancer. It was this news that convinced me that the idea of bringing the enemy to trial for war crimes was folly. Without the declaration of war, without an absolute invasion and occupation that reached down into that bunker and pulled him out by his nose hair, the likelihood of bringing him anywhere was nil. Why was anybody in the Capitol wasting their time thinking about it, unless only as a brain teaser? This whole civilian bunker thing demonstrated the impossibility of total warfare.

That night in my dream, I entered a crowded room. I was among people for whom I had great respect, though I could not tell you now who they were. Their hair was cropped short to their scalps and they were dressed in robes. The gaze of each of those men was evocative, slow, sweeping, and distinct. I know because they each looked at me as I entered. They looked at me in turns it seemed, and noticed that I had seen this. Not knowing my place there, I sat myself down on the end of a bench. The light in the room was not bright but alluring, and distracted me until I noticed quite suddenly that they were all silent and looking toward me. Their leader, a large man, sat in the middle of the room.

"Have you ever placed your life in the hands of another man, son?" he said directly to me.

"No. I haven't."

"If you can't give yourself up to another, how can you be trusted?"

"I don't understand you."

He looked at me square on. "No noble purpose is served without a higher authority. Actions must be total and committed. This requires a relinquishment of the self to a higher authority. A person requires an emotional reference for such a thing, the trust required in putting one's life in the hands of another; the other representing the higher authority. If you cannot do this, then you have not accepted a higher authority. If you cannot trust, you cannot be trusted."

"And once this occurs...?"

"You are committed."

"And if I rebuke you afterwards?"

"You will rot from the inside."

"And if I make no commitment?"

"Then nothing you do will matter."

"Who are you to condemn me?"

"I am no one to condemn you. But if you ask me to hold your life in my hands, I will accept the challenge at risk to my own. And afterwards I will turn

my life over to you. For anyone to understand their charge, this must occur."
And they all looked upon me, each iris' gaze.

"What are you saying?" I said to him. They all smiled and looked around to
one another.

CHAPTER 26

▼

To track an enemy.

The next two days were intense working days for which I had to relinquish my daily exercises. There had been two homeless youth shelters in the city but because of the cuts, the Agency was consolidating programs, doubling the number of beds in mine and also making it more difficult to be allowed in. Lawrence was out in the street again, no longer armed. From a Community Relations point of view this had no significance because in my discourse with the neighbors I was told that nobody gave a God damn. I spent my time running my ass off making adjustments, counseling people I had no qualifications to counsel, and filling out reports and assessments in order to protect the agency from possible lawsuits. On most of these there was no place to lie. I was moving furniture, knocking down walls, and trying to smile at people I had never met, nor cared to. These were people from the office who seemed to be there only to overcrowd an already overcrowded situation. I had never thought of furniture as a burden. But it was, an anchor, a weight one must bear to move, a deterrent to movement. Sunday and Monday melded. I did not distinguish between the two. Why would I, anyway? They were both just days of the week. My actions—what were they? Just things I did. What would distinguish them from one another? I was doing this today. I would do that tomorrow. Perhaps, I would do this again.

I didn't make policy. I had no input on the budget cuts or the consolidation. As a Community Relations Officer in a neighborhood without community, it was difficult to give the illusion that I was having any impact. Fortunately for me, no one at the Agency gave a damn. During these two days the Boss collapsed with some sort of pneumonia. "Don't worry," I told her. "I'll take care of everything." Not that I thought I could take care of everything. It was falling to hell. But I figured she should get some rest.

I did hear small pieces during that time, that child-abuse reports were up seventeen percent in the state. The Russkies were falling more in line; probably real-

izing they'd been trying to get into bed with a maggot. Downtown, there had
been a big antiwar protest. It was a silent march reportedly to honor those killed
in the war. At a nearby Air Force base, protesters had been arrested. They were
obviously committed people. I think more Scuds had been fired without meaningful result.

On Tuesday, I was forced by an administrator to take half the day off as com-
pensation for extra hours worked in the previous two days. During my run, I
headed into the wind and rain, which soaked me and made me feel majestic. I
was alone around the water, which was covered with mist. I finished with a sprint
out to the end of the floating dock and sucked down the damp air. I breathed
down deep into the heels of my feet. I was winded, but I tried to take control,
breathing slowly. My lungs screamed, but I wouldn't let them dictate my needs. I
imagined inhaling all the mist from the top of the Pond. All I could hear was the
traffic and the breathing. I was alone out there trying to control myself, trying to
control it all, and I thought I was finally beginning to understand something I'd
tried long ago to stop thinking about. It used to keep me up at night. It used to
occupy me on long trips in the car. Eventually, my thoughts about it just seemed
stuck in a loop, and in an effort to break the cycle, I worked hard to forget it all
together.

It was a story my father used to tell me when I was little. A lot of times he'd
explain stories, but with this one he'd say he didn't know. Every time he told it,
he'd say we had to figure this one out together. It was about a boy who lives in a
part of the world with huge underground caverns. Worlds exist there that human
beings don't know about, places too fantastic for our timid imaginations. In these
caverns live the bats, swarms of them, that black out the sky at dusk as they
emerge. The boy, walking the countryside one evening, witnessed this for the first
time. He had seen bats before but never millions of them all at once. It immediately struck him that they must be fleeing, that from under the ground something
more immense than a swarm of bats was coming, something so hideous that its
terror pierced the bats' erratic senses. So he ran home to tell his father, crying and
afraid.

When his father calmed the boy down and realized the cause of his terror, he
explained the bats; that they were rushing toward the open air to feed in the
absence of the sun; that the bats had a clock within them keeping time, telling
them to emerge from the enclosed darkness to the open, and back again. "Would
the bats die in the sunlight?" he asked. "Yes, they would."

As he received the explanation of what he had seen, the boy began to resent
the bats for having frightened him, and his terror became a seed of hatred which

grew with him into his adolescence. Every night he would go and watch the bats, first out of curiosity, and then out of cunning. As he watched them night after night, he would cultivate his hatred. The bats were ugly and made horrible noises. He had dreams of their swarms attacking him, covering him completely, eating him, or carrying him down into the caverns where the darkness was as thick as a fortress wall. He captured one every so often and, after studying it, would set it out to burn in the hot sun. It was not pleasure he felt in doing so, but satisfaction that his enemy could be vanquished.

As he watched the swarm at dusk fly out each night, he would imagine watching them all drop dead, though he could never imagine from what. He thought how wonderful it would be if they all flew out during the day by accident, how relieved he would feel to watch them all die, for by this time he hated them passionately, and feared them for their numbers. He wished he could rip the Earth open at midday. He hated that they were so much on his mind, and he wanted them all dead.

As he grew into manhood, he spent his time figuring ways to trick the bats, getting them to fly out on their own while the sun was high. He had many elaborate projects that involved making calls at the mouth of the cave, nighttime noises; he tried covering the cave mouth with huge blankets to fool them. He tried lighting fires in the caves as far down as his fear would allow him. But the extent of the caves gave the bats fantastic recourse, and their clocks were infallible. Over the course of twenty years, none of these efforts inspired the death of even one bat.

Working in the fields one day under the sun, which no longer burned his skin after the years of exposure, he looked up at it and thought, "To kill them, I must control that thing." He imagined himself holding back the sun with a long rope above the horizon, turning the bats' own infallible clocks against them. This image, he felt, was brilliant, and set him to thinking on how he would capture the sun.

Months and months went by as he patiently thought of the task inspired by the image of himself holding back the sun. He knew from hunting that to capture prey, one must stalk it and study its movements. One must inhale as the prey does and exhale on the same beat. Take steps only in image of the prey. And so, his thinking slowly turned to stalking. He slept from the moment the sun went down, slept in the field, and jumped to his feet awake at the moment it peered over the horizon. He abandoned his observations of bats, for, he felt, he knew their movements like he knew his own, and could afford to do so for the greater good of his scheme.

The boy, now a man for half his lifetime, took the midday hours to observe the sun, when it was most directly visible to him. He watched it day after day, trying to see into it, to understand it as he understood the ways of wild boar. After months of stalking he noticed that, more and more, all that he could see was the sun, even when he wasn't looking at it. This, he felt, was a very good sign. It showed him focused and harmonizing with his prey. Images of other people and things on the earth became fainter and fainter in its glare.

So it came one day that he awoke with his vision of the sun but nothing else. He could not honestly say whether it were night or day. But all this time stalking had given him an internal clock which put him to sleep at sundown and put him on his feet at sunup. He never saw a bat again, and after some years forgot about them altogether. For, he went inside at dusk when his old blind enemy came out, and he came out after dawn as the bats settled back in the cavern.

"Where are you?" I said out loud, and I thought of my father.

As I headed back home, someone I didn't recognize was driving on the busy road around the water, honking their horn and waving to me. When I waved back, they flipped me off. "Gun control," I thought.

CHAPTER 27

▼

Ring Time

Work was much the same. My boss had been admitted to the hospital. More consolidation had kids tripling in single rooms. "It's just temporary," they told me as they closed their doors and drove off. Just temporary. Madness is always temporary. George, from down the street, walked by as I stood there on the stoop of the shelter. He glanced through me as he might any stranger.

"Hello," I said.

"Good afternoon." He spoke without taking his cigar out of his mouth.

Jake called. He wanted me to pick him up downtown on my way home and go for a drink. I told him I wouldn't be out until midnight. That was fine with him. We'd go for a drink and then get something to eat.

We just managed to get a pint at a closet of a pub downtown. It was typical in these places for them to make last call, give you your drink, take your money, and then tell you to chug it and get the hell out. They were bastards, but what could you say if you knew that going in. We went to a restaurant Jake knew in China-town, one he said was open all night. Jake didn't know exactly where it was, so we had to drive around awhile. We got a booth. For some reason, at two in the morning in a city that died at nine o'clock, this place was busy. The waiter gave us exactly a minute and a half to look over the menu. Jake spoke harshly to him, "We need more time." The waiter asked us in a heavy accent if we wanted anything to drink.

"Yes. We want cold tea."

"Cold tea?" asked the waiter.

"Yes. Cold tea."

"I don't want cold tea," I said.

"Trust me," said Jake. Then to the waiter, "Cold tea."

"But I don't want cold tea," I said.

"Yes, you do. Why are you such a dick about everything?"

I spoke harshly to him. "I do not want cold tea."

"All right, fine," said Jake, turning to the waiter. "I'll have cold tea. Bring him regular tea." The waiter sped off.

"I don't want tea at all."

"Well, you can order whatever else you want when he gets back. What are you getting?"

"Some chicken stuff with rice."

"Yeah, that's for me, too."

"How come you yell at the waiter like that?"

He smirked. "You have to in this place, or they try to fuck with you."

The waiter came back, put two tea pitchers on the table and then took our order, repeating it as we gave it to him, and then ran off like he was missing his flight. Jake took the cold pot and poured a glass for me.

"That's beer," I said.

"No. That would be against the law at this hour. This is cold tea." He smirked.

"Forgive me."

He smirked again and shifted in his chair to face me squarely. "So what's been going on with you?"

"Nothing."

"You say that like you don't want to talk about it. That's okay." He put his elbow on the table like he was doing something naughty.

"I don't know what you mean." I didn't.

"Well, fighting with the neighbors, stealing Georgia's newspapers. She chewed my ear about that. She thought I was in on it, and I didn't know anything about it. She's into Voo Doo, you know. She was going to put a hex on you."

"You talked her out of it?" I said. There was a Chinese scream from the kitchen like someone being boiled. No one in the restaurant seemed to hear it.

"I didn't have to," said Jake. By this time he was slumped and pouring more beer. "She said it would be bad karma."

"Isn't that like mixing metaphors?"

"What do you mean?"

"Voo Doo is Afro-Caribbean. Karma is from India. It's Buddhist."

"You want me to see if she'll reconsider?" he said with a sneer.

"Anyway, I paid her for the papers. It was just an oversight" I said.

"I thought it might have something to do with work." He squared again.

"Why what's going on with work?" The waiter stopped next to our table and yelled across the room to a teenager working the register. Jake flinched, but I didn't move. I looked at his hands. His fingernails were long, like a musician's. His face was healing. The bruise had spread, but the swelling had gone.

He started talking like a spy, like he was being chased, like he thought I might be the last person who would ever see him alive. "I've got it on good authority that our place is going to be closing down. Have you heard anything?"

"No. They just moved more people in on us. If nothing else, I guess that's a good indication we'll be open for a while. Who told you you'd be closing?"

"I can't say. I had to have sex for the information."

"Was it really that important to you?"

"No, but the sex was. It added something to it for her. You meet all types in this business. You know."

"All grey and beat up like that? She thought she had to extort you for sex?"

"Like I said, you meet all types."

"What are they going to do with the clients? There's no place to put them."

"I know," he said. "But I can't think about that right now. I'm going to lose my job. I don't know what they're going to do."

"What are you going to do?"

"I don't know. This is the first job I ever liked. I mean, this is the first time I'm going to be fired without trying."

"Are you prepared to lose your job?"

"Yeah, right. I haven't even paid this month's rent yet."

"Have they said anything to you about it?"

"No."

"Ah, they're lazy fucks, anyway. You've got that going for you. Maybe they won't get to it for a while."

"What are you talking about?" he said. "The money dries up and it's over. If the state cuts funding tomorrow morning, we'll be packing it up by noon!"

"So, get another job. You should be used to this."

He was really slumping now. "I don't want another job. I like this job." More people came in. It was getting crowded, the vampire crowd, all safe in numbers, safe in the buzz of florescent light. Every time the door opened, cold air flooded the place, and the napkins blew off the table. "I thought maybe I could get a job at your place," he said.

"I'm sure you could if there were any. It's not like they're viciously screening applicants, Jake. It's the same agency. They should be able to find you something."

"I'm not going to worry about it. The decision hasn't been made yet. I just know they're talking about it." He finished off the beer.

"Did anyone from the office say anything to you?" I started to realize that he was going to want me to pay for the meal. I didn't mind. I'd just charge it, pay it later.

"No. I'm a fucking staff person. The way they look at you sometimes, it's like you're a giant bug. I had to pump a few people." Jake shouted to the waiter, "More cold tea!"

"A few people?" I said.

"Well, literally only one but I wanted to confirm it. So I just went down to the office and wouldn't leave till somebody told me something. By the way," he said, "do you recall the other day, someone calling you, and you said you'd be right over to pick him up?"

"Oh, yeah. Where the hell was he?"

"He was at the train station."

"North Station?"

"South Station. Why would he be at North Station?"

"I don't know. He said the train station."

"North Station's a freaking subway stop. Why would I just say the train station if I meant North Station?"

"I don't know. I thought your directions were a little vague. What did you wind up doing?"

"Well, first I called around, but I couldn't get anybody else. Then, I had a lot of shit with me, so I took a cab."

"Well, why didn't you tell me you needed a ride beforehand?"

"I didn't think of it. Cabs ain't cheap. Plus, the driver was a hillbilly."

"Ah. I'll buy you a couple beers. You'll forget it." He agreed. The truth was I'd totally forgotten Jake had called as soon as I'd hung up the phone.

When I got home, I turned the radio on as I was falling asleep. I caught the news that a man in Amherst had poured paint thinner all over himself and set himself ablaze. There were interviews with people who had seen it. He had set a sign down on the ground which said "Peace." Frankly, I had no sympathy for this moron. It was speculated that his message was one about the charred bodies in the bunker. And for what impact? The man just tossed his life away to make a flash in the dark statement about what? He left that for interpretation; a visual aid for all the crybaby wannabe martyrs. Here was a man who took on the problems of the world, who had indulged himself in the terror that is the condition of humanity, because he either had no problems or had refused to face them. That he should levy this violence on those acquainted with him, his family, friends, on those who had to witness it, on the community that had to clean up his remains,

I found despicable. I thought if I'd been walking by as he poured on the paint thinner and he asked me for a match, I'd have kicked him in the teeth and had him arrested for stupidity.

The big news of the next day was that the President had rejected the Soviet Peace Plan. No shit. Calls for a cease-fire from the Old Nemesis were denied publicly by everyone with any say. It was said that if the Opposition took this opportunity to pull out unconditionally, they would still have the most powerful military in the region, despite the daily bombing. The General said that while their military was on the verge of collapse it still appeared to be very capable for that part of the world or something like that.

Yevgeny Primakov, the Soviet Middle East envoy, was quoted as saying, "We've thrown off all attributes of the Cold War in our relations with the United States. Please don't worry about us doing something against you." That's right Russky. It was said that Moscow and the U.S. were in harmony on the key point of the accord. Hopes for a quick resolution to the conflict were quelled in light of the President's response.

Iranian President Hashemi Rafsanjani asked the Coalition to delay the Ground War during diplomacy sessions with Tariq Aziz. Yeah, right. Assessments of the enemy military held it as hurting and demoralized; deserters reportedly braved execution squads to desert. Allied forces were ready for the Ground War, the General said, though he refused to speculate publicly about when that might occur. The enemy, in the guise of their state-controlled papers, made expressions of high hopes for peace in response to the Moscow initiative but also warned that "the army had prepared all necessary means and power to make the Ground War a killing zone and a graveyard for all the invaders dispatched to the region," and that Iraq's "…all-powerful weapons…will explode in their faces." Having no other choice, I resolved myself to sit and wait for ring time.

At work everybody had their heads spinning. The kids didn't know which end was up. Suddenly, the house had been invaded by all these people no one knew anything about. There was at least one other staff person with me, and the boss was to come out of the hospital on Saturday. We never heard from the top unless they came by to take something or to move something in. If I had had time to analyze them, I would have. But I didn't. I knew that as a counselor, I was standing right next to the kids at the end of the poop shoot. Perhaps care was a limited commodity in the human rationale. "We do not have the time or money to care for you. Times are tough." I didn't know the administrators personally, but I began to hate them. I began, too, to understand that before I even realized a fight existed, I had been beaten. The best I could do was try to ensure that the victor couldn't shake my carcass loose. In a way, I thought, society is a system by which people determine acceptable parameters of violence and the mechanisms by which it will be imposed. Power is the manipulation of responsibility to maintain this system.

In reading the papers I felt immensely powerful. I was supremely American; young, righteous, more powerful than my forefathers, unapologetic, more determined by my past, more damning of dissenters, more embracing of those with what I deemed a respectable vision, disdaining of those who lacked it, and absolutely intolerant of those who put themselves above the Manifest World Order. Yes, this was my disposition and how I approached the people with whom I had contact. Yet, in the scope of my immediate personal world, the problems and their solutions had been definitely played out without a glance toward me for input.

Operations at the front had begun. These were preliminary assaults before the launch of the Ground War which resulted in the capture of over four hundred enemy soldiers. Talk was tough. Speaking at the U.N., the Secretary of State said, "One way or another, the Iraqi army of occupation will leave Kuwait soon. And so Kuwait will be liberated. Soon." Finally some words with flavor and bite.

In talk of strengths of the enemy, it was presented that the enemy was well dug in, hunkered down, and that the Allied approach would probably consist of concentrated strikes at strategic points on a massive front, which would seek to isolate and confuse the Enemy, destroying whatever remaining means of communications they had, ultimately encircling the Enemy and closing in while air support bombed and strafed Enemy positions within the circle. With the addition of air support, this was textbook Chingis Kahn strategy. The Soviet Peace Plan was getting bantered around. The enemy responded to it by saying he would respond soon. U.S. officials stated that the plan did not include anything contrary to the U.N. resolutions but it did not either include them all; leaving, it was said, the potential for the enemy to remain in power with much of his "war machine" intact. Arab diplomats stated that it was precisely the plan's lack of a guarantee of this that delayed an affirmative response from the wretch. Medical personnel were said to be gearing up for the "flood" of casualties they expected. Decontamination units were set up. All the injured would have to be decontaminated before being treated. The process was estimated at taking about six minutes. The contamination expected would be from chemical and possibly nuclear warheads. Injuries expected were massive burns, and missing body parts from the myriad of land mines that were reportedly planted everywhere. It sounded as if the Iraqis wouldn't even have to move to kill a few hundred of us, as if we could just start counting from there.

The Saudis were said to have said that the oil slick on the Gulf, originally estimated at about 11 million barrels, was now thought to be only about 1.5 to 3 million. Well, that was a relief. Reportedly, there was no imminent danger to the water supply. Coalition forces were said to be a bit shocked by the number of surrendering Iraqis, and speculation pointed to the pamphlets dropped by Coalition warplanes urging surrender, as well as to starvation and mounting casualties. Some Europeans were endorsing the Soviet Peace Plan. I wondered who had orchestrated their support and for what purpose. The Chairman of the Federal Reserve was said to be confident that the current recession would be a mild one and would be followed by a modest recovery.

Within the next twenty-four hours the enemy decided to respond positively to the Soviet Peace Plan. Of course, this caused a tsunami of political seesawing and commentary, everybody and their monkey was willing to put on a tie and a tag, "Political Analyst." On the few opportunities I had to watch television, I found the Military Analysts the most engaging. They used those video pencil things like John Madden. At least they could tell you something. I was interested to know what these guys really did for a living. None of them had mentioned Chingis Khan. Certainly, there was some need for historical analysis. But nobody really had the stomach to speak about war properly. Funny we should all be so engaged in it. As for the response of the Opposition—Yeah, right. The Soviets were gloating over this whole thing, acting like they'd done something. Congressmen were urging the consideration of a cease-fire. "Bullshit! We're going in," I said. We were committed to it at this point. We were waiting on our toes for six months, and we're going forward. If they kill one of us, they'll pay with thousands. China, who had veto power in the United Nations, said the Opposition response was promising. Fuck you, China. You're as bad as they are. Watch your step or we'll be ousting your communist ass out of Tibet. Who cares what China says? Go now! Suggestions were made here and there that after the war the Enemy might be the victim of a bloody coup. My feeling was that we should go in and blow his head off. That way we could be a little more sure of things.

An Army Lt. Colonel violated division guidelines that commanding officers were not to personally engage enemy forces and was relieved of his command of a battalion of Apache helicopters after an incident in which he mistakenly fired on two U.S. armored vehicles which left two American soldiers dead. The loss of any life is a tragedy…The Administration estimated that the cost of the Persian Gulf War would top off at somewhere between $58 billion and $77 billion. Depending on the type of combat involved, the combat phase of the operation through March 31 would top $25 to $44 billion. As if that was something. We had pledges from the rest of the world totaling $51 billion, and we had a deficit in the trillions. It wasn't as if we didn't see numbers like this every day.

There was a smattering of reports about war protesters. Hundreds had stopped traffic, protested at the stock exchange and at a television station. "The way to support the troops is to bring the troops home—alive!" That kind of thing. People were arrested for disorderly conduct. Students across the country were said to be staging rallies and teach-ins. Well, that was okay, I supposed. They weren't doing any harm. Every effort needed nay-sayers to deepen its perspective. Of course, they weren't having any effect on the real situation. God forbid. The President's mandate from the people was perfectly clear as far as I understood. In, out, and not too many of our people get hurt. So, you bomb the crap out of them. It was going according to plan. The President's demeanor assumed the authority that had been given him by the world in their consent to the war, and especially in light of this dissenter cease-fire talk coming from the Russkies, this was the card to lay down. During the course of Friday night, the President gave the deadline of noon. After that, we would damn them. A showdown. Ring time? High noon. Such assertive poetry. Haiku was Japanese. This was American.

CHAPTER 28

▼

Win or lose, it's your enemies who define you.

After a few hours' sleep, I woke up in the morning and went back to work just like the old days. Parts of me waited cautiously to hear the toll of American Dead. Ideally, I wanted none of us to get killed, though I felt the conflict would be deadly. I felt myself personally committed to something that I knew was going to hurt. The boss came in during the evening sometime and told me to go home. "Okay." On the ride home I heard the President on the radio announcing that the Ground War had begun. The announcer mentioned that the Ground War was expected to be the bloodiest part of the conflict. Hours before the final assault began, the Opposition denounced the President for having set the shameful ultimatum and announced that he was turning to the Soviets and the U.N. to work out a peaceful solution. I finally understood that he had no qualms about making a fool out of himself. His antics were redolent of the World Wrestling Federation. He also denied that his forces had engaged in what the President termed a "scorched earth" tactic by setting ablaze 160 oil wells in Kuwait. The U.S. military was anticipating a collapse of the Iraqi army, and it was speculated that it was this assessment, arrived at in the previous few days, that contributed to the decision to undertake the Ground War rather than consider the Soviet Peace Plan.

Reports from all over the country were coming in that antiwar demonstrators were being beaten up. A comment on the radio came that they were leftover hippies from the 'sixties. A person couldn't have an intelligent, honest opinion against war, it seemed. It bothered people. People were afraid to think they might be wrong in their own support for the war. They compensated for that fear by attacking people who thought differently. Leftover hippies from the 'sixties? As if war had never been protested before the 'sixties. You'd wish people that stupid would join the other side. A poll announced that sixty-three percent of us felt it was a bad thing to have people protesting against war when U.S. troops were fighting. Thirty-one percent would support a law banning antiwar demonstrations during wartime. I thought, "The public is ripe for an ambitious fascist." I noticed in the newspaper the next morning that war protesters were repeatedly referred to as "peace protesters," which made no sense, and they were referred to as an extreme minority. Personally, of course, the point of ideology was mute.

By Monday, Allies were reporting 5,500 Enemy POW's, with one Marine killed and eight wounded. Marines had taken up position west of Kuwait City. Intelligence reports were said to reveal that the Iraqi military was randomly executing Kuwaiti citizens. The General said that the invading troops had achieved all their first-day objectives by mid-afternoon. He also affirmed that the deadliest fighting had yet to occur. The Enemy charged his troops to show no mercy. The Deputy National Security Adviser announced that the Iraqi people would hold Saddam Hussein accountable for these crimes against Iraq. The paper said the government was resting its hopes on a bloody coup to oust the Opposition. A Scud was fired that night on Allied troops and landed in a military barracks of U.S. personnel, killing twenty-seven, injuring ninety-eight. The Scud was reportedly breaking up in flight and, therefore, no Patriot was fired to intercept. There's your blood, Saddam baby. On the home front, a man out walking with his five-year-old son was fatally stabbed in the heart and robbed. The boy was unharmed.

The rout continued for the next two days. There had been impatience to get all this done. It had been disregarded by the leadership, who had its eye on the battle, as a requirement for victory. The war was a rout. The elevated mobility of the Allied forces over its enemy rivaled that of the Mongols. If they had taken the Mongol tack and slaughtered all those they ran across, it would have been even quicker. But they were slowed by taking prisoners in the hundreds. Starved enemy soldiers, only too happy to give up their arms, kissing their captors. Such a rout it was that had it been a Mongol operation, there would have been no survivors. With the exception of the dissidents, the Kurds, the Iraqis would have been slaughtered down to nothing. No people would be left to define Iraq. Just their empty buildings and hapless possessions.

By Wednesday night, the President announced a halt to the offensive, saying the enemy had been beaten. It was day forty-two. I didn't really give a damn about the rest of the news. 50,000 enemy troops had been taken prisoner. 700 tanks destroyed, twenty-nine Iraqi divisions totaling 300,000 Iraqi troops had been "knocked out." Twenty-eight Americans had been killed in the Ground War, with 213 wounded since Sunday. Thirteen Brits had been reported killed in the invasion, including nine killed on Tuesday when two U.S. A-10 jets fired on

British armored vehicles. "Any loss of life is regrettable…etc., etc." As for enemy killed in action, the General refused to estimate, saying only that it was a "very, very large number." This was all filler to me. It was clear that my concern had no effect one way or the other, and I felt strongly that the men in government, and those in command of the military, having been paid very well to perform, would do so, that they would clean up and come home. Now, we'd be able to focus on progress again. Now, we'd be able to address a few problems, the solutions to which would re-fortify our muscle, our fortitude, our character.

The atrocities of the Iraqi occupation in Kuwait were thrown all around to be seen and listened to wherever we turned. What a good people we were. I was not concerned. I felt a soothing relief from the burden of my personal obsession with "the news." My posture was completely revitalized, like a coil springing back into place. A piece of news was once again as significant to the landscape as a vacant lot. The turmoil at work, too, caused me pain no longer. The bureaucracy, the institutional contradictions, the know-nothings with their bloated asses anchored to a seat in their personal fantasies of "public service." It seemed to me that we could all start again, begin the next day from scratch; that I could begin to work again in the turmoil, assured that, though the ultimate goals worth struggling for were eons away, each day would be a step toward something beyond the hedonism of the moment.

It was with this stoned, mild elation that I drove to work on Thursday afternoon and found a scene of company vans in the driveway of the Shelter. Men were moving furniture. The kids were wandering around smoking cigarettes. Some were defiantly putting their stuff back in the house. Emilia was out on the front lawn trying to comfort everybody. She said they could live with her. The boss was sitting in the office looking out the window.

"What's going on?" I said.

She glanced up at me as if I had risen from the dead. She stood up and looked hard across the desk. "You're fired," she said.

"What the fuck did I do?" I blurted.

"We're all fired." I didn't feel like yelling, but I felt like I should and I couldn't. I heard people in the house. Heavy feet and moving furniture.

"Where are they putting the kids? We're just dumping them out in the street?"

"I don't know. Different places. Bigger places."

"Jail?"

"Will you shut up! They can hear you!" She whispered now. "I don't know. This is your last day."

"Who made that decision?"

"I don't know," she said. We stood in silence and I looked at her, and I thought about all the crap she'd had to put up with to keep this place going.

"What am I expected to do on my last day?" I looked around the room, "Normally, I'd booby trap the place, maybe put a snake in your pocket book."

She was quiet. "Say goodbye, I guess."

Without even knowing there was a fight, I'd been beaten. This was an artist at work.

"I'm going for a walk," I said. "I don't want to take this out on you."

I had never conceived that I could be demoralized in this way, that I would be beaten by the Administrator without even perceiving a fight. Why would he tell anyone about the closing? He'd just have a fight on his hands. We'd all get worked up for nothing.

I turned the corner and headed up the drag. Vinny called from the bank across the street. He waved like I was his best friend. I managed a nod. I wasn't pissed at him, after all. I smelled the pizza place and walked past the crowded pharmacy parking lot. The amount of stores got thinner as I walked. There were more houses and more empty buildings. People seemed to scurry into the cracks of the neighborhood. I walked the streets like I was in a hurry. I was trying to work off the feeling in my stomach and as I saw more garbage on the sidewalk, it seemed to propel me. There were cups with straws and cigarette butts. There was a small plastic bag with a tear in the bottom and toilet paper dribbling out. The people outside seemed to change. Their heads bent forward, and their shoulders drooped like melting wax figures. They stood in groups with their hoods over their eyes. They didn't look at me, but I knew they could see me. They looked like prisoners finding strength in numbers, listless, distant, and waiting. The buildings looked like crack houses. Windows were boarded up, but I could see light coming through the rotted window sill. It was the neighborhood of The Office of Administration. I put my head down like the prisoners, trying to work through the anger when a belt came around my neck. It pulled me back and swung me to the ground. There was broken green glass everywhere, and I wondered whether my face was in it. My forehead and nose scraped the pavement, and someone stood on the space between my shoulder blades. "Give me what you got, nature boy!" he said. He moved his foot up a bit and pulled on the belt as he took my wallet from my back pocket. I did not speak. I felt him kick me in the kidney as he pulled again on the belt, then he took a step off my head as he leaped into a sprint down the block.

I watched him turn the corner as I got up and caught my breath. I brushed away some pebbles and sand and little bits of glass. My face was scraped up, but only bleeding a little. It occurred to me that I now had license to kill. I ran after him and followed him from a couple blocks back. To watch him you'd never know he had just assaulted someone. He took a left off Broadway. I took a left two blocks behind him and ran up to an alley one block up. I ran as fast as I could up the alley and closed the gap between us. When he stepped off the curb into the passageway, he had no time to react, and the force with which I hit him carried us into the street. I got on top of him and began driving my right fist into his face. I knew I'd hurt him, but when I didn't draw blood I got angry. I grabbed his throat with my left hand and hit him harder. He flailed at me, but it was weak. Just then a car turning the corner came to a quick stop to avoid hitting us. It broke my concentration, and when I stood up to confront it, the driver just swerved around us and kept going. There was no movement for a second, and in that moment I realized who he was. This was the reason I never wanted to get close to these kids. You never knew just how badly they were going to blow up in your face. It was Web lying in the street. He was trying to sit up. Now I knew why I hadn't seen him at the shelter. He had gone off and become what everyone expected him to become. For all I knew he had been stalking me. For all I knew, that time he'd run into me outside of D's was just practice. I told him to give me my wallet. He was slow to move.

"Give me my wallet!" I shouted.

"Yo, man. What you do that for? I could have shot you, motherfucker."

"Give me my wallet!" I was standing over him. I could have kicked him in the chin and knocked his teeth out.

"I don't have your wallet, man! I don't know what you're talking about!"

I grabbed him by the hair, and I came down with my knee on his chest. He lost his wind, and he was gasping for air with my weight on him. I held my fist up. "Deny it one more time! I want to hear you deny it one more fucking time!"

Web looked at me, and I could tell one more beating wasn't going to make a difference to him. All those times I had done favors for him or given him money, all the times he'd pissed me off with his attitude and surly mouth, and here he was in my sights and giving me complete justification to beat him up. I would beat him up, and he would go to jail. He reached into his coat, and I came down on his arm.

"You want it or not?" he said. I let up, and he slowly pulled the wallet out of his pocket. I grabbed it out of his hand, and I got with him face to face. "You're not my enemy!" I told him. Where were my enemies? Yes, I would go find them.

978-0-595-34769-8
0-595-34769-X

Printed in the United States
63983LVS00004B/169-186